Clare stood at the wall phone in the kitchen, her forehead puckered in a frown. "Are you absolutely certain there is no Michael Duffy in your directory?" she asked the switchboard operator again. "Could you please ring the laboratory?"

"We have no laboratories here, madam. This is a business office only."

Hadn't Michael told her he was in research medicine? Where else did researchers work, if not in labs? "Dr. Duffy is on temporary assignment from the main office in Washington," she explained.

"The main office is in Geneva, Switzerland. Are you sure you have the right pharmaceutical company? This is Schoenfeld-Loewe."

Of course she had the right company! She'd seen Michael go into the firm's office building that morning, so he had to be there now. The operator had obviously made a mistake....

ABOUT THE AUTHOR

Deirdre Mardon is a full-time writer who often draws from her own experiences to bring her characters and stories to life. When she's not writing, Deirdre does needlepoint and enjoys collecting American antiques. She and her husband live with their two daughters in rural Connecticut.

Books by Deirdre Mardon

HARLEQUIN INTRIGUE
2—IN FOR A PENNY
15—RELUCTANT LOVER
20—WITH PENALTY AND INTEREST

HARLEQUIN AMERICAN ROMANCE
9—CANVAS OF PASSION
33—DESTINY'S SWEET ERRAND

HARLEQUIN TEMPTATION
15—A JEALOUS MISTRESS
31—A TOUCH OF MADNESS

These books may be available at your local bookseller.

Don't miss any of our special offers. Write to us at the following address for information on our newest releases.

Harlequin Reader Service
P.O. Box 52040, Phoenix, AZ 85072-2040
Canadian address: P.O. Box 2800, Postal Station A,
5170 Yonge St., Willowdale, Ont. M2N 6J3

WITH PENALTY AND INTEREST

DEIRDRE MARDON

Harlequin Books

TORONTO • NEW YORK • LONDON
AMSTERDAM • PARIS • SYDNEY • HAMBURG
STOCKHOLM • ATHENS • TOKYO • MILAN

For
B.E.M.

Harlequin Intrigue edition published June 1985

ISBN 0-373-22020-0

Chapter One

Clare Eckert hated scenes.

She also hated braggarts, loud noises, social pretense and her brother-in-law, Jonas Hahn, a man who epitomized her list of dislikes. Staring at Jonas across the table of the outdoor restaurant, she willed the paving stones of the courtyard in which they sat to open and swallow him forever. When nothing happened, she smiled automatically, nodded at something her sister, Emily, murmured in her ear, and took another sip of the exotic tequila concoction a waiter had placed before her several minutes before. Her face was beginning to feel as if it would crack from the stiff smile that had been plastered on it ever since dinner had ended and the seemingly endless rounds of after-dinner drinks had begun.

"Mexico is a backward country," Jonas was saying, "with backward people, hopeless economics, inedible cuisine and lousy service. I can't imagine why I wanted to come here!" He slammed his drink down with such force that its pale green liquid sloshed onto the magenta cloth and puddled for a moment before sinking out of sight, to leave only a damp spot around the base of his glass. Despite the blare of raucous mariachi music that surrounded their small party, Jonas's resonant voice carried clearly to Clare's ears, and to those of the other customers in the patio restaurant. A few heads turned their way, and Clare was aware of expressions of disapproval on the quickly averted faces of other American tourists who were guests at El Tapatio, one of the most luxurious hotels in the city of Guadalajara.

Clare leaned slightly to her right. "Let's get out of here, Emily." The quick aside was delivered to her sister when Jonas turned his head to summon the waiter, whom he called "boy," much to Clare's discomfort.

"I can't leave," Emily replied. "You know how Jonas hates it if I leave." Emily's delicate face, so much like Clare's—the same green eyes, the same dark brows and lashes, the same generous mouth—had the too-frequent pinched and nervous look Clare had learned to recognize during the past three months that she had been living with her sister and Jonas. In fact, there were new, distinct lines on Emily's face—across her forehead, half hidden by shiny blond bangs, and running from the sides of her nose to her mouth—lines that made Clare suddenly aware of the inexorable passage of time. She wondered if she looked as defeated and worried as her sister, whom she resembled physically as well as in personality.

Clare was twenty-nine, two years younger than Emily, but never before, not even during the last two troublesome years of her life, had she been so acutely conscious of the loss of their girlhood.

Clare's gaze caught the eye of the man who had joined their party ten minutes earlier. Jonas had introduced the stranger to her—somewhat vaguely, Clare recalled. He was a doctor, as was her brother-in-law, but she hadn't caught his name because of the raucous music. The man smiled—it seemed almost a conspiratorial smile of sympathy—and she found herself studying him for the first time, grateful that he sensed her discomfort and hoping he wouldn't associate her with her boorish brother-in-law—even though it was obvious that Clare was traveling with the Hahns and was, however unwillingly, Jonas's guest.

The stranger wasn't handsome by her standards—not by anyone's, perhaps. His face was too serious, although its features were pleasantly regular. His eyes were blue, an ordinary blue. His hair was a nondescript color, a light brown. Although it was trimmed neatly, she knew he used a barber and not one of the overpriced stylists Jonas patronized. His clothes were, if not somber, quietly traditional. He wore a dark blue blazer of summer-weight wool with a light beige shirt and a cotton tie of muted stripes. Very appropriate for the mild February night in Guadalajara, she thought, but hardly the earnest, trendy resort wear of Jonas's madras sports jacket and coordinating slacks that picked up a pale raspberry tint in the plaid and reminded Clare of an ice-cream cone. The stranger sported a plain gold watch with a black leather band and no other jewelry; Jonas had on a chunky Rolex, eighteen karat gold, and a heavy gold signet ring from Tiffany & Company, with a crest carved deeply into its face.

Jonas looked like the affluent, hotshot plastic surgeon he was, but the other doctor looked like...like...an accountant. That was a calling Clare recognized, having been trained as one herself, even though she hadn't worked at her profession for the last half of her six-year marriage, which had ended in divorce eight months before.

Clare decided she preferred the tasteful way the stranger was dressed, although it was clear the newcomer hadn't spent anywhere near the money on his attire that Jonas had.

The mariachi trio drifted away, Jonas having determined not to tip them because *he* hadn't requested any songs. The musicians took a break, and a band in one corner of the patio began to play a rhythmic romantic melody that Clare vaguely recognized. She had enjoyed hearing the mariachi music ever since her arrival in Guadalajara three days before, finding something appealing in the naïveté of the dissonant sounds created by violins and cornets. The joyful noise provided an added benefit: It made conversation at their table, stilted at best, nearly impossible. In fact, Clare liked everything she had seen in Mexico since their arrival—the people, the food and the vibrant colors splashed at every turn.

"Do you mind if I go to bed, Emily? I hate to leave you alone with..." *I might as well say it,* Clare thought. *It can't come as a surprise to poor Emily. After all, she has to live with him.* She couldn't say Jonas's name, however, because she felt guilty for wanting to desert her sister, who had been so kind and welcoming to her. The Hahns were paying for Clare's trip to Mexico. They had opened their luxurious home to her when she had nowhere else to turn and were helping her get back on her feet, financially and emotionally, after several years of pain and difficulty.

Emily glanced at Clare, her eyes clearly begging her sister to stay. "Go ahead," she said instead. "I'll be all right."

Clare hesitated, torn between wanting the peace and quiet of her hotel room and her imagined duty to Emily.

"Would you care to dance?" The doctor-accountant was at her side, leaning toward her ear. She hadn't even noticed that he had left his seat and come around the table. His hand was extended palm up in a gesture of invitation, and Clare felt the warmth of his body next to hers.

"I was just going to bed," she said.

"Only one dance."

"Yes. Of course." She stood up and smoothed the front of her dress before taking the hand he held out; then she allowed him to lead her to the small dance floor in the center of the patio.

"I didn't get your name," he said, slipping one hand around her back and laying it lightly and quite properly on the wide cummerbund of her thin cotton dress. She stepped into his arms and was surprised to feel his body warmth again. She also noticed with pleasure that he was more muscular to the touch than she had been led to believe by his clothes. His shoulder was hard under her palm. The hand in hers was firm and dry, and the top of her head came up to his nose. They stepped slowly to the music without that minute of awkwardness that often characterized the first dance between new partners.

"Clare Eckert," she replied. "Jonas's wife, Emily, is my sister. And I didn't get yours, either. The mariachis..."

"Michael Duffy. Call me Mike."

"And you're a doctor, isn't that right? Are you a surgeon, too, like Jonas?" Clare was wary. She had nothing against doctors, but she had found some of the members of Jonas and Emily's set hard to stomach. A few of them seemed to have more interest in money than in healing.

"Yes, I'm a doctor, but a researcher, not a practicing physician."

"Does that mean you're a Ph.D.?"

"No, a medical doctor," he explained. "Just one who doesn't deal with patients. I'm associated with a drug company, Schoenfeld-Loewe." The name was familiar to her. While it was not as well known as Lederle or Eli Lilly, nevertheless Clare had heard of the pharmaceutical house, which had modern offices in Stamford, Connecticut. She lived only a few miles away, in a small apartment on the second floor of the stone carriage house on Jonas and Emily's Greenwich estate, which overlooked Long Island Sound. The Hahns owned one of the choicest pieces of real estate on the East Coast.

"That explains why you don't look like Jonas," she said. *Or act like him,* she thought.

"Don't I? What does that mean?" he asked mildly, yet she knew her observation had piqued his curiosity.

"Nothing." But it did mean something to Clare. Somehow the fact that this man spent his time with test tubes, instead of with adoring patients who deified him more than was healthy for any human being, made his personality more refreshing to her. "How do you and Jonas know each other?" She couldn't imagine that Jonas was interested in medical research.

Michael hesitated briefly before replying. "We both went to medical school here in Guadalajara, but I haven't seen him in years and years. I was sitting across the patio, and I thought I recognized him, although he's put on a little weight since those days. I must admit he didn't recognize me at all."

"And what are you doing in Guadalajara?"

"Just taking a short winter vacation," he replied. "How about you?" The music had stopped, and they stood talking in the middle of the dance floor. Clare found chatting with Michael Duffy infinitely preferable to returning to the table. When the band began to play again, he took her into his arms once more, and she imagined that he held her a little closer. But the song was slower this time, with a different tempo altogether, so it might have been only her imagination.

"We aren't supposed to be here," she said. "We're supposed to be in some enormous resort in Puerto Vallarta on the Pacific Coast, but there was a mix-up in the reservations or Jonas didn't book early enough—I don't know the details—so we ended up here. He hates it."

"But it's a lovely hotel and an even lovelier city. Do you hate it, too?"

"I haven't seen much of Guadalajara, but I love what I've seen so far—the Orozco Museum, a tequila factory.... Jonas likes to lie around the pool." Clare closed her eyes in misery when she recalled the fiasco of their aborted city tour the day before. Emily's three-year-old twins crying; Jonas complaining about the heat, the hired car, the driver whose English was less than perfect, the fact that Emily apparently had not remembered to pack a certain silk shirt he favored. . . .

"And you? Do you like to lie around the pool?"

"Not much. My skin's too fair. I burn."

"Yes, your skin is fair. And soft, too," he added, raising the hand that rested on the small of her back so that it came into contact with the bare skin above her sundress. Clare stiffened slightly. Not that his touch on her skin wasn't nice. It was very nice, indeed, and had sent a quick thrill through her. She was confused by the long-forgotten reaction of her body to a man's. She hadn't been this close to any man since. . . Clare tried to remember when she had last made love with her former husband. A long time ago. Too long, she realized, to be without a man's company.

She relaxed somewhat and leaned slightly into the warm bulk of Michael Duffy, enjoying the light touch of her breasts against his chest. In response, his grip on her palm increased, and he spread the fingers of his other hand on her bare back. Clare deliberately slowed her breathing so he wouldn't hear it.

"Are you married, Clare?" His breath tickled her ear as he posed the quiet question.

"No, single," she replied. "Divorced, actually," she added after a moment. "And you?"

"Bachelor. Never married. Never met the right girl," he said quickly, as if to forestall the inevitable question.

"Yet," she said. " 'Never' makes a person sound so old, as if your life is over already."

" 'Yet,' then. I'm thirty-seven."

She nodded. She had figured that to be his age, because he said he had gone to school with Jonas. Laughing lightly, she snuggled just a millimeter closer into his chest and closed her eyes, resting her cheek against his shoulder. Dancing slowly was such a sensual pleasure, she mused, such a personal thing. An activity that brought one immediately close to another body, even that of a virtual stranger. She tried to recall Michael Duffy's face but was unable to do so, remembering only that he was a pleasant-looking man who appeared to be very, very clean, as if he had just stepped from a shower. And he smelled clean, too, she realized as she inhaled his natural scent, which was one of fresh laundry and only the merest hint of newly mown grass on a lazy summer afternoon.

He was a good dancer, a man with an innate rhythm who responded naturally to the music coming from the corner of the patio canopied with stars. Clare found that she was thoroughly enjoying herself in his arms. She stopped concentrating on the way her feet moved and let the touch of his body against her lull her into a sort of somnolence. If just a dance or two could relax her so. . .

Her mind drifted away from the patio of the Hotel El Tapatio and to abstracts that had been niggling at the back of her consciousness: time to start dating again, time to enlarge her circle of friends. Past time to look for a new job that would enable her to leave Jonas Hahn's carriage house and the unhealthy atmosphere that permeated his marriage to her sister. Life had become so much simpler since the day Emily and Jonas had taken her in, and yet the price she paid was high. Now that she felt stronger, the price was proving to be too high.

"A penny for your thoughts," Michael Duffy whispered in her ear.

"Not thinking at all," she replied, allowing herself to drift to the surface from the depths of her reverie. "Just feeling good."

"I'm glad. Would you like to see some of the real Guadalajara tomorrow?"

"I. . .we have plans to drive out to Lake Chapala for lunch tomorrow. Perhaps you'd like to join us?" Immediately Clare regretted the invitation that had slipped from her lips. She would have enjoyed spending a day with Michael Duffy, but she had a quick, painful vision of the morrow. Jonas would show his famous temper; the twins, Ian and Kevin, would burst into tears and whimper intermittently during the entire day; Emily would become quiet and miserable. And Clare would squirm with shame and embarrassment in front of this pleasant stranger.

Why, *why* had she ever agreed to accompany the Hahns to Mexico when she could be enjoying the solitude of her own apartment, despite the Connecticut winter weather?

"Is there room in your car?"

He was giving her an out, she realized. Michael Duffy was an intelligent man who, in ten short minutes with the Hahns, had sized up the situation. He, too, had no desire to torture himself with an afternoon of Jonas. She wished she were as free as Michael Duffy.

"No, not really."

"Why don't you come with *me* instead?" he suggested. "We can rent a car, and I'll show you the cathedral—very beautiful, with an original Murillo—and the *barrancas*—the main market."

Tempting. It was all very tempting. But she couldn't desert Emily so easily.

"Oh, I couldn't. Emily . . . needs me."

"Why do you have to stay with her?"

Clare was too reserved to explain herself to a virtual stranger. How could she relate that Emily had come out to California to pick her up and carry her back to Connecticut after her divorce? How could she tell him that she had owned nothing after the bankruptcy—not her lovely Spanish-style house, not a stick of furniture, not even a decent winter coat? Or that Emily had promised to take care of her until she was back on her feet?

"I just do, that's all," Clare said with a sigh. "I'm sorry, Michael. I'd like to come with you tomorrow, but I can't. Maybe another time. Back in Connecticut, perhaps."

"You have to live your own life, Clare. It's too easy to be taken over by others."

Clare stiffened and stood back a few inches so she could see into Michael Duffy's eyes. *What a strange thing for him to say,* she thought. This man didn't know her from Adam, knew nothing about her past, had spent but a few short minutes at their table—yet he was telling her the exact truth, both as he perceived it and as it existed.

"That's one of my failings," she admitted. "Or was, in the past. I'm working on it." She looked into his eyes, which weren't the ordinary blue she had thought they were at first but, rather, were flecked with glints of gold and shadows of navy. Nice eyes, she thought, serious and honest. Appraising, but compassionate. The kind of eyes a doctor should have, but seldom, in her recent experience, did. He held her gaze for a long minute, and she felt something dissolve within her.

"How are you working on it?"

She was confused, more by the intensity of his stare than by the simple question she barely heard.

"How?" he repeated.

"I...I don't know. I just am." She had vowed she would never trust a man again, but when she looked into Michael Duffy's eyes, she felt her resolve weaken. Anyway, that vow had been an exaggerated reaction to the unimaginable horror of the breakup of her marriage. She knew, intellectually at least, that there were men in the world who were trustworthy. She just hadn't met any lately, but perhaps Michael Duffy was one of those men.

"Be more specific."

What a strange conversation, she thought. His intensity caused a chill flutter in her breast. They were no longer bantering like strangers on a dance floor. He was asking her real questions and clearly demanding real answers. They had stopped dancing, although couples all around them swayed to the beat of a muted bossa nova. *Lighten up, Dr. Duffy,* she said silently. "I'll never again sign anything without reading the fine print," she said with a laugh calculated to lighten the tension.

He put his arms around her, both of them this time, and picked up the rhythm of the dance, slipping easily back into the melody. "Forget Emily for a moment. What do *you* want to do tomorrow?"

"Go back to Greenwich," Clare answered immediately, without thinking that he was comparing a city tour to lunch at Lake Chapala.

"Why don't you?"

"Oh, I couldn't! I'm their guest, Jonas and Emily's. She needs me." Even as Clare mouthed the excuse, she knew it wasn't true. She had told herself she was accompanying Emily to help her out with the twins, but upon their arrival at the hotel, Emily had hired a local woman to care for the boys and had paid her in advance with American money. Clare found Emily's habit of always carrying cash incongruous with her sister's cool and elegant exterior. It was easier to envision Emily airily signing her name to receipts, or telling a merchant to send her the bill. Not only that, they all lived in a credit-card society, something Clare was only too lamentably aware of, yet Emily seemed to pay cash for everything.

"To protect her from Jonas, is that what you mean?"

"Really, Michael. You don't even know us." Truth was truth, but Clare was stunned by his bluntness.

"Yes, you're right. I spoke out of turn." Contrite words, but no note of contrition in his voice.

"No, that's all right. Jonas is difficult, that's for certain. Emily—and I suppose Jonas, as well—was exceedingly kind to me when I most needed friends, and now I feel I owe both of them something in return. I can't just walk out on her in a bad situation. You can understand that, can't you?"

"I think they're using you in a sick game some married

people get into at times. I *know* they are. Can you understand that?"

"Are you sure you're not a psychiatrist?" she asked with another mirthless laugh, attempting again to lighten the conversation.

"I don't have to be a psychiatrist to see that you're allowing yourself to be a victim in their complicated family dynamics."

Victim! Clare stiffened in earnest this time and pulled away, leaving him to drop his arms awkwardly at his sides. If there was one tag Clare despised, it was the word "victim," perhaps because its nearness to the truth was too uncomfortable to contemplate. Yes, she had been a victim, but she had begun a new life now, and she didn't need Michael Duffy to remind her of her old one.

And why should Michael Duffy suddenly be so interested in her psyche? Why couldn't he have kept the evening light and pleasant? A few dances and a few superficial comments about the weather, the hotel, the exquisite city of Guadalajara, known as the Pearl of the West? There were at least a dozen bland topics they could be discussing instead. She would have welcomed even some of the hackneyed questions single people asked each other—what her astrological sign was, for instance—rather than his totally unexpected seriousness. The last thing Clare wanted was an amateur analyst poking into her life and into that of her sister. Really, the man had gone too far!

"I don't think the dynamics of our family are any of your business, Dr. Duffy. I'd like to go back to the table now." Her words were firm and carried conviction, although there was nothing less appealing than returning to the table to face Jonas, unless it was continuing the dissection of family neuroses that Michael Duffy had begun. She glanced over at their table just in time to see Emily dab at her eyes with one of the lace-trimmed handkerchiefs she always carried in her handbag.

"Fine," he said amiably. "But if I were you, I'd go home. What kind of vacation leaves you feeling more tired and anxious than you felt before you left home?" He gave her a gentle smile, and she almost imagined that he shrugged his shoulders, although his body did not move.

Indeed, she thought, knowing he had unerringly unmasked her own sentiments. But she said nothing, turning her back on him and making her way to the table.

TEN MINUTES LATER Michael Duffy mouthed polite excuses and retired. Clare had made an effort not to look at him again and an even mightier effort to keep the conversation flowing smoothly, an almost impossible task because Jonas was clearly in high dudgeon over something Emily had done or forgotten to do. Emily was as silent as a stone. Every so often she emitted a small, discreet sigh and looked as if she wanted to be elsewhere—Afghanistan, perhaps.

Twenty minutes later Clare announced that she, too, was going to bed. Incensed that her sister was unwilling or unable to stand up to Jonas's bullying, she found herself unable to listen to her abusive brother-in-law for another minute. Jonas was settling the bill as Clare said good night, pulling from the pocket of his trousers the unsavory-looking roll of American money—mostly tens and twenties—that he always carried. He had refused to change his dollars into Mexican pesos, claiming that Mexican money smelled as if it were printed on sheets of raw bacteria and that there was no reason for him to learn the filthy currency when he never planned to return to Mexico in any case. The waiter sighed and accepted Jonas's money with an impassive expression on his broad and placid Indian face. The plastic surgeon was known as a big tipper; besides, everyone remembered the scene that had ensued in the hotel's restaurant the first morning Jonas had insisted on paying with dollars.

Jonas also refused to use bankcards or traveler's checks, complaining vociferously about the interest rates charged by the credit card companies. He himself didn't have a personal checking account, although he insisted that Emily keep the household accounts in absolutely perfect balance at all times. Emily was a disaster at the chore, being much more inclined to artistic and literary pursuits. Clare, who was a trained bookkeeper, had promised to balance the books in secret upon their return to Connecticut.

Clare gathered up her handbag and the light shawl she had thrown over the back of her chair when Michael had asked her to dance. She bade Emily good night for the second time, but her sister only nodded an acknowledgment.

"You meeting that Duffy character in his room?" Jonas's words elicited a small gasp of shock from Emily.

Clare turned back to the table and stared at her brother-in-law. "No, Jonas, I am not. And if I were, it would be none of your business, would it?" Three months before, she would have been wounded and insulted by his innuendo, but she was learning not to be offended by Jonas's words or insinuations. Almost immediately she had realized that he did not dislike her personally, although she actively disliked him. It was clear to Clare that Jonas used her to anger Emily, who, in the beginning, had jumped to her sister's defense, until Clare explained to her that all Jonas wanted was a rise out of his wife.

"Then why are you going in the opposite direction of your room?" he queried with a grin of triumph.

"Because I need toothpaste, and the shop in the lobby is open until midnight. That's why."

"Have a good night, Clare," Jonas said, with the emphasis on "good."

A way from you, it will be, she thought. She understood that he didn't believe her and was thinking salacious thoughts about her and Michael Duffy. But Clare was a fully paid guest of her brother-in-law, so she said nothing.

Nevertheless, she couldn't manage the sweet, knowing smile she wanted to give him.

She turned away and walked toward the lobby, self-consciously aware of the stares of interest and sexual invitation that came from the waiters lined up against the wall of the hotel. She was trying to relax under the scrutiny of the flashing dark eyes of the handsome Guadalajarans—Tapatios, they were called, just like the hotel—but it was difficult for a woman who was basically shy and inhibited, and who had spent the past several years feeling very bad about herself. No man had ever looked at Clare the way the Mexicans did, with an air of lusty appreciation that sometimes bordered on reverence. She had heard that Mexicans fancied blondes, and Clare was anything but blonde; her dark brown hair was nearly black when the light was right. She had also thought that Latins liked a woman to have a little meat on their bones, and Clare had little enough. Even she considered herself too thin.

But she did have nice legs, long and shapely and nearly perfect. Her sundress, chosen to show off her legs, had what the saleswoman in Greenwich called a handkerchief hem, a finish that dipped to deep points that accented her calves and drew the eye away from her rather flat chest.

Every woman coming out of a bad marriage should visit Latin America, she mused, if only for the whistles of admiration and for the melodious, whispered invitations from strange men on the street. Their intentions were unmistakable, even if their Spanish murmurs were incomprehensible to Clare's untrained ears. In Mexico a woman was made to feel like a woman, was treated by men as if she were part madonna and part chippy, and was admired for her assets, as skimpy as they might be. Whatever the implication of the Latin males' attitudes was for the progress of women's liberation, she had to admit the trip had been good for her battered ego.

She crossed the almost deserted hotel lobby and turned a corner that led to the *farmacia*, her destination. But despite the fact that the wall clock in the lobby read barely eleven-fifteen, the small shop was closed. Another aspect of Mexican life she had noted was that nothing opened on time, stores were closed at the oddest hours in the middle of the day, and apparently only *gringos*—Americans— paid attention to clocks anyway. She found the relaxed attitude another definite plus after the hectic routine of life at home.

Clare supposed she wouldn't lose any molars if she didn't brush her teeth for once.

However, in a tiny travel agency next to the pharmacy, lights were still burning. A young woman sat at a cluttered desk near the agency's plate-glass window, on which was taped a large poster depicting the Manhattan skyline at night. The photograph transformed New York City into a glittering and fabled paradise. Clare studied the picture. A photograph, while purporting to represent reality, could also be deceptive. Maybe nothing in life was what it seemed to be.

She looked again through the window of the travel agency. Yes, it was really open. How crazy—the drugstore was closed, but the travel agency was open. It was ludicrous, but it was also very Mexican and almost. . .almost prophetic.

Clare was not at all superstitious, not particularly imaginative and not in the least whimsical. She worried at times that she was too methodical, sometimes verging on the dull, and she knew she had probably never, not once in her nearly thirty years of life, done anything that could truly be called spontaneous. And yet she found herself pulling open the heavy plate-glass door of the agency without another thought.

"Are you really open?" she asked the young attendant, whose long-fingered hands were wrapped around a stack of ticket coupons she had been counting.

"No, not really," the woman replied in adequate but heavily accented English. "I'm working—what do you call it?"

"Overtime."

"Yes, that is the word. The IATA reports are due tomorrow. But if I can help you, I'd be happy to do so, señorita."

Clare, who had no idea what an IATA report was, found herself saying words that she hadn't even thought before that very moment.

"I'd like to go back to New York tomorrow. Is there a flight?"

"There are two flights a day, one in the morning, one in the late afternoon. You have to change planes in Texas, however. There are no direct flights at present." The woman rolled her chair over to a small computer and flicked on the power switch. "Won't you have a seat?"

Clare perched on the edge of a chair in front of the desk and looked nervously over her shoulder. The hall and the lobby beyond were empty of people. At least they were empty of Jonas, who was her only concern. As for Emily... Well, she could explain herself to Emily before she left for the airport, and she was certain her sister would understand. Clare was an adult. She should be able to do what she wanted to do, even if Jonas and Emily *had* bought her a ticket. What she wanted now was to return to Greenwich and her rooms above the carriage house. She could use her time alone to search for another, better-paying job, one that would allow her to get her own apartment. That way she could be alone and not have to watch how Jonas treated Emily and the children—even more to the point, how Emily allowed herself to be treated. She'd think of something to tell Emily.

"How many passengers?"

"Oh, just for myself," Clare answered.

"The afternoon flight is sold out, but there are seats on the seven-thirty flight."

"In the evening?"

"No, in the morning. Shall I book a seat for you?"

"Mmm..." Did she dare? Well, why not? When was she going to be independent if she couldn't make up her mind about the smallest details? "Yes, go ahead," she said after a moment's hesitation. "What time do I have to be at the airport?"

"Six o'clock."

Six o'clock? She wouldn't have an opportunity to talk to Emily before leaving. "So early? I have my ticket already. I'm certain everything is in order." *Call Emily from the airport,* an internal voice ordered. *Leave a note for her in the Hahns' message box at the desk.*

"Those are the rules, señorita. It is high season for the tourists, after all. Many people making reservations they don't use."

And airlines promising seats they don't have, the internal voice whispered, but so quietly that Clare did not pay conscious attention. The woman's dark eyes were watching Clare for some sign that she had changed her mind. Was that a flicker of impatience in their depths? Clare glanced at her wristwatch and decided she could pack in less than ten minutes and still get enough sleep to be functional the following day.

"Please book me a seat." Clare gave the agent her name and room number but, when asked for her ticket, could not produce it, since it was upstairs in her room with her tourist card and identification.

"It's not important," the agent said. "At the airport they have the same computer, and your name is registered now. Please do not forget your tourist card when you leave."

"I won't," Clare assured her. When she stood up, she felt slightly dizzy with daring at what she had done. The agent showed Clare out of the office and closed and locked the plate-glass door behind her.

Yes, she was being rude to the Hahns, she acknowledged. Ungrateful, too. But what kind of vacation was it, anyhow? That doctor, Michael Duffy, had been correct, after all: She was caught up in the middle of Jonas's sick dynamics, and she was playing a hopelessly frustrating maternal role with Emily. She decided that a phone call from the airport was the best way to handle the situation.

If she ever saw Michael Duffy again, she owed him an apology.

Chapter Two

The sky was still pitch-dark the following morning at five forty-five when Clare, having checked out, emerged from the hotel into predawn air that was fresh and cool. She felt a moment's regret at leaving Guadalajara's balmy climate and its pleasant tropical air scented with bougainvillea and sweet-smelling wood smoke—mesquite, she had been told. She knew what ferocious weather might be awaiting her in Connecticut.

One of the Hotel El Tapatio's many advantages was its close proximity to the Guadalajara International Airport. The desk clerk had assured Clare that the trip would take less than fifteen minutes at such an early hour and offered to call a taxi for her. She had thanked him, then given him the note she had written for Emily the previous night.

While she waited for the taxi, Clare paged through a brochure that listed the delights of Guadalajara for tourists, regretting that she had been able to see so little of the city during her short stay. At the time, she had no reason to suspect that her trip to New York would not go off without a hitch. She was calm. Jonas and Emily wouldn't be up for hours, so there was no chance they would see Clare in the process of leaving.

The taxi pulled up to the door of the hotel, and the driver loaded her bags in the trunk. Clare got in the man's yellow-and-blue vintage Chevrolet, sinking back on the cracked leather seat and seeking a comfortable place where the springs near the surface of the upholstery weren't too obtrusive. She sat back with a jerk as the driver accelerated out of the cobblestone courtyard and took his place among the sporadic traffic on the highway to the airport.

Clare remembered that, immediately outside the city limits, a long winding hill descended to flat, unfenced farm and grazing land. Even as she recalled their hair-raising arrival from the airport several days before, a pair of horses strayed across the road, and the driver had to swerve and brake to avoid them. Then, halfway down the grade, the taxi suddenly entered a bank of heavy, rolling fog; in response, the driver slowed the car to a crawl and turned on the headlights. Their bright beams reflected off droplets of moisture suspended in the air, all but blinding Clare and the driver to their surroundings.

"Turn down your lights," she told him. Having lived most of her married life in a California seacoast community, Clare had had plenty of experience driving in fog. "Your lights," she repeated. "Put on your dim lights."

"*No hablo inglés*," he answered.

"Lights...beams...headlamps... Too strong. *Muy grande*." She had all but exhausted her Spanish vocabulary, and yet she was certain she wasn't communicating.

He turned to look at Clare, incomprehension written across friendly dark features. She saw his shoulders elevate in a classic shrug at the very moment she became aware of the small donkey looming before the Chevrolet. Clare let out a squeak. The driver turned back to the road just in time to yank the steering wheel violently to the right. The taxi careened off the road, dipped into a ditch that ran alongside, righted itself and, with a crash, turned, recrossed the ditch and jerked back up on the macadam. The abrupt maneuver threw Clare from left to right in the backseat. Her hurtling body came to rest in a half sprawl just as an invisible truck emitted a deafening blast from its air horn, followed by a long earsplitting second wail as it pulled into the totally opaque oncoming lane and passed the taxi. An acrid odor of cattle filled the backseat. Clare's stomach clutched, and she found that her hands were squeezed together in a death grip. Her legs went weak.

The driver continued unperturbed as Clare tried to relax, breathing shakily and sneaking a covert look at her watch. Already six o'clock. She wasn't worried about missing the plane, which didn't leave until seven-thirty, but about losing her life on a highway shrouded with fog in western Mexico. She glanced at the speedometer—ten miles an hour, and unsafe at that speed. She couldn't fault the man's driving; it was the invisible menace all around them that worried Clare.

"*Mucha niebla*," the driver said. "Many clouds." He smiled at his attempt at English.

That's a romantic way of putting it, she thought. "Foggy," she agreed, surprised to find her voice almost normal.

Twenty uneventful minutes later, the Chevy pulled up in front of the terminal. Clare stumbled from the car. She paid the driver and watched a porter load her luggage on a cart and wheel it into the modern airport building. She followed, still counting her change in the unfamiliar peso bills.

Once inside, Clare was unprepared for the scene worthy of Dante's *Inferno* that greeted her. If she hadn't known better, she would have suspected that war had broken out in Jalisco during the night and that every possible citizen was attempting to evacuate. Three long lines of passengers crowded in front of the check-in counters.

At least two suitcases and assorted ill-shaped hand luggage—she saw charro hats, enormous wicker baskets, giant flowers of riotously colored crepe paper, a large papier-mâché bird—accompanied each person. A baby wailed, a vendor screamed the name of the morning newspaper in a harsh falsetto, an airline employee was attempting to make an announcement without benefit of electronic amplification, and in two languages four people were vociferously exhorting the crowd to silence. Clare took her place at the end of the shortest line, optimistically hoping that it would move the fastest.

After an interminable announcement in Spanish, followed by shrieks and groans on all sides of her, Clare, along with a boisterous knot of travelers who were obviously foreign tourists like herself, pushed forward to hear the translation into English.

"Ladies and gentlemen, Flight 407 is now full, with the exception of two first-class seats. If there are any first-class passengers not yet checked in, come forward now. Those people holding economy seats, please wait on the right and we will try to accommodate you on tomorrow's flight."

A collective groan, the exact echo of the one that had followed the Spanish announcement, rose to the vaulted ceiling of the terminal. Everyone waited for the first-class passengers to identify themselves. When none did, pandemonium broke loose. All the passengers, native and foreign alike, surged forward to claim the last two seats on the plane.

Clare fought down a feeling of momentary panic. What would she do if she couldn't leave? Could she return hangdog to the hotel? No, she couldn't face Jonas again, not after she had made up her mind to leave Guadalajara. Could she go to another hotel and spend the night? Did she have enough money to take care of herself until the next day? She didn't think she did. Oh, what now?

Gradually, she took a grip on herself as she realized that being stranded in a foreign airport probably happened to lots of travelers. There had to be some formalized method for dealing with such an emergency. She agonized for a moment until a plan half formed in her mind. She would ask the ticket agent to recommend an inexpensive hotel near the airport.

Clare pushed her way against the surging crowd to retrieve her luggage, then headed toward the area the agent had pointed out. She decided that if she couldn't get on that morning's flight, at least she could assure herself of the first seat on the next day's plane. She had no desire to fight the maddened crowd that pushed and shoved toward the counter. Anyway, it was obvious who would get the last two seats. A tall, balding American, expensively if flashily dressed and bejeweled, had already arrived first at the head of the line forming before the ticket agent, having pushed a toddler to the floor in his careless haste. The small child exploded in tearful outrage, while its mother began to beat her fists on the back of the American's camel hair sports jacket. He ignored them both.

No wonder we're known as ugly Americans, Clare lamented, turning her head away in shame and embarrassment at her countryman's behavior. By then he had resorted to tapping a red credit card on the counter with such vehemence that she heard its harsh staccato from fifteen feet away.

Creating her own line at the extreme right of the ticket counter, Clare became aware that one of the other passengers had taken his place behind her. A few other travelers fell in behind him.

Clare couldn't resist watching the altercation that continued to her left. The American man was shouting his important credentials to the perspiring ticket agent. The mother, having abandoned her futile physical assault, scooped up her wailing baby and resorted to verbal invective—in Spanish, thank goodness. Clare could tell from the sudden silence of the crowd that the woman's vocabulary was both extensive and imaginative; it drew coos of admiration mixed with gasps of shock from the fascinated onlookers. The vilification continued in high-pitched Spanish that cut the air like a knife. Yet the woman had no effect on the American until she loosed her major weapon: a short, ugly Anglo-Saxon noun that brought a crimson flush to the man's ears.

But apparently the American knew an appropriate retort in Spanish, for he turned and spat it at her. At that, the crowd began to babble as it surged forward. It was one thing, barely tolerable, to see a baby pushed to the floor; quite another to hear its mother's supposed indecent means of employment shouted in public. Clare wondered if there was going to be a riot, and a sudden assault of panic paralyzed her. With her back against the wall, there was nowhere to run if the frustrated crowd turned ugly.

"He'll get his seats for certain now," said a familiar voice at her side.

"What?" She turned to see Michael Duffy standing directly behind her in line. Her mouth fell open in surprise.

"I said he'll get what he wants now," he said with a smile. "They'll give the man the last two seats just to get rid of him. It's always the squeaky wheel that gets the oil. Haven't you noticed?" He nodded his head toward the tall American. Her gaze followed, only to see the ticket agent hastily writing on the man's and his wife's boarding passes and directing him toward the gate.

"How right you are. And what an awful comment on our society," Clare added. She was about to ask Michael what had brought him to the airport; hadn't he asked her to spend the day with him? But his words had made her think ruefully of Jonas. Certainly Jonas always got what he wanted by dint of his obnoxious behavior, which badgered everyone around him to compliance, if only to buy a bit of peace. What was it her mother had always said? *You'll catch more flies with honey than vinegar.* A nice sentiment, perhaps, but totally unrealistic in a world where passengers were bumped, where reserved tables in chic restaurants were conveniently given to others, where husbands ran roughshod over submissive women. Perhaps the lesson had been wrong; certainly it hadn't made her life—or Emily's—any easier.

"You look a bit peaked, Clare."

She laughed. "Peaked! What a word! What a morning!"

"I assume you're on your way to New York."

She nodded.

"Look, there's no sense in both of us standing here in line. Why don't you give me your ticket, and I'll take care of everything. There's a restaurant upstairs on the second floor where you can have some breakfast. I'll join you as soon as the arrangements for tomorrow are made."

Clare hesitated. There was no question that she wanted to sit down; her legs still felt shaky after the horrible taxi ride to the airport. And she wouldn't mind some coffee and one of those delicious Mexican rolls—what were they called again? *Birotes*, that was it.

"Go on," he added kindly. "I've been in this pickle before."

"Thank you, I will take you up on your offer, but please make certain the connecting flight arrives early enough for me to catch a limousine to Connecticut. I have no other way to get home."

"Don't worry about getting home. I left my car at Kennedy. I'll give you a ride."

She pointed out her luggage to Michael, picked up her carry-on bag and made her way in the direction he had indicated. She was grateful for the escalator; she didn't think her weak knees would have carried her up the stairs.

The waitress had filled her coffee cup twice before Michael arrived at the second-floor restaurant. Pretending not to, Clare watched as he approached her table by the window. His jacket was a double-breasted dark blue with gold-colored buttons, and it fit him well. Around his neck, below the open collar of his shirt, he had tied, ascot style, a red paisley silk scarf. The combination made him look well-dressed, affluent and distinguished. For the first time she realized that his light brown hair had a slight curl to it that she liked. Funny, the night before she hadn't noticed the way it fell in a gentle wave. Yes, he seemed more handsome than he had the previous evening. She wondered if the surprise of seeing him, if his unexpected gallantry, had colored her judgment. Or maybe he had always been as attractive as he was that morning, and the previous evening's discomfort had made her unappreciative.

"Table with a view," he said with a laugh as he took the seat opposite her. His face was actually handsome when he smiled. Not in a conventional sense, not like a male model's, but he was a man whose features were well-proportioned and pleasing to the eye. She hadn't realized how good-looking he actually was. She imagined he had been a winning young boy, the kind of kid who wore his baseball cap sideways and carried a slingshot in his back pocket, much to the disgust of the neighbors.

"I'll say," she agreed. There was no view. Although the sky had lightened, the runways were covered with fog, and they could see barely ten feet from the building.

A waitress took Michael's order and left them alone.

"What an odious man!" Clare said, thinking back on the scene at the ticket counter. "Did you see him push that child to the floor?" Now that the excitement had died, she felt ill at ease, remembering that she had left Michael Duffy on not-too-friendly terms the previous evening. She fussed with the place setting on the table, then looked out the window. "But I have a feeling he won't be gloating in an hour or so. Do you realize this airport is totally socked in? He may have got the last two seats, but that plane's not going anywhere for a while."

"Sure, they'll sit on the runway for two hours, he'll miss his connection in Texas, and he'll be out in the cold when he asks for a hotel room. 'Act of God,' they'll tell him. He'll be furious."

"Serves him right."

"I agree," Michael replied. "The fog comes up often in the winter, but only in the lowlands near the airport. The city will be clear. What are you doing here? I thought you were going to Lake Chapala today."

Clare looked down at her hands. "Well, I got to thinking about what you said, and I decided to return to New York. I guess I owe you an apology. I shouldn't have taken offense at your words last night. I came to the conclusion that I don't have to suffer Jonas, even if Emily does. And what about you? You weren't planning to go home today, were you?"

"I . . . I had a call from my office," he said quickly.

"An emergency?"

"Ah . . . yes. There was an accident in one of the labs. Probably not too serious, but one never knows." His face flushed slightly, and his eyes slid away to stare at the fog. After a moment he said, "Do you realize we have the whole day to look around the city? I can show you some interesting things, if you're willing."

Why not? she thought. What else would she do until the following morning? Michael Duffy was an attractive man, not to mention very self-assured, and whatever arrangements he had made, his ability to handle the unfortunate situation had saved her a lot of trouble. She wasn't accustomed to making her own travel arrangements; she wasn't accustomed to caring for herself at all. That was one of the character weaknesses she had determined to change after her divorce. She thought back with discomfort on the paralyzing panic that had overtaken her in the airport terminal and realized that she couldn't imagine Michael's being frightened into inaction. She hadn't yet thanked him properly.

"I...I really appreciate what you did down there, Michael. I was worried about how I'd handle the situation," she admitted.

"All in a day's work," he replied easily. His blue eyes twinkled with laughter. "Saving a damsel in distress."

Clare laughed, too, and sat back in her chair. "I'd love to spend the day with you," she replied. "What shall we do?"

"First let me tell you about the arrangements I've made. We're confirmed on tomorrow's flight. The airline will put us up in a hotel overnight—"

"Not the Tapatio, I hope."

"Oh, no. I requested the Hotel Frances, a small colonial hotel with lots of atmosphere, right in the center of the city. The Tapatio is rather sanitized, don't you think? You could be anyplace in the world in a hotel like that. I prefer a place with a Mexican atmosphere. It's probably a bit shabby, but it has *ambiente*, as they say here."

Clare wondered why he had stayed at the Tapatio if he preferred the other. But maybe he hadn't. Maybe he'd only been there for dinner and dancing. She would have asked him about it, but the waitress came with his order, and he began to eat. He had ordered *huevos rancheros*, two eggs on a corn tortilla, smothered in a red chili sauce that Clare knew from experience was very, very spicy.

"The airline agreed to pay for our meals, including this one, and our taxis in and out of town. We also got a big fat compensation check."

"We did?" Her eyes opened in surprise.

"Yes. Double your ticket value." He reached into an inside pocket of his jacket and handed Clare her ticket, baggage claim checks and a check made out to her.

"Why?"

"Because they bumped us. They can't do that without compensating you. That's the law."

"But I checked in late. The travel agent warned me to be here at six, but because of the fog I was delayed.'

"I doubt they could have accommodated you even if you had arrived at five-thirty. I was here before six, and believe me, the line didn't move two feet."

As Michael spoke, Clare decided that if Schoenfeld-Loewe had called him in the middle of the night to tell him about a laboratory emergency, the problem must be a serious one, clearly too serious to be discussed lightly with a woman he barely knew. Yet he seemed so calm, a man whom little bothered. She herself wouldn't have been too pleased to be summoned back to Connecticut, bumped from a plane and saddled with the problems of a virtual stranger.

She watched him butter a piece of toast. He had nice hands, she noticed, and she liked the way his hair grew, a little curly, a little bit disordered, although he had tried to slick it down and make it behave. It would be better if he grew it longer, she thought, but maybe patients preferred their doctors to be conservative. Then she remembered that he didn't have any patients; he was in research. Anyway, all the men she had met on the East Coast wore their hair shorter than Californians. Since her own hair was as straight as a poker, she had always been a bit envious of those blessed with a natural wave.

She placed the papers he had given her into her purse, thinking how nice it was that everything was arranged. She easily saw that he was a man a woman could trust to take care of things.

"You realize I'll have to give the check to Jonas. He bought my ticket for me."

"What did you tell him and your sister?"

"Only that I was going back to New York. I didn't actually tell them, I left Emily a note."

"Afraid there would be a scene?"

"Well, you know Jonas," she replied. Michael's expression was noncommittal, but she didn't want to get too personal with him, most especially since they would be spending the day together and the night in the same hotel. She hoped he wasn't assuming that she would... Just because he had made the arrangements... She wondered if he would try to seduce her, and the thought brought two spots of color to her cheeks. At the same moment she heard a telltale rushing in her ears. *Don't blush*, she commanded herself. Oh, it was so hard to be divorced and to begin the single life all over again. One really lost the knack, and the world had changed so much during the six years of her marriage. Today everyone was so liberal, so sexually available, so...so... She felt like an old fuddy-duddy at times, but her standards were her standards, and she couldn't pretend she was someone she wasn't.

"What are you thinking about? You have quite a scowl on your face, Clare." His blue eyes studied her mercilessly.

Clare felt her cheeks flash crimson. "Oh, just about Jonas," she lied. "He *does* have a temper!"

"You can't give him this check, you know. If you do, he and Emily will know you spent another day in town and didn't tell them. Then they *will* be insulted."

"I never thought of that. You're right," she agreed.

"Salt it away for an emergency. Anyway, you earned it. Or you will."

"What a strange idea," she said, but she spoke lightly. Did he mean because of the inconvenience of postponing her trip? Or was he referring to her relationship with Jonas and Emily? She hoped he didn't mean anything else by the casual remark.

Michael smiled enigmatically and picked up his cup of coffee, which he sipped slowly, all the while watching Clare's face. Clare liked the way the skin around his eyes crinkled when he smiled. She liked the shadows in his blue eyes, the gradations of color she saw there. In fact, she was beginning to like him very much.

AN HOUR LATER Clare stood in the old-fashioned, colonnaded lobby of the Hotel Frances. She was still in awe of the contrast between the noisy streets outside and the colonial atmosphere, faded but still splendid, of the hotel's enclosed courtyard, ornamented with blue and white tiles and accented with carved wooden balustrades. In the middle of the quiet lobby a marble fountain played melodically.

While Michael made the arrangements for their rooms, she sat on a heavily carved wooden chair that she was certain was an antique. The hotel was built Spanish-style, in a gallery with open halls surrounding the space that overlooked the lobby. Glass now covered the roof, but she guessed that the center of the building had been open to the air in the past. After the heat of the streets, the coolness and the shadowy gloom inside the hotel were pleasantly welcome.

"We'll have to walk," Michael told her. "The elevator doesn't work, and as far as I can determine, it never has. Ah, Mexico."

"This is what I thought the country would be like," she said when they followed a bellhop up curving stairs fashioned of hand-carved granite slabs that had been worn smooth over the years. They climbed to the third floor. "It's like going back to the last century."

Michael turned and smiled at her. "No, the one before, the eighteenth century. This was the palace of a Spanish viceroy. And here's your room."

The bellboy opened a tall wood door to reveal a small suite with a sitting room so tiny it was little more than an anteroom. Victorian furniture—not the correct period for an eighteenth-century palace, but appropriate in scale to the twelve-foot ceiling of the room—crowded the tiny space. In the bedroom itself, a high double bed sat on a dais, its head surrounded by heavy red-velvet hangings that extended to the tile floor. On the far side of the bed, floor-to-ceiling French doors led to a small balcony that overlooked the roofs of colonial buildings in the old sector of the city. A heavy bell tolled mournfully in the distance, calling the faithful to church. Crossing to the window, Clare imagined that, except for the electricity wires, the city had not changed since the days when the Spanish had ruled Mexico. The street below her had been permanently closed to traffic, and pedestrians strolled on its cobbled surface.

"I *love* this! I wish we'd stayed here before instead of at that modern place." But even as she spoke, she imagined that Jonas would hate the Frances, calling it austere and shabby and hopelessly out-of-date. No ice machines, no room service, no wall-to-wall carpets. Yes, the hotel lacked modern amenities, but it was so romantic and so evocative of another era that its shortcomings paled to nothing in Clare's mind.

"Why don't you get settled here and I'll pick you up in half an hour," Michael suggested. "That'll give me a chance to rent a car and map out our itinerary for the rest of the day."

"Fine," she replied. Michael and the bellhop left, and Clare hung two dresses in a tall armoire that dominated one wall of the bedroom. She wandered into the bathroom to inspect an enormous claw-footed bathtub with polished brass taps and a cloudy, full-length beveled mirror, its glass crazed with a thousand tiny spidered lines, in an ornately carved frame. In the sitting room she discovered a small refrigerator, its two shelves stocked with soft drinks, wine and snacks, all of which were available to her on the honor system. She sat down on the stiff, high-backed couch—not too comfortable, she admitted as its horsehair stuffing crackled beneath her weight, but nice. She wished she were wearing a long dress with a bustle, and a mantilla with one of those wildly ornate combs Spanish ladies used to put in their hair. She would need a fan, too.

She was still seated on the sofa, allowing her imagination to transport her back a hundred or more years, when Michael returned for her twenty minutes later. He had changed into a short-sleeved cotton knit shirt, and his hair was wet, as if he had combed it again to tame its slight wave. His efforts were unsuccessful, however. Again she was tempted to tell him to grow his hair a bit longer and to let it curl, but she said nothing. Such a remark was too personal to utter to a man she had known for so short a time.

"How's your room?" she asked him, immediately regretting the impulse. He would probably invite her to inspect it.

"All right. Ordinary, really, not a suite like this one. I've got a car, so shall we go?"

Clare grabbed her purse and they made their way back to the lobby. Outside on the street, a new Ford awaited them.

"I thought we'd see the main market first, since it's only a short drive from here," he said. "It's called the Libertad, and thousands of people still shop there, although supermarkets have really replaced the function of the market, especially in the suburbs."

They left the car on the street, something he told her was impossible to do on a weekday, and entered the market. The sour smell of rotting fruit and fresh meat smothered Clare's senses as soon as they went through the large open door. She tried not to wrinkle her nose as they walked through narrow aisles where butchered carcasses hung on all sides.

"You thought meat always came wrapped in plastic,

didn't you, Clare?'' His hand was firm and warm on her elbow as they negotiated one particularly crowded aisle where women dressed in Indian costume bargained in shrill voices for cuts of beef that Clare had never seen before.

"You read my mind," she agreed.

"Be happy this isn't the fish market. That's interesting only during Lent. Come over this way to see the produce—it doesn't smell as bad."

Suddenly they were in a wider aisle illuminated by muted green sunlight that filtered through a wavy plastic skylight high above. As they walked through passages lined with open bins, he explained the various fruits for sale—cactus, guava, nutmeg melon—each one strange to Clare's eyes.

Michael stopped and lifted a small green vegetable covered with spiky hairs. "This is a prickly pear. And this," he said, picking up an ugly brown thing, in size halfway between seed and fruit, "this is a tamarind. It's made into candy or can be crushed for an unusual beverage."

"If it tastes anything like it looks, tamarind juice must be very unusual indeed," she replied. "How do you know so much about these things, Michael?"

He smiled at some faraway memory. "Clare, when I was in med school here, I was so poor I couldn't even afford a cook—they were only about twenty dollars a month in those days—and I had to learn to cook or starve. I was forced to eat like a native, to shop here in the main market, where the prices are about half that of the chain stores. You know those cute little Italian restaurants in Greenwich Village with a dripping candle in a bottle on the table, the kind of place people always look back on fondly while they reminisce about how poor they were in the old days?"

She nodded. She and her husband had patronized just that type of place while he was in law school; it was all she had been able to afford on her meager salary as a book-keeper. Clare still remembered the delicious aroma of food that she hadn't been forced to cook herself after a long day at the office. She also remembered coming home from work and opening the door to the inevitable mess Teddy left in the apartment. No smell of dinner cooking, no dishes set on the table, dirty laundry on the floor of the tiny bedroom, Teddy stretched out on the couch sound asleep.

A sinking feeling, accompanied by a familiar, swallowed anger now muted by the passage of time, filled her breast. "Had to study, babe," he would say on a good day, and his eyes would twinkle in the special way that had first attracted Clare to him. On a bad day, a day she dared to complain that she worked eight hours and commuted two on the bus so the car would be at Teddy's disposal, he'd say, "Your job is nothing, nothing! For God's sake, Clare, I'm in law school! What I'm doing is important, competitive. I have to have my wits about me or else I'll be left in the dust. Not everyone passes law school, you know. If they did, every Tom, Dick and Harry would be a lawyer already. I can't be bothered with shopping and cooking. That's women's work!" And fool that she was, she saw his argument, she swallowed the anger, and she cooked dinner. She should have known then what life with Teddy was going to be like.

"Well, on a really grand occasion," Michael was saying, "I would have dinner at a little stand-up taco stand in my neighborhood. Four kinds of tacos, a glass of tamarind juice and a paper napkin for thirty-five cents. That was a big night out for me, usually enjoyed when I couldn't stand my own cooking anymore!"

Why hadn't she stood up to Teddy in those days? Why hadn't she pointed out that her job fed them, housed them, clothed them? Why hadn't she forced him to participate in running the house? What a doormat she had been! What a fool!

"Clare, are you all right?"

She blinked her eyes and stared at Michael Duffy as if he were a stranger. "What?"

"You're a million miles away, Clare. What's wrong?"

She ran an open hand down the side of one cheek. Her fingers were as cold as ice. "Was I? I'm sorry, Michael. It's. . .it's the heat and the smell in here, I guess. I think I need some fresh air."

"It *is* pretty overwhelming," he agreed. "Especially for a gringo's nose. Let's go, then. The rest of the market is pretty dull at that: cheap shoes, horrible gimmicks for tourists—like stuffed iguanas. I thought you might be interested in how the other half lives."

"The other half? I *am* interested in the market," she insisted. "But don't get me mixed up with my sister and her husband. I'm the poor branch of the family. I haven't a cent to my name."

"Sure," he said, with thinly veiled sarcasm.

"I don't like the way you said that, Michael." Clare's quick retort surprised even herself. He must have been *very* poor when he was young, she thought. Clearly he had a terrific hang-up about money, especially other people's money. "I was Jonas and Emily's guest here in Mexico. My usual idea of a vacation is taking a sick day from work. I'm flat broke myself." She said the words almost with pride, inwardly laughing that she would ever brag to anyone that she had nothing. How life had changed for her!

"Okay, I'm sorry," he answered, immediately confirming her speculation with his following words. "When you come from nothing, it's hard to let go of your resentment of the rich."

"Emily and I were never rich," she explained. "We come from a perfectly ordinary middle-class family. Our father was in minor, and I mean minor, management in the telephone company. Our mother never worked; it just wasn't done. We were brought up in a small town, we went to a local junior college. . . . Emily made a fortunate marriage, that's all." "Fortunate" was not the correct word, Clare realized as soon as it left her mouth. "Well, she married someone with more money than *we* ever saw before."

"And you?"

"Me?"

"Whom did you marry?"

"A law student."

"That's all, a law student?"

They were outside the market now, standing ten feet away from a lovely fountain that splashed musically and caught the sparkle of sunlight. He had dropped his hold on her elbow, and she missed the warmth of his hand, but the personal turn the conversation had again taken agitated her, even though she felt a need to explain herself and distance her life from Emily's. A gust of wind blew minute droplets of water that showered like a thousand diamond chips from the fountain to where they stood, cooling Clare and reminding her that the Moors had invented the fountain a thousand years before for just such a purpose.

"Well, eventually he became a lawyer," she added reluctantly.

"How come you're divorced now?"

"You don't want to hear such a boring story, Michael. Even I don't want to hear it. That's like bending someone's ear about your operation."

"I guess you're right," he agreed with a smile. "C'mon, we'll walk around downtown for a while." Again he took her elbow, dropped it, and took her hand instead. Clare fell into step beside him, noticing immediately that their strides matched in a most comfortable way.

They ambled through the main square of the city, past a theater he told her was modeled after La Scala opera house in Milan, and under seemingly endless vaulted arches that formed an arcade around the main square. In this protected passage were tucked scores of tiny shops, all closed now, since it was Sunday. After a walking tour of downtown, Michael showed her two baroque churches, so tiny they seemed to be private chapels. He tried to teach her the pronunciation of their names, but Clare found the words too difficult.

"Where would you like to have lunch?" he asked her. "I know a place with wonderful violin music. It's not too far from here."

"Frankly, I'd like to try your taco restaurant, the one with four tacos and a glass of tamarind juice for thirty-five cents." *There, you reverse snob,* she said to herself, *try that one on for size.*

"You would?" His blue eyes gazed into hers. There was no hiding the surprise on his face, but there was something else there, too. Something more intense, more moving, than what she expected to elicit from the simple conciliatory words she had uttered. Within her breast, Clare felt her heart turn over in a most unfamiliar way.

"That's a deal."

The open-air taco stand was about twenty minutes away by car, located in a quiet residential neighborhood near the previous site of the medical school. Michael pointed it out to her, explaining that the school had moved to new and modern quarters after Jonas's and his time there. The taco stand huddled under a canvas shelter, its crude reality even worse than Michael's description had implied; but the tacos were delicious, so small and so succulent that Clare ate six of them.

"If the truth be told, I'm not crazy about tamarind juice. The tacos, though, were terrific," she said when they had returned to the car and were once again driving toward the downtown area. "And now I'd like a siesta." The late hour of the meal they had eaten, the heat and the walking had taken their toll on her energy, and she understood why everything came to a halt in the afternoon in Guadalajara. She was surprised to see it was after five by the time he pulled the car up in front of the Hotel Frances.

They made a date to meet for dinner in the lobby at eight.

Clare slept for an hour, then read a book about Mexican painters she had bought at the Orozco Museum several days before. Every so often she gazed at the telephone and wondered if she should call Emily, who would probably be trying to reach her in Greenwich, but she finally decided not to bother. If she called now, she would certainly have to explain that she was still in Guadalajara, and she had no desire to do that.

For dinner, she chose to wear the finest dress she had brought with her, a black silk with a clinging bodice and full skirt. Undulating ruffles at the wrists and around the hem were the dress's only relief from severity. Gazing at herself critically in the bathroom mirror, she knew the dress, which she had bought only at Emily's persistent urging, had been the right purchase, even though its price was too extravagant for her budget. It fit perfectly, and the tight bodice accentuated her small but rounded breasts. The effect was ladylike, yet alluring. She hoped that Michael would like the way she looked.

Before she left the suite, she returned to the bathroom and sprayed an extra spurt of her favorite perfume behind each ear. An inner voice told Clare that tonight was going to be special, that in an as-yet-undefined manner her past was behind her and a new life was beginning. She felt poised on the edge of an adventure. The feeling, inchoate and very, very tenuous, was nearly unconscious, but it was strong enough to be acknowledged. Nothing concrete had transpired to signal the change she knew was evolving within her, but in some confusing way Michael Duffy was responsible for it.

Chapter Three

At eight o'clock sharp, Clare descended the stairs to the lobby. She stood a bit straighter and walked a bit more sedately than usual, imagining herself a Spanish vicereine on her way to a ball on the first floor of her own palace. She knew her thoughts were silly, but there was something so atmospheric about the old hotel that she couldn't help herself.

There he was at the bottom of the stairs, leaning against a pillar with his hands in the pockets of his slacks. She went up to him and impulsively took his arm. "Can we eat here, Michael? I love this place."

"Done, señorita," he said, leading her to a corner table half hidden by potted palms and stone pillars. At Clare's request, he ordered, in Spanish, a dinner of Mexican specialties. Fried squash blossoms in warm, home-made flour tortillas as soft and plump as bread fresh from the oven were followed by chicken *mole poblano*, which he told her took three days to make and contained chocolate. Clare could discern no taste of chocolate whatsoever in the smooth brown sauce. For dessert, they ate a candied fruit that he finally admitted, after Clare pronounced it delicious, was fresh tamarind—seeded, softened and rolled in sugar and cinnamon.

After dinner they rode in an open cabriolet through the cobblestone main square, permanently closed to motor traffic and now artfully lighted to show to advantage the architectural splendors of what in Mexico's colonial past had been the capital of Nueva Galicia. Downtown was nearly deserted on this quiet Sunday night. Without the noise of traffic, Clare could again imagine herself as an eighteenth-century Spanish lady riding with a romantic gentleman. She slipped her arm through Michael's and gave herself over to a lazy contentment evoked by the monotonous clip-clop of the horse's hooves.

"My name is Elena, the year is eighteen-fourteen, and you are a Spanish grandee. We're coming home from the opera at the Degollado Theater," she said. "No, no— you're Zorro, a nobleman disguised as a bandit, and you're taking me away from the evil duke who has claimed me. We're riding in your carriage trimmed with silver."

Michael took Clare's hand between both of his, laughing at her fantasies. "I hate to tell you, but the theater didn't exist until at least fifty years later, and you would have had a chaperone, a dueña, with you. No Spanish lady—no Mexican lady, for that matter—was ever alone with a man—not until she was married to him."

"You're too practical, Michael. And a chaperone! Such a custom must have inhibited the rites of courtship a bit." She laughed. "Wait, what about Don Juan? He must have been alone with the ladies."

"But he is punished for his sin, if you recall, consumed by the fires of hell when he keeps a date to meet the statue of a dead man in a cemetery."

"No, I didn't know that," Clare admitted. "All I know is that Don Juan is supposed to represent the degenerate roué in literature. I've never actually read *Don Juan*."

"Offhand I can think of at least half a dozen versions— Byron, Shaw and Mozart among them, and the original in Spanish by Tirso de Molina. That's the one I was actually thinking of."

"You're the most unusual doctor I ever met!" Clare exclaimed. "I thought doctors read only the financial pages of *The New York Times*."

"You're awfully hard on the profession, aren't you? What did doctors ever do to you?"

"To me, nothing," she admitted. "My experience with doctors consists of a general physical now and again, nothing more. I was thinking of Jonas and Emily's crowd. When they get together, they talk about their investments and their latest trips to Bermuda or Sun Valley. I've never heard one of them discuss an idea, a book or a patient. But you aren't like them, Michael. You're their exact opposite. Why is that, do you suppose?"

"Everyone's different," he said. "Anyway, I'm not part of your fancy Greenwich crowd."

"There you go again. I *told* you I'm not even on the fringes of that crowd." Clare heard her voice rise a note or two in irritation and determined to change the subject immediately. After such a thoroughly pleasant evening, it seemed a shame to ruin it by returning to the persistently unpleasant topic of their imagined economic differences.

The cabriolet pulled up in front of the Hotel Frances, and Michael helped Clare down its steep drop to the street. She watched him pay the driver, admiring his facility in Spanish and his easy understanding of the Mexican currency, which still confused her.

He took her arm and led her into the hotel. As they climbed the stairs, she withdrew a large old-fashioned room key from her clutch purse and asked him, "What made you go into research? Didn't you want your own practice?"

"Yes, I did, but I couldn't afford to set one up. And I couldn't afford to spend the extra time specializing that a doctor needs." There was no note of regret in Michael's voice, however.

"But aren't there group practices like those medical cooperatives? You go to work for a salary paid by the cooperative.'' They were nearing her room. Outside her door, he stopped and leaned casually against the wall.

"Yes, that's true now, but it wasn't true ten or fifteen years ago. Anyway, everyone is a specialist these days, even in cooperatives.''

"So you went into research by default? What a shame. You needed a wife to support you while you studied. Then you could have done what you wanted, and you wouldn't have any regrets today.''

"Is that what you did, Clare? Supported your husband?''

"Yes,'' she admitted. "Yes, that's what I did.''

"And now he's a successful lawyer, while you have nothing to show for your time and trouble.''

"Not so successful. You see, he. . .'' On the brink of an explanation, Clare hesitated, then looked directly at Michael's face. "Why do you always deflect the conversation back to me? Why don't you want to talk about your past?''

"And why don't you?'' he countered. "What's the big secret?''

"Because today is today. There's no sense regretting the past. I'm tired of thinking about it. And besides, my past is boring!''

"And painful, I wager.''

"Yes, that's true. It was, that is, but I don't think about it much anymore.''

"Let's talk about us instead.'' His voice lowered, changing from its normal tone to a new and husky intensity.

"Us?''

Before she knew what was happening, he had slipped his arms around Clare's waist and pulled her toward him. His sudden move surprised her, and she lost her balance, teetering uncertainly on the high heels of her shoes. Involuntarily she leaned against him, one open palm coming to rest on the smooth cotton of his white shirt. His chest was warm and solid, the beat of his heart strong but irregular beneath her hand.

"Michael..."

He buried his lips on her neck. She felt them nibble on the sensitive skin there, and she stiffened. "Michael, I've had a lovely day, but I'd like to say good night now."

"Clare, I need you and want you. You want me, too— admit it." The words were a hoarse whisper, his breathing as irregular as his heartbeat. He drew her so close to him that she could not avoid the sudden stirring maleness of his body against hers.

"Michael, please..." She pushed against his chest with her open palm, raising the hand that held the key and her clutch purse to keep his arm from enfolding her. The key dug into the flesh of her fingers. "You're out of order—"

His lips covered hers, silencing the words. He had her at a disadvantage, his power and girth exceeding hers, his arms firmly around her, while she was off balance and trapped by him, her head thrust back by the passion of his unexpected kiss. His tongue stroked the stiff contours of her lips, increasing its pressure until her unyielding lips were forced to open beneath it, and its tip entered her mouth and searched it intimately. Clare sought to deny the warmth that filled her body at his touch; she refused to admit that her legs were threatening to buckle beneath her, that her own breathing was becoming as irregular as his.

She moved her hands to grasp his sleeves in a vain attempt to pull him away. At the same time he raised his palms to cover her cheeks, holding her face firmly while he continued to kiss her for a seemingly endless moment. Finally he took his mouth from hers, and she inhaled unevenly.

"Invite me into your room," he said, the words low

and hoarse, gravelly, nearly a whisper. "Let me come in. Let me make love to you."

No, she wasn't ready, she would probably never be ready. Why did he have to push himself on her so unexpectedly? Everything had been wonderful until his unwelcome move. "Certainly not!" she exclaimed, breaking away from the now gentle grasp of his hands on her face. "Thank you for a lovely day. Thank you for dinner, but it's time to say good night now. We have to be at the airport at six o'clock." She turned, swiftly unlocking the door to her room with trembling fingers that fumbled disobediently, infuriating her with their clumsiness. Rushing inside, she slammed the heavy door behind her and leaned against it, still trying to catch her breath.

"Good night, Clare," he called softly from the hall.

Clare didn't answer. She stood for a moment, listening to the thump of her heart. In a moment his footsteps echoed on the tile floor as he went to his room.

THERE WAS NO FOG the next morning, and the plane to Dallas, with Clare and Michael safely aboard, departed on time. When the seat belt sign went off, Clare looked around and recognized several of the passengers who had been bumped from the plane on Sunday. In the strong morning light, she thought that Michael looked tired, although it hadn't been that late when she had bidden him good night the previous evening. She had a window seat, and Michael the seat by the aisle. The one between them held her purse and a selection of magazines he had purchased at the airport. They had been courteous but not particularly friendly to each other during the long drive to the airport and the wait to board the plane.

"Clare, about last night..." he began as soon as the plane was in the air.

"Yes?" Oh, Lord, she didn't want to talk about last night. He didn't seem angry, but it was so hard to tell; she barely knew Michael Duffy, although they had spent a day together. He was probably going to tell her that she was hopelessly old-fashioned, that most women these days went to bed as a matter of course with a man who had just bought them dinner. She had heard that line already; heaven knew she had heard it enough from the first men she had gone out with after the divorce. In fact, that sentiment was one of the main reasons she had decided not to date for a while. Men expected so much from a woman now. Certainly life had been simpler before she married Teddy, hadn't it? *Was* she hopelessly old-fashioned?

She held her breath and waited for him to speak. She hated postmortems; why did Michael want to discuss last night at all? Usually a man would simply never call again after she turned him down, but this time she was locked into a jet, seated next to a man she had rejected. Clare gripped her hands together and held her breath.

"I want to apologize. I came on too strong, I guess." He stared straight ahead, which must have made it easier for him to explain himself to her. It certainly made it easier for her to listen.

So he wasn't going to give her a hard time. She exhaled her relief. "That's all right, Michael. You didn't do anything wrong."

"No, really," he continued. "You looked so beautiful in that dress, you moved so gracefully...you smelled so good. You're nothing like what I expected you to be. I couldn't help myself. It's not like me to rush a woman like that, and I'm sorry."

"You're used to giving your women a little time, is that it?" Clare teased him. What a relief to receive an apology! And here she thought she was the one who had done something wrong. She no longer had to be embarrassed that she had been unable to stop thinking about him the night before while she searched unsuccessfully for the sleep that had eluded her for hours.

"Now you make me sound like a man who has a hundred women in his life. I assure you it's not true." He sounded serious and a bit stuffy.

Clare decided to ignore the comment. "How did you expect me to be?"

"Very Greenwich, Connecticut," he replied immediately. "Snobby, pretty, interested in where people went to school, in how much money they have in the bank, in whether they buy their clothes from J. Press or Brooks Brothers. I expected you only went out with men who had little dead sheep hanging on their breast pockets, like the Brooks Brothers logo."

"One step up from the alligators, you mean?"

"In certain circles."

"You're describing Jonas Hahn to a T. Or to a dead sheep."

"I know I am. I don't shop at J. Press, I went to totally undistinguished schools, and I've hardly a penny in the bank, Clare."

"I've told you before that I'm the poor relation, Michael."

"I like you better this way," he said. Then he picked up everything on the seat between them and awkwardly moved over next to her. He took her hand almost shyly, and she allowed his hand to close over hers.

"I'm glad you do," she said. "I really am. I like you, too, and I'd like to start off on a new footing. Yesterday we seemed to run into a few hurdles. In fact, since the first night we met." Suddenly it was simple to talk to him. Everything was going to be very simple.

She freely acknowledged the warmth that spread through her body at the touch of his hand, and she knew what that warmth signified. He had been right last night—oh, how right he had been! Yes, she wanted him. Yes, she would have an affair with Michael Duffy, she realized, but on her own terms, in her own good time. She was very attracted to him; what was more, his apology had endeared him to her as nothing else could have done. She gave his hand a squeeze and was pleased to see an answering flicker in his blue eyes. Merely admitting to herself that she wanted to sleep with this man set off a clamor within Clare's breast. She dropped her gaze to the back of his hand, uncertain that she wanted him to read the emotions racing through her blood.

"We did get off to a bad start, and my big mouth is to blame. Let me tell you how I see you, Clare."

"Will it hurt?" Clare looked up from his hand into blue eyes that seemed to soften with affection. Blue eyes, kind eyes . . . but eyes without dreams.

"I don't think so. First of all, you have an active imagination. A fantasy life—"

"Oh, no, Michael. I'm a trained accountant. I assure you there's nothing more prosaic in the world." She blushed as she denied the truth of his words. He was right, of course. All that talk about Spanish grandees and Zorro and palaces of the viceroy. He'd be blind not to have noticed.

"And you're a very private person. People think you're shy, but it's more a reserve than basic shyness."

"That's true." It pleased Clare to know that he had spent time analyzing her.

"You're maternal. You're very maternal toward your sister, did you know that?"

"Yes, but she's older than I am, and she doesn't pay any attention to her kid sister, so I've decided not to be that way anymore. She has to look out for herself, since I can't help her."

"A good decision. Okay, there's more. I see you as a woman who is afraid—"

"To get involved, is that what you were going to say?" The analysis disappointed her, not because it was inaccurate, since it was not, but because it had been so overused. "Really, that's a cliché! I expected more from you, Dr. Duffy. You were doing so well. Are you certain you are what you seem?"

"What do you mean?" he asked quickly.

"Are you certain you're not a psychiatrist?"

He grinned broadly. "No, I'm not a psychiatrist, just a man who prides himself on observing people. But it's true, isn't it? About getting involved, I mean. How long have you been divorced?"

"Eight months. However, we were separated a long time before the divorce, so it's more like two years."

"It's time to get back into circulation. Not all men are like your husband, whatever that was. You have to get over the once-burned-twice-shy attitude you have."

Was it so obvious? His assessment displeased her until she decided that he was wrong. No, he was right about her attitude, but wrong that she wore it on her sleeve. "Do I really come across like that?"

"Oh, Clare. You know you do."

"All right, I know it's time to socialize again," she replied, suddenly serious. "And I've tried, but it's difficult for me. I...I'm simply unable to get used to the new morality. Take last night, for instance. It's not that I don't find you immensely attractive. I *do*. It's only that relationships these days simply go too fast for me. I'd...I'd like to know you better."

"You mean there's a chance for me, after all?"

"Yes, I mean that," she answered after a moment's hesitation. So now the die was cast, and he knew what she was thinking. She wanted to be closer to Michael Duffy; she was, in fact, becoming quite fond of him. Even if he was a doctor, he was totally unlike some of Jonas's boringly egotistical friends.

"Halleluiah!" he said in such a loud voice that Clare blushed, and a man seated in front of them turned around to give Michael a strange look.

Michael cleared his throat and leaned toward Clare. "Let's order champagne," he whispered into her ear. She felt his lips warm and very close to her skin.

"Champagne! It's not even ten o'clock in the morning."

"But what a morning!" He signaled for a flight attendant, who quickly came to their seats and took his order for two splits of champagne, which she delivered almost immediately.

"To us," he said, holding a plastic glass up and toward Clare.

"To the future," she answered. They both sipped, Clare feeling slightly wicked with abandon at the idea of drinking champagne at such an early hour. The bubbles of the wine tickled her nose and the sensitive skin of her upper lip. "A person shouldn't drink in the morning," she added.

"I know. That's how you become a hopeless alcoholic. Your mother told you that, I assume."

"Yes."

"I'm certain if you started drinking champagne before ten in the morning on a daily basis, well, then you'd have a problem. I bet your mother told you a lot of things that don't necessarily apply to your life today."

"It's true," Clare replied.

"Like what?"

"Like 'Your husband is the boss in the family. Do what he asks without question.' Like 'You made your bed, now go lie in it.' Like 'Always be a lady, turn the other cheek, there's a better tomorrow.' What about yours? What did your mother tell you?"

"Oh, plenty!" he said bitterly. " 'You're too big for your own britches. What's wrong with your home? Are you ashamed of us, is that why you want to go away and leave us?' Lots of nice inhibiting ideas guaranteed to give a poor kid the guilts."

"Didn't your parents want you to be a doctor? I should think they would be very proud."

"A doctor? Fat chance!" He laughed harshly. "They didn't even want me to go beyond high school. As it was, I was the first person in my family even to go to college, which they considered an enormous waste of time to begin with. They thought I should get a job on the railroad like my father had and start contributing to the family."

"Where was that? How did you end up in Guadalajara?"

"In Pennsylvania. A little town called Berwick, in coal-mining country. I worked in the mines to get money for college."

"In the mines!" Clare exclaimed, imagining the heavy labor necessary to pay for medical school. "But med school is so expensive."

"Y-yes—that's why I ended up in Guadalajara," he said quickly. "Both tuition and living expenses were cheaper in Mexico. Even if I had been accepted at an American medical school, I couldn't have afforded to go."

Things must have changed drastically in the fifteen or more years since he and Jonas were in school, Clare thought. Jonas was always bragging that the medical school tuition in Guadalajara was the most expensive in the world, conservatively four times the cost of its counterparts in the United States, or even in Florence, Italy, where so many American hopefuls studied medicine. It pleased her to realize that Jonas's braggadocio was out-of-date, that his education had actually been a bargain and not the killing outlay of funds he had claimed.

"Funny, I thought it cost an arm and a leg to attend medical school there—'The Guad,' Jonas calls it. I never realized you had done it on your own. You must have been very determined."

"It was cheap then," Michael insisted. "Everything in Mexico was cheap in those days. They've been bled by inflation during the last two political administrations." He looked away, biting his lips as if he had already said more than he'd intended.

She had meant her words to be complimentary, but she assumed from the way he clammed up that she had offended him. Could he guess what she was actually thinking—that his demeanor, his actions and the way he dressed did not betray the humble origins he claimed? Anyway, it was clear Michael was through discussing his past. He gazed past Clare and out the window, as if to dismiss the subject.

"Parents," she said. "I guess they mean well, but. . ." Suddenly she was thinking of Emily again. How Emily loved her twins, Ian and Kevin! She would do anything for them, anything but what Clare thought was best—to get them, and herself, away from Jonas.

There was a murmur of voices from the forward section of the plane, and Clare became aware of quick movements in the aisle. One, then two, flight attendants hurried forward. She craned across Michael to peer up the aisle to discover what was going on, but she could see little except the backs of the crew.

"I think there's a man lying in the aisle," he said after glancing at the forward commotion.

"Lying in the aisle?"

A disembodied male voice came over the public address system. "This is the captain speaking. Is there a doctor on board? Is any of the passengers a doctor?"

Clare looked quickly at Michael, but he didn't move. His face was turned toward the aisle, and she could see only the strong line of his jaw where a muscle worked.

"Aren't you going to respond?" she whispered.

"No, I can't."

"Is there a doctor aboard? Please identify yourself by means of the call button above your seat." The voice of the captain boomed from the loudspeaker. "A nurse trained in CPR?"

"Why can't you? I don't understand, Michael. They're asking for CPR training—someone's having a heart attack!" She willed him to turn his head toward her. After a long hesitation, he did, but he refused to meet her eyes. His lips were set in a grim, tight line.

"I can't, Clare. Don't ask me to."

"Why not?" He didn't answer her. "What about your oath, Michael? Didn't you promise to help people, never to do anything to hurt them? What kind of doctor are you, anyway?" Her eyes narrowed. She couldn't believe he was sitting so calmly in his seat while, not twenty feet away, a man was lying on the airplane floor and might be dying.

"I'm a research doctor, Clare. Research doctors don't carry malpractice insurance, so there's no way I can help a stranger as a physician. Especially a stranger, Clare. If that man dies, his widow might sue me, bleed me white, and I'd never come back from it. The whole country is crazy to sue doctors these days, don't you know that? I can't afford to take the chance."

Clare was speechless. How she had misread him! He seemed so kind and compassionate, so willing to swallow his pride to apologize to her. She couldn't believe the change that had come over him. When she had partially recovered, she looked him straight in the face. "What I *do* know," she retorted, "is that you're more like Jonas than I thought you were. Your attitude stinks, Michael Duffy. Stinks! If that man dies, I hope you'll never forget it. I'll make certain you find out, too," she added.

"I'm a nurse!" shouted a stout woman seated several rows behind Clare and Michael. "Let me through—I'm a nurse."

"It's all right," he said, patting Clare's hand, which lay forgotten in his. She snatched it away in anger. "Someone else will attend to him."

"Don't patronize me!"

"Clare, you don't understand anything," he said sadly. "I—"

"You're damn right I don't," she said. "Save your explanations, if you will. If I knew CPR, I'd be up there helping him, and you know in your heart *you* ought to be there, not that nurse. Some doctor you are!"

"Shh, keep your voice down," he urged her, but it was too late. The man in front of them turned around again and gave Michael a withering look.

"Clare," he whispered urgently, "Jonas pays more in malpractice insurance than I earn in an entire year. Clare, please listen to me."

"I don't want to hear about it," she said. "Excuse me, I have to go to the ladies' room." She shoved her glass of champagne into his hand, shot out of her seat and climbed over him, trying unsuccessfully not to touch him. She stamped down the aisle toward the rear of the plane.

Inside the dimly lit cubicle, she saw herself in the mirror and was astonished at how she looked. Her cheeks aflame with anger, her hair mussed, she resembled a vengeful harpy. She couldn't remember ever having been so angry with anyone, not even with Teddy in their worst days together. But then, she had never shown Teddy her anger, had barely admitted to herself that her anger existed. A lady didn't. Besides, she had been so afraid that Teddy would leave her if she wasn't nice.

"So what's the problem?" she asked her reflection. "This man is nothing to you." She splashed cold water on her face. With no thought for her makeup, she patted her cheeks dry with some rough paper towels she found in a dispenser to the side of the soap-spotted stainless-steel sink. Thank goodness she hadn't already committed herself to him in some way. That *would* have been awkward. She must learn to follow her instincts, she told herself. There had been something wrong with Michael Duffy right from the start, something a bit out of sorts, something she couldn't quite put her finger on. She should have stayed away from him.

But he had pursued her, hadn't he? She hadn't arranged to meet him in the Guadalajara airport, or to spend a long day together. Well, that was over. She would accept his ride back to Greenwich; it seemed silly to pay twenty dollars to the limousine service and wait around for a car when Michael's awaited him at the New York airport. Then, in Greenwich, she would need a taxi to the house. But after that, she was finished with Michael Duffy.

"WELCOME HOME, Mr. Duffy," the immigration officer in Dallas said. "Welcome home, Mrs. Eckert."

Just behind Michael in line at the glass-walled immigration booth, Clare was gratified that the federal officer had called him "mister"; she knew it drove doctors crazy when their medical degrees were not acknowledged by an adoring public. But a sidelong glance at Michael told her he had barely heard the greeting, and he didn't seem insulted in the slightest.

After immigration, they went through customs. Luckily there was a very short connection for the flight to New York, so Clare didn't have to make conversation with him at the Dallas airport. Their next flight was full and, although they sat next to each other, the presence of another person in the third seat made communication stilted and painful. Clare lost herself in a paperback novel she had purchased in Dallas and did not put it down until the plane landed.

The ride home to Greenwich was made in near-silence. Clare commented once on the new-fallen snow that had been pushed to the sides of the Connecticut Turnpike. As they pulled up to the closed gates of the driveway that led to the Hahn's estate on Long Island Sound, Michael told her that the sick passenger had been taken to a hospital in Dallas, conscious and smiling when the ambulance left the airport. He jumped from the car to open the gates.

"Aren't you happy he's all right?" he asked her on his return. When they reached the house, he turned off the ignition, and the sound of restless waves slapping against the dock behind the house penetrated the uneasy tension of the car.

"That's nice to know, but it doesn't change anything," she answered.

"No, I guess it doesn't. May I call you sometime, Clare?"

"I'm busy, Michael. I can't believe you think there could be anything between us after this morning."

"That's not what you told me on the plane. As a matter of fact, you led me to believe something quite different." There was a new hard edge to his voice, an edge that frightened Clare, but she shook off the fear. The anger that had overcome her on the plane returned and intensified. She had made a mistake about him, that was all. And there was nothing to salvage. If his ego was wounded, well, so be it. She wasn't getting involved with a man who was incapable of reaching out a hand to a fellow human being. She'd had enough of that in her life.

"That was before," she answered. "Before you showed yourself to be selfish and arrogant. I'm just coming out of a marriage with the most selfish, arrogant man alive, and believe me, I have no intention of getting involved with another one. I wasted six years of my life with him, worked myself half to death putting him through law school so we could have a wonderful future together, and he went crazy making hotshot investments behind my back that pushed us into bankruptcy and left us owing a couple of years' salary to the Internal Revenue Service. They took our house and our cars, all my jewelry—even my wedding ring, Michael. The IRS also took my grandmother's engagement ring, the only thing of hers I had! Then, on top of everything, my husband ran off and left me holding the bag. I'm still paying off his debts—never get married in a community property state—and the last thing in the world I need is a selfish man. Do you think I want to live here?'' she shouted, waving her hand in the general direction of the house.

"It looks fabulous to me," he said, glancing around at the exquisitely landscaped grounds that sloped down to a small dock on the Sound. His gaze took in the bleached shingles of the house, a sprawling mansion that boasted seven bedrooms plus servants' quarters, an enormous solarium and a game room larger than Clare's entire apartment above the carriage house.

"I've been taking their charity," she retorted, "and eating my heart out listening to my brother-in-law browbeat his wife and his kids and his servants. It's not nice having to take charity, but what would you know? You're a doctor with a viable career. I'm almost thirty years old, and I have nothing. Not even a decent job." Against her will, Clare burst into tears. She fumbled for the door handle, but Michael put his hand on hers to stay her.

"Did he run off with another woman?"

"Who?"

"Your husband."

"How do I know? I never heard from him again."

"Clare, I'm terribly sorry about what happened on the plane. You really don't understand, but there's nothing I can do about that. Forgive me for offending you. I know how unfeeling I must have looked to you, but I also know that you and I have something very special between us. I hate to see it end this way." He handed her a handkerchief.

"I'm mortified at my outburst," she choked out, taking the cotton square from him. "Oh, Lord." She blew her nose into the handkerchief. "No, don't call me. It would never work, Michael. Thanks for the ride." She opened the door and stood in the snow, oblivious to the cold that penetrated the thin summer shoes she wore, while he left the car. She watched him in silence as he took her luggage from the trunk.

"Where do you want your bags?"

"Just leave them at the bottom of the steps to the carriage house," she said. "Someone will bring them up for me." She didn't want him to know there was no one in the house at the moment. The Hahns' housekeeper, another innocent victim of Jonas's tirades, had quit several weeks before. Although Emily had hired a new one—a fat, friendly woman from Barbados—she was not due to begin her job until the Hahns returned from vacation. Clare would carry her luggage up to her second-floor apartment herself after he had gone.

"Thanks again for the ride," she said tonelessly, watching him trudge through the snow to his car, which was a vintage Volkswagen that had probably been blue at one time but was now faded to a nondescript pale gray.

At the side of the house, there was a clink of metal against metal. The Dobermans! She had completely forgotten about the guard dogs. "Get in the car quickly, Michael," she shouted. "The dogs are loose!" He stopped and turned with a quizzical look on his face, as if he had heard the urgency, but not the sense, of her words.

Two sleek black Dobermans roared around the side of the house. Snarling, they leaped in unison and landed on Michael's chest, knocking him into a snowbank alongside the driveway.

"Stop! Rolf, down! Heidi, down!" Clare screamed their names and ran across the snow. "Down!" She grabbed at Heidi's choke chain. "Down, I say. Get down, there's a good dog." With all her might she pulled Heidi off a cowering Michael. Heidi was the leader of the two.

Rolf was nothing but a cream puff, but if Heidi attacked, he did, too.

Heidi licked Clare's bare hand. Her tail began to wag enthusiastically.

"You'd better get in the car before they change their minds," Clare said, never taking her eyes from the dogs. She fumbled for Rolf's chain. Michael stood up and brushed off snow from his jacket. "They obey me, but they're trained to keep strangers away."

"You certainly have a way with them. They look like killers to me." His voice quavered.

"They're attack-trained. There are a lot of robberies around here, despite the police protection. Jonas likes to protect his possessions."

"I imagine," Michael answered. Before he entered the car, Clare got a glance at his pale face. He might be arrogant and selfish, but no one deserved the scare he had just experienced. She felt a twinge of compassion for him.

The engine caught after two tries, and he nosed the car gently over the brick turnaround in front of the house. At the back of her mind, Clare thought this was probably the most disreputable-looking automobile that had ever graced the front entrance of Jonas's mammoth house. It was probably six months since the VW had been washed, and the entire back was spattered in mud. Someone had wiped off the marker plate, and she could see the word "Virginia," but the numbers were totally illegible.

Both dogs strained at her hands, yanking unmercifully against the choke chains that bit into her fingers. She spoke to them in soothing tones until they quieted. When she was certain Michael had left the grounds, she let them go. They ran to the back of the main house, and Clare returned to the carriage house.

What a waste, she thought. Would she ever see Michael Duffy again?

"Who cares!" she mumbled aloud as she trudged up the stairs to the door of her apartment. A doctor who wouldn't doctor—even if he *was* in research—was as bad as Jonas; worse, perhaps. At least Jonas was practicing medicine. At least Jonas took care of his patients, even if Clare suspected that most of them were spoiled rich women who could afford to purchase thighs that were thinner or breasts that were fuller or a nose that was picked from a photograph in a catalog. Michael Duffy didn't have any patients, and it was clear he was happy with that arrangement.

"I never want to see you again, Michael Duffy," she said. But even as she spoke, she knew they would meet again. The social life of Fairfield County doctors was too inbred for a future meeting to be all but inevitable.

Chapter Four

Nine days of solitude was just the vacation Clare needed. She dismissed the gardener, who had agreed to come by twice a day to care for the Doberman pinschers, and visited the library to borrow the latest espionage thrillers, her favorite type of escapist book. At night she watched old movies on the black-and-white television in the carriage house.

Since coming to stay with her sister, Clare had been keeping the books on a weekly basis for a variety of small businesses located in Greenwich and Stamford. After she had insured her health and paid a minimum toward the enormous debts still outstanding, she had little left of her hourly-rate earnings. Her purchases were minimal: basic cosmetics and a few items for her wardrobe. But every week she'd salted away a fraction toward the day she could afford to move to her own apartment.

Since she had told all her clients that she would be away until the end of February, Clare was able to devote her energy to looking for a full-time job. She owned no car, but Emily's buttercup-yellow Mercedes-Benz station wagon was always at her disposal. She never used the luxury automobile when Emily was around, feeling that borrowing it would place an inconvenience on her sister, whose days were full of errands dictated by Jonas's champagne-and-caviar tastes. Although the bus service in

Greenwich was efficient, if sometimes erratic, waiting in the February wind and snow was agony, so she was relieved to have use of the station wagon in Emily's absence. Clare knew she should buy herself a car soon, maybe even before searching for an apartment; she decided to look for something appropriate at a used-car dealer the following week.

There were jobs available, but none in her specialty, accounting. Nor did they pay enough for her to consider spending forty hours a week locked in an office from where she would be unable to find truly viable employment. Making the rounds of the personnel offices of the many firms located in Stamford's spanking-new buildings depressed and frustrated her. Only one firm, Pierce and Pierce, had a position that offered a future, but Clare didn't think she would get the job. She was not a certified public accountant, although Pierce and Pierce sometimes took on people who were studying for the national test necessary for certification. Unfortunately, she was missing several college credits that would qualify her, and she totally lacked the one-year employment requirement for a C.P.A.

She left the number of Jonas's answering service with the personnel offices. Having no telephone in the guest house was a distinct disadvantage. On the other hand, it had twice saved her from the discomfort of speaking to Michael Duffy, who had called and left messages for her to call him either at a Stamford number, which Clare assumed was his office, or at a New Canaan exchange, where she knew he lived. She might be alone, her ears might sometimes ache from the silence of not speaking to another person, but she was not lonely. She was almost enjoying the winter solitude; and anyway, she didn't want to see Michael Duffy again.

Emily called once, also leaving a message with the answering service. "Tell Mrs. Eckert that I understand, and

I hope she is well." The words were formal because they were filtered through a stranger, but Clare had smiled, knowing Emily had meant just what she said. Emily had always been the forgive-and-forget type, one of her very best qualities, and one that she needed in order to live with Jonas Hahn.

During the short winter afternoons Clare exercised the dogs with long runs on the beach near Jonas's estate. She knew that taking them away from the rambling house left it vulnerable to robbery, one of her brother-in-law's greatest fears. But the house had a sophisticated electronic alarm system hooked directly to the Greenwich police station. The protection it offered was not only against breaking and entering, but against smoke, heat and even the cold, in case the furnace failed.

One afternoon on the beach, after a long run with the dogs, Clare was on her way back to the house. She had borrowed a thigh-length down jacket from Emily's closet; her head was wrapped in a beige-and-brown plaid wool scarf, also Emily's, and covered with the hood of the jacket. Since her arrival from California, Clare had been forced to purchase a winter coat; she had found an attractive one of dark green loden cloth in a consignment shop that specialized in exclusive used clothes. At the time, she'd calculated that she needed a dress coat more than a jacket, so she had taken to borrowing, with Emily's permission, her casual outer wear. She and her sister wore the same size, were the same height and looked very much like each other, except that Clare's hair was dark and Emily's was a dull gold.

Heidi and Rolf caught sight of a man walking toward them from the direction of the house and ran ahead with the exuberance of puppies. Clare quickened her step, afraid the dogs would attack, even though they were not on Hahn property. The Dobermans were spirited and unpredictable. Emily hated them, fearing they would hurt Ian or Kevin, but Clare had always been able to control them. It wasn't that she was expert with dogs; she merely had no fear of Heidi and Rolf, and they seemed to sense that assurance in her, taking it for mastery.

Clare called their names, but the icy February wind that blew off the Sound whipped the words from her mouth and carried them away. Hampered by the heavy winter boots she wore, Clare began to run in earnest. Heidi caught up to the stranger near the end of Jonas's dock and jumped on him, her head nearly reaching his as she extended her sleek, black body.

"Heidi, down!"

Rolf ran in circles around the man, who stood still, apparently talking quietly to Heidi.

"Emily, when did you get home?" the man called over Heidi's head, pushing her down gently as he spoke. Heidi was now at his feet, sniffing his boots and then nuzzling against the knees of the wool trousers he wore beneath a heavy down jacket.

As Clare came up to him, his face showed surprise, then a distinct look of disappointment. "You're not Emily," he said, eyes wide. "I could have sworn..."

He was a big man, his bulk accentuated by the plump down jacket. Despite the weather, he was hatless, and his iron-gray hair was brushed back from his forehead like crinkly wire. His eyes were kind and serious, his skin tanned to a weather-beaten leather.

"I'm her sister, Clare Eckert. People say we look alike." She extended a hand covered by a fur-lined leather glove. He gripped it in his, causing Clare to wince at his strength, although he, too, wore gloves.

"Gene Janklow," he said. His eyes were gray, but a darker shade than his hair. "Emily told me you were here. You're your sister's twin," he exclaimed, "but up close I see you're a brunette. You walk just like her; even your voices are the same." Nevertheless, it was clear he wished she had been Emily.

"I can't hear the resemblance, though we've often been told that. I hope the dogs haven't bothered you."

"Oh, no—I'm old friends with Heidi and Rolf." He gazed at the animals fondly as they ran off down the beach to explore a chunk of seaweed-draped wood that had washed up on the sand during the night.

"You're Gene Janklow, the historian?" What was the name of his latest book, the one with the picture of the jousting tournament on the cover? She could see the illustration in her mind's eye, but the title would not come clear.

"You've heard of me?" He looked at her with renewed interest.

Clare realized immediately that he wanted her to say she had read his books, all three of which sat unopened on a night table in her bedroom. Emily had lent her the books when she first arrived from California, but there was nothing about the thirteenth and fourteenth centuries that Clare wanted to know. To her surprise, Emily had spoken enthusiastically about Janklow's work. Clare had never suspected that her sister had an interest in medieval history.

"Emily told me about you," she admitted, never one to lie and be caught immediately after having said something pretentious. The most she would venture was a bland social lie. "No, I haven't read your work yet. I've been too busy."

Disappointment showed on his face again. "Where's Emily? I've been in Italy for several months doing research, and I tried to call her, but there's no answer at the house."

"They're still in Mexico, in Guadalajara. They should be back on Sunday. That's the plan, anyway."

"Ah, yes, she did mention they were going away in February. And you? Didn't Emily tell me you were going to Mexico, too?"

"I came back early," Clare explained, slightly surprised he knew so much about her, even more surprised that a man who had been in Italy for months would know of Emily's trip to Mexico. Did her sister and Janklow keep up a correspondence, then? "I'm staying at their house until I can find a place of my own, and I came back to look for a job to hurry up the process."

"And get away from Jonas, I wager."

"I won't take that bet," Clare said with a laugh. "Too easy to lose."

He nodded as if he understood everything. "I...I came by to see Emily because I'm having trouble with my furnace. I rent a house from the Hahns not far from here, you see, and I know there's a man who takes care of the furnace, but for the life of me, I can't remember his name. I'm certain Emily wouldn't want me to call just anyone. When I saw you on the beach, I thought you were your sister."

"Why don't you come in the house? I know Emily keeps a file with all the service people's names in it. Perhaps I can find the name for you. Would you recognize it if you heard it?"

"Probably."

With the dogs following, they climbed wooden steps that led to a terrace behind the house. Clare unlocked the door with a key she carried, expertly turning off the alarm system once they were inside. She led him to the kitchen, where she located the small phone book immediately and gave Janklow the phone number he sought.

"Don't you want to call from here?" she asked him when he pocketed the number.

"No, I'll call from home. There's no urgency."

"Is the heat off at your place?" In the gathering gloom of an early twilight, Emily's empty, rambling house seemed as cold as death to Clare, although she knew the thermostats were set at fifty-five. She couldn't imagine how Janklow could stand his place if the heat had gone off. The temperature outside could not have risen above twenty during the entire week.

"No, just erratic," he answered.

Clare remembered her vow to socialize more. Should she invite him for a cup of tea, she wondered. He was an attractive man, and now that he had doffed his gloves, she noticed he wore no wedding ring, although that meant nothing. Jonas didn't wear a wedding ring, either. No, she had better not. He *said* he was a tenant of Emily's, and while Clare was already aware that the Hahns owned several houses as investments, her sister had never mentioned that Janklow was one of the tenants. Better to wait until Emily came home and gave her further information, she decided.

"Tell Emily to give me a call when she gets back, will you?" He was putting his gloves on and heading for the kitchen door without another personal word. "Thanks for your help, Mrs. Eckert."

Mrs. Eckert. She, who was used to the informality of California and had found Easterners to be taciturn to the point of frigidity, was nevertheless stung by his studied formality. He seemed to be in a hurry to leave, too. Obviously he was not interested in Clare.

"You're welcome, Mr. Janklow."

TO HER SURPRISE AND DELIGHT, Pierce and Pierce called Clare back for a second interview. Their offices were located in the Federal Building, one of the newest architectural wonders in Stamford. She was grilled thoroughly on the courses in accounting she had taken at the University of California after Teddy had begun to practice law. The personnel director then dismissed Clare with a soupçon of hope: they *did* hire accountants who were not yet C.P.A.s, and would she care to do some homework, three hypothetical cases to work on independently? Would she! Clare took the manila envelope and tucked it into her briefcase.

AT THE SAME MOMENT, in the same building, in offices as Spartan as those of Pierce and Pierce were affluently fitted out in the latest corporate modern style, another meeting was breaking up. Seven men and one woman sat in a large conference room. Upstairs at the prestigious accounting firm, it would have been called the board room. But on the fourth floor, it was known as the think tank, because that was where the agents of the Internal Revenue Service assigned to a specific case gathered weekly to brainstorm, in order to bring their undercover investigations to a speedy and efficacious close.

The men were in shirt sleeves, their jackets abandoned at gray, government-issue steel desks in a large outer office whose windows afforded a panoramic view of Long Island Sound. There was no carefully chosen art on the pale green walls, no heavy-duty, neutral gray or beige wall-to-wall carpeting on the dark green synthetic tile floors—nothing but an occasional poster exhorting the employee to give blood.

Within the glass walls of the think tank, the conference table was littered with neglected and nearly empty paper cups that now contained an inch or two of cold coffee. In front of two of the agents, overflowing ashtrays attested to the length of that morning's meeting.

The sole woman was speaking; she was the last of the agents assigned to the ongoing criminal investigation to give a progress report, having waited until the end of the meeting because she had little to impart. She had been brought in on the case only recently.

She was impeccably dressed, wearing an expensive two-piece suit of gray flannel and a cream-colored silk blouse with thin white stripes woven into its soft material. The only color in her ensemble came from a pair of red enameled earrings and a matching necklace. Clothes were her self-admitted weakness, and she wore them well. Male heads had turned in outright admiration when she first arrived at the Stamford office on temporary assignment from Washington, despite the fact that she was seriously overweight. But she was a tall woman who carried herself with grace, and on her the added girth looked good.

Her accent was educated, neutral and thoroughly American; as her report continued, there were traces, simply whispers, of a Southern background that had not been eliminated by six years of college in the Northeast. Her education had been funded, in part, by a generous scholarship from the United Negro College Fund.

"As far as expenses go," she said, "I have bought four white uniforms and two cardigan sweaters, total cost $158.60. I'm living at the Holiday Inn and paying for my meals from the expense account, although the hotel is billing this office for the room. I'll be going back to Washington this afternoon but plan to be in the hotel on Sunday night, if anyone needs to talk to me before I move to the Hahns, where my job begins on Monday."

"You'll never pass as a Jamaican, Harriet. You sound just like a New Yorker," a man said. He sat back in his chair and studied her. On his face, his thoughts were obvious. She was too classy to pass as a domestic, most especially a foreign one working as an illegal.

"I'm to be a Barbadian, not a Jamaican. A lot you know, mon," Harriet Alpert said in a thick, lilting Caribbean accent that broke up the agents sitting at the table.

"Where did you learn to talk that way?" one asked, incredulous at the transformation.

"I've always had a facility for languages. Accents are merely a variation of that."

"All right, people, I think we're ready now," said a gray-haired man named Paul Marcone, who, like Harriet, had been imported from Washington to supervise the operation. "That does it for today. Let's say we leave the timing of the next meeting open, since Harriet won't have freedom of movement once her part of the operation begins." He closed the file folder lying before him and stood up. The agents followed suit, some stretching, some breaking into small groups to chat. "Duffy, I want to talk to you."

Michael Duffy, in the midst of inviting Harriet to join him for lunch, approached his boss. "Yes, sir?"

"How's it really going, Duffy?" Marcone's face reflected the incisive acumen about his personnel that had brought him to the position he now held.

"Everything's fine, sir. You heard my report. I've already met the Hahns, and I'm certain I can maintain a relationship there."

"You don't sound convinced. What's the problem?"

There was a frown on Michael's face, and two lines had appeared between his eyebrows. "I don't know. I think I'm getting over the hill for this work. At first I believed in the entire concept—"

"You've always been terrific at it, too."

"Thank you. But now it seems... I don't know. It gives me a sick feeling sometimes."

"Too deceptive?" When Michael nodded, Marcone continued, his voice rising with emotion. If anything, Marcone believed in the validity of what they were doing. "What about the perpetrators? How can you feel we're too deceptive when *they* are insidiously dishonest? What we're doing is simply dosing them with their own medicine."

"It isn't that," Michael said. "It's the risk that an in-

dividual will be led into a professional or confidential relationship with an undercover employee. The responsibility
is a heavy one.''

"You're not actually practicing medicine, Duffy. You
aren't even authorized to put a Band-Aid on a scraped
knee.''

"I know. The truth is I'd like to be removed from the
case.''

"Look, you're an ambitious guy, Duffy. You're good
at what you do—the best, as far as I'm concerned. The entire concept of this operation is yours; we've got a good
month invested already and plenty of expenses, so you
can't quit now—it would be disastrous for your career. I
don't suppose I have to remind you of that aspect. Besides,
you're holding all the reins on this one. We have no one to
replace you with.''

"I guess I should forget my scruples until this job is
over. But after that. . .'' Michael said the correct words,
but his voice lacked total conviction.

"After that, we'll see about getting you assigned to
something different,'' his boss promised. "In the mean-
time, you're the best doctor the department has.''

Michael gave a short, bitter laugh. "Michael Duffy,
M.D.—Master Deceiver.''

He and Harriet rode down in the elevator together. She
was unable to join him for lunch because she wanted to be
on the two o'clock shuttle to Washington, but she promised to phone him that night in order to work out the last-
minute details of their plan for the following week.

After Harriet had left the building, Michael stood in the
lobby, his hands in the pockets of his trousers, his
thoughts far away. He didn't like the situation he found
himself in, didn't like it at all, but he wasn't about to confide in Marcone the fact that, for the first time in his career
as an agent, he had become personally involved in a case.

It had started out innocently enough, he knew that. He

had approached Clare because he knew she was close to the Hahns. She looked enough like Emily to be her twin, and he had realized immediately that they were sisters.

Nothing was supposed to grow between him and Clare. It was to be business, strictly business. One look across the table at her, however, and he just *knew*. There existed a special flash between two people when they first met, a current that was not to be denied. Michael was aware of the existence of that almost physical flash, although the phenomenon had never happened to him before. He'd felt that lightning strike him with a shock that shook him from head to toe when, like a fool, he'd asked Clare to dance. At the time, he was still telling himself it was all business.

He should have backed out right then. He should have taken a chair next to Hahn himself, invited him to play golf the following day, done anything to avoid those sad green eyes of Clare's.

But he hadn't. No, he'd danced with her. Not just to one number, either, but to three or four. Playing with fire, he'd let himself be drawn in to the point where he was actually giving her perfectly unsolicited advice about her personal life, of which he knew nothing at that time. Then he had followed her home the next day, rather than staying with his prey. And tried to kiss her when he *knew* she wasn't ready.

He couldn't help himself, he admitted. The hardest thing he had ever done in his life was to try to keep his hands off her during the day they had spent touring Guadalajara. He'd felt like a teenage kid—palms itching, hormones coursing through his body—as if he'd just discovered girls. He'd also been tongue-tied, making one mistake after another and practically jeopardizing his cover.

Clare had, correctly, been put off by his kiss. And later, could he blame her for thinking him a worm? He would despise any doctor who ignored a mortally ill person. Yes, he thought, she had every right in the world to consider Michael Duffy despicable.

UPON LEAVING PIERCE AND PIERCE, Clare took the elevator to the street level and began to search in her purse for the parking stub. She had left the Mercedes at an indoor garage a block away. Parking in downtown Stamford was nearly impossible now that the town had exploded into the business and commerce center of southern Connecticut.

The radio had warned that a snowstorm of major proportions would hit the Northeast, and during the two hours she had been upstairs, the sky had changed from a thin shade of blue to the threatening grayish yellow that Clare now associated with oncoming snow. Fat snowflakes swirled thickly, impeding her view through the lobby windows of the opposite side of Summer Street, whose sidewalks already wore a coat of white powder.

Clare's fingers fumbled in a zippered compartment of her purse, betraying her anxiety to return to her apartment before the roads became clogged with commuters leaving work early and school buses rushing their passengers home.

"Clare Eckert—is that you?"

She turned in surprise at the sound of her name. Involuntarily, her mouth fell open. *Michael Duffy again. The man was like a bad penny, turning up at the most unexpected moments.* A dimple she had never before noticed appeared with a flash at the side of his mouth. Although she told herself that his presence was unwelcome, her heart did an abrupt little flip when she realized she stood face to face with him again. Suddenly the lobby felt warm and cloying.

"Hello, Michael," she said calmly, making a studied effort to still her fingers, which had begun, unaccountably, to tremble. She found the parking ticket at last and jammed it into a pocket of her loden coat. *It's simply the shock of seeing him,* she told herself without conviction. But she was pleased that she was dressed for the unexpected meeting. Her stylish loden coat, the new boots she'd been forced to purchase when the crisp autumn weather had given way to the misery that was known as winter in Connecticut, the extra care she had taken with her makeup that morning because of the interview at Pierce and Pierce—all combined to give her an air of professional competence that she knew suited her.

"What a coincidence! I'm on my way to lunch—care to join me?"

"I don't think so, Dr. Duffy. I want to get home before the snow gets worse." She noticed he wasn't wearing a coat, just a conservative dark gray suit with a matching vest and a sedate, dark red tie, and she wondered where he planned to eat.

"A quick cup of coffee, then. How about it, Clare? There's a coffee shop downstairs in the basement."

She was tempted to say yes to his invitation, not because she wanted to be with him, but because she wanted to share the news of her interview with someone, even someone she disliked as much as Michael Duffy As she hesitated, his grin vanished, and with it his dimple, and she saw him bite his lower lip. Clare had a fleeting thought that Michael was as nervous as she. She shifted her briefcase from one hand to the other, suddenly feeling awkward like an abashed schoolgirl. *Fool,* she told herself. *He's not even a nice guy—remember?*

"You owe me one for not returning my phone calls."

"What phone calls?" she asked. Why should she explain herself to him? If he pressed, she'd tell him she hadn't been checking with Jonas's service since her return from Mexico.

"Didn't you get my messages? I've called three times."

"Only twice," she said without thinking, then immediately realized her mistake and clamped her mouth shut. There was a roaring in Clare's ears. Her lips were dry, her throat was parched, and she sighed with exasperation and embarrassment. She'd been a fool for even considering his invitation. Lies, lies—they always got her into trouble. She hated lies, whether her own or someone else's. Lies always reminded her of Teddy.

"Hoist by her own petard," Michael said with a laugh, taking her free arm and drawing a furiously blushing Clare toward an escalator that led to the lower level of the office building. He left her no choice but to follow, her body responding almost hypnotically to his touch, not just in its movement, but in the overwhelming warmth that shot through her. "Now you *have* to eat lunch with me!"

"But—"

"You don't agree you have to expiate that sin, Clare? I thought you were a woman whose morality was honed to a keen edge."

A keen edge—that was what she heard in his voice, an edge of sarcasm that made Clare see red, as angry at her own involuntary consciousness of the nearness of his body as she was at his words. She stopped just short of the escalator, causing Michael to step painfully on the tip of one of her boots as she wrenched her elbow from his hand. She was through with being pushed around by men—by Teddy, by Jonas and by this persistent doctor. She was not about to be manipulated into something she definitely did not want to do, even if her body seemed to want to follow his.

"You're very sure of yourself, aren't you? Did it ever occur to you that I simply don't care to be with you? Not for lunch, not for a cup of coffee, not for—"

"C'mon, Clare. Let's have a new start, shall we?" He smiled winningly, but she remained unmoved.

"Again? It didn't work last time, so why should it work now? I'm already *having* a new start, Michael, and you're distinctly not part of it. Good day."

She left him standing alone, a still, single man in a lobby crowded with scurrying people. She turned once and glanced back as she went out the revolving door that led to the street. He had a pensive expression on his face.

He was a quite ordinary-looking man, she thought—nothing special, even if the three-piece suit he wore made him look serious and almost distinguished. But, she reminded herself, he was a man who turned his back on his fellow human beings, and she didn't believe she could accept his reason for it. Every instinct told her to forget him.

Her mind was operating efficiently; she applauded its clarity of thought. But her body betrayed her. Clare could not deny the unaccustomed sexual stirring within her. She had thought that part of Clare Eckert dead forever.

EMILY, JONAS AND THE CHILDREN arrived home in a private limousine late Sunday night. Clare was already in bed, reading, but she turned off her light when she heard the car pull into the driveway. Although she had no desire to see Jonas, she was anxious to talk with Emily. She decided to wait until tomorrow, when she knew he would be at his medical office.

The following morning, her coat thrown over a two-piece running suit, Clare took the flagstone path that led from her quarters to the main house. A light snow was falling, softly blanketing the graying piles of old snow on either side of the path with a fresh coat of white. She stuck out her tongue to taste a snowflake. Although she hated to drive in it, all the years she lived in California she had missed the sight of falling snow and the silence it brought with it. Now a muffled peace seemed to cover the world, muting the noise of traffic in the distance and even the rhythmic slap of small waves on the dock at the end of the property.

Inside the kitchen, she found Emily seated alone at a round table set in the recess of a bay window that over-looked the Sound, which was barely visible through the lightly falling snow. In front of her was a half-drunk cup of coffee. The sisters embraced, and Clare admired Emily's golden tan.

"Where is everyone? It's so quiet. Where are the boys?"

"The new cook is out marketing, and I've enrolled the boys in a local nursery school. I took them over this morning about eight-thirty."

"Aren't they awfully young?" Clare asked.

"There's no one their age to play with here in the neighborhood, Clare. They need other children."

"But they have each other, just as we did. *We* never needed to go to nursery school."

"All children go now. It helps them adjust to real school later." Without another word, Emily went over to an antique Welsh sideboard and prepared Clare a cup of coffee—black, the way Clare preferred it—from a fancy digital coffee maker that turned itself on, ground the beans, and poured, all without benefit of human hands. She set a porcelain cup and saucer in front of her sister and returned to her chair. The flat gray light particular to snowy days made Emily look thin and tired, despite her even tan. There was a permanent sadness to her eyes that wrenched Clare's heart.

"How was your trip home, Clare?"

"Uneventful," she lied. "I hope you don't mind that I took over the care of the dogs. I couldn't see any sense having someone come in while I was already here."

"You're welcome to the monsters! You know how I feel about them," Emily frowned, clearly thinking about another subject. "We have to do the books, Clare. Jonas was on my back about them all during vacation. You remember that you promised to help with the ledger? Well, I told him everything was shipshape. One of these days he's going to ask to see it, and when he does, he'll hit the ceiling. You know how he gets about money."

"Yes, I know. I would have started while you were gone, but I don't know where you keep your records. Besides, there would have been too many questions to ask you, so I decided to wait until you came home."

Clare knew that Emily was almost backward when dealing with figures; her interests lay more in the arts. She painted rather well in a style that was naive, almost primitive, although she had taken art lessons for years. Clare, on the other hand, had a natural gift for mathematics.

"Well, I'm ready when you are," she said, "so if you have time this morning, let's get started. I don't have to be anywhere today. My usual Monday appointment canceled."

"Oh, I have time. I won't have to go for the boys until noon." Emily picked up her coffee cup and led Clare through the kitchen and into a small office in the rear of the house. "I keep everything in here," she said, pointing at a desk in the corner of the room. The desk was covered with papers—receipts, unanswered personal letters, booklets of instruction for the incredible number of household appliances and gadgets the Hahns owned, fliers from the various activities in which Emily participated. "March fifteenth will be here before you know it," she said vaguely.

"What does March fifteenth have to do with the books?"

"Jonas wants all the household books for last year ready to go to the accountant by then. You know how stringent the IRS is with doctors. Everything has to be absolutely perfect."

"Where's your ledger?"

"Somewhere here." Emily shifted the confetti of papers on the desk until she found a book covered in dark red leather, the previous year stamped in gold on its cover. Clare took the book and opened it, riffling through the pages. A cold sinking feeling suddenly filled her breast.

"The pages are blank, Emily." She looked directly at her sister.

"Yes, I know," Emily said, shamefaced.

"Do you mean we're going to have to re-create the entire year?"

"No, not everything," Emily replied brightly. "Only the things I paid for with checks. It's not so difficult—really, Clare. I did it last year with the help of a friend, and it took us only a week. He—my friend—wasn't trained the way you are, so I'm certain it won't take us that long. My checks are all in order." As she spoke, Emily opened a drawer and took out twelve gray envelopes held together with a rubber band. She extended the packet upside down to Clare.

"You haven't even opened your bank statements!" Clare exclaimed, dumbfounded. "Emily, I can't believe it! How do you know how much money is in your account?"

"I always have enough." At the look on Clare's face, she hastened to add, "Oh, that sounds so snooty. I don't mean it that way. All I mean is, every so often, after I've written a bunch of checks, I deposit a couple of thousand dollars, and it all works out. It always has. So far."

"Does Jonas know what a mess this is? Who takes care of the household bills?"

"I do."

"Why doesn't his accountant take care of everything? I assume he has someone to do the books for his office."

"Yes, he does, but he wants *me* to do ours. Don't tell

him you've seen anything, all right? He'd have a fit! He's pathologically private, you know."

Simply pathological, Clare thought. "Of course not," she replied instead. She had promised this help to Emily. Emily was housing her, often feeding her, and all for nothing. The least she could do was set Emily's finances in order.

"Okay, bring me another cup of coffee and I'll get started. I'll come over every morning until we're finished."

"Oh, good. I'll get a phone and bring it in here while you work. I'm planning a dinner party for a week from Saturday. That way you can ask me questions about the books, and I can ask your advice about the party." Emily hurried back to the kitchen, and Clare heard the low moan of the coffee grinder at work, pulverizing the black Jamaican beans that Jonas preferred to order from a gourmet food store in Manhattan.

"And bring me your checkbook," Clare called.

"It's in the top drawer," came Emily's voice from the kitchen.

Emily loved to entertain, and she did it well, using it as a creative outlet. Jonas wouldn't permit her to work, and he had forbidden her to sell her paintings, telling her that he earned so much that they certainly didn't need the few extra dollars her scratchings might bring in. Both Clare and Emily were aware that the money wasn't the point of selling the paintings; any artist appreciated payment in the coin of the realm. What good was painting without an audience? So Emily had donated her best paintings to the Greenwich Hospital, the public library and several other public buildings, where they brought a lovely spot of primitive New England color to the walls.

Clare opened the bank statements and balanced them, only half listening to Emily's voice on the phone behind her. Emily sat in a leather chair next to the window, one finger playing with her long blond hair, and charmed her potential guests. It would be a big party, Clare figured, after Emily had made at least a dozen calls. She recognized the names of several doctors' wives and that of Myra Randolph, a well-known local antiques dealer whom Clare had met once before at a party given by another member of the Hahns' set. She knew Emily had bought several pieces of furniture from the woman.

She was done with the bank statements before Emily had to leave to pick up the boys. Emily's balance was comfortable, not exorbitant, but enough to make Clare sigh with envy. With the few thousand that Emily had, Clare could buy a used car, find a decent apartment, and reduce her debt. Well, she had no one to blame but herself, she mused for the hundredth time. She should have been aware of what Teddy was doing with their money. She was a trained bookkeeper, after all, with plenty of accounting courses under her belt. Love had blinded her. But never again.

While Emily was gone, Clare began to prepare the ledger. A few minutes later she pushed the leather book aside, realizing that some of the papers she needed were missing. From the kitchen came the sounds and smells of a meal under preparation, and she wandered out to find Harriet, the cook-housekeeper, stirring a pot of home-made soup, the perfect repast for a snowy day. While they waited for Emily to return, Clare set the table and made sandwiches of peanut butter and banana for the twins.

After Emily had taken the boys to their room for an afternoon nap, Clare returned to the office. Emily joined her within a few moments.

"I'm going to invite a bachelor I know for you."

Clare was still looking for the missing records in the stack of papers on the right side of the desk, and she didn't reply.

"To the dinner party, I mean. Remember the party?" Emily paged through her wine-colored Mark Cross address book as she spoke.

"Whos' that?"

"That historian I told you about, Gene Janklow. He should be back from Italy before Saturday."

"Oh, Emily, he's already back. I forget to tell you that he stopped by to see you last week. Something about his furnace being out of order."

"He did?" Emily looked up from her address book with interest. "How is he? Didn't you think he was nice? I knew you'd hit it off with him."

"He looked fit—suntanned, interesting. We didn't exactly hit it off, if it's matchmaking you're planning, but, yes, I found him congenial. So he isn't married?"

"No, not now. He was divorced once and widowed once."

"He's too old for me, anyway." Clare bent her head over the ledger.

"He's not that old, only forty-two. I don't think he's too old."

"He looks older somehow."

"It's his gray hair. And he sails a lot; that makes his skin tough. But he's very young at heart. He's a lot of fun, actually, and he knows something about everything!" Clare had never heard Emily so enthusiastic about any man, and she began to suspect that Gene Janklow was being invited in Emily's behalf, not in hers. Well, she couldn't blame her sister for liking another man.

"He wasn't taken with me." *Nor I with him*, she added silently.

"How do you know?"

"There's a certain spark when you meet someone who is going to mean something to you, and that spark was missing when I met Gene Janklow." The spark that crackled between her and Michael Duffy, she realized. It was palpable, a physical presence, even when he wasn't touching her. Surprisingly, the warmth she had felt when he took her arm in the Federal Building came back with a rush. She stood up and opened the window a crack. "Hot in here, don't you think?" she said in explanation.

"Yes, I know what you mean. I saw it when you met that man in Mexico. What was his name again?"

Clare's heart leaped at Emily's mention of Michael. It was almost as if Emily had read her mind. "I...I don't remember his name."

"I'll ask Jonas; he should remember. They went to school together, didn't they? Why don't I ask *him* to the party, too? I'm certain he'll mix well with our friends. As a matter of fact, he mentioned that he belonged to the same country club we do—and didn't he say he lived in New Canaan?"

"I don't remember," Clare said again. *I knew it! I knew this would happen! All these doctors run in the same group.*

"Yes, I'm sure he said New Canaan. Wait—Duffy, that was his name. Michael Duffy." Emily picked up the telephone and dialed information for New Canaan.

Clare felt a sinking feeling in the pit of her stomach.

Chapter Five

In a moment Emily was carefully entering Michael Duffy's telephone number in her address book. As she wrote, she hummed a tuneless air. Clare emitted a quiet snort of disgust. For a woman who didn't even open her bank statements, Emily certainly was meticulous about her social paperwork. "I'll call him tonight."

"Emily..."

"He was attractive, wasn't he? And you just told me that you and Gene didn't hit it off. If I have Myra for Gene and Michael for you, we'll have an even number at the table. What do you think about Caribbean food? That's always unusual, and since Harriet is from Barbados, it should be no problem."

"But, Emily—"

"What's the matter?" Emily's green eyes under dark brows stared at Clare.

"Nothing." What could she tell her? Since she had already lied, since she had never explained that she and Michael had spent that day and night in Guadalajara, had met again one snowy noon in Stamford, had clashed in a most distasteful manner, she couldn't very well tell Emily now. Emily would ask a lot of questions—questions that would cause Clare to regret having spoken at all. So far, Emily had not brought up Clare's precipitous departure from Mexico, and Clare did not want to, so perhaps it was best to be silent and allow her sister to invite Michael to the party. Maybe he would have another date; maybe he would be out of town; maybe... "Nothing is the matter. Go ahead and invite him, if you want to. I'm certain he will like Myra, and maybe Gene and I will hit it off better the next time we meet. Seat me next to Gene, all right?"

"You want to play hard to get, is that it?"

"No, that's not it," Clare snapped.

"But you're so right, Clare—Gene isn't your type. Michael Duffy is the man for you. I could tell from the way you two looked at each other."

"Horsefeathers, Emily. I wasn't impressed with him at all." Clare longed to change the subject. "By the way, I can't find any checks for household help, child care, entertainment or—"

"No, you'll just find checks for the groceries, for service for the cars, for dry cleaning. Real estate taxes, the mortgage. Things like that."

"What about the other things? Where shall I put them?"

"Oh, nowhere," Emily replied, waving a hand airily. "I pay those in cash. Jonas gives me a thousand dollars every two weeks, and I pay everything else out of that money."

"In cash?"

"Yes."

"Why?"

"I don't know why. We've always done it that way. That's how Jonas wants it, I guess."

"You must keep a lot of cash around the house, Emily. Is that wise?"

"The money's secure. We keep it in a wall safe behind the painting in the bedroom. No one even knows the safe is there."

"All right." Clare began to fill in the entries in the ledger, frowning slightly as she did so. She couldn't imagine why Emily wanted the bother of dealing with cash. Cash was hard to keep track of and easy to lose. Credit cards were simplicity itself. Clare still missed the credit cards she had lost in the divorce—all the dangerous pieces of plastic that had brought her to her knees when Teddy had pulled the financial rug out from under her. It seemed almost un-American to pay cash. Everyone everywhere bought on credit these days, so why didn't Emily?

Clare thought of the check she had been issued by the airline in Mexico and realized that the tickets Jonas had bought must have been paid in cash, too. Otherwise, the airline would have credited an account, rather than issuing her a refund check. What was she going to do with the check? She realized that what Michael Duffy had suggested before was true; it was too late to give the money back to Jonas. She would only compound the lie she had told.

The check was for more than four hundred dollars. She could probably find a junky used car for the money. Or she could look for an apartment on a bus line. The four hundred dollars, plus what she had saved, would go a long way toward a deposit and the first month's rent on a furnished apartment.

As the afternoon darkened to an early twilight, she found her thoughts straying back to the check, which rested in the top drawer of the dresser in her bedroom. The closer the hour of Jonas's return from his office came, the more her stomach clutched, and the more she favored the idea of finding her own apartment. Maybe if she found a place that was really cheap, she could afford a car *and* an apartment.

Ten minutes before Jonas was expected, Clare asked to borrow the Mercedes. She wanted to drive into town and pick up the local paper; she was determined to check the classified ads for an inexpensive apartment in Greenwich or Stamford. She was on her way to the kitchen closet for her coat when the door that led to the attached garage opened and Jonas walked in. He bumped into her, but ignored her.

"Good evening, Jonas," she said.

"Where's Emily?" His face was a storm cloud.

"Right here, dear," Emily said, coming in from the dining room, where she had been setting the table. She tried to kiss him, but Jonas turned his head aside petulantly, so that Emily's kiss landed on his jaw.

"I've been trying to get you all day." His voice was tight with irritation.

"I've been here. What's the problem?"

"I *know* you've been here. The line was busy for hours!"

Emily blinked rapidly, her fingers moving up and down on the napkins she held in her hands. "I've been putting together the dinner party you and I discussed. I had to call and invite people, because it's too late for written invitations. Why did you need to talk to me?"

"To remind you to pick up my mohair sports jacket from the cleaner's. I have to go out tonight, to a meeting. Did you get it?"

"Oh, Jonas, no. I never thought to go for it." Emily bit her lower lip. Clare held her breath.

"I knew it! Blast, Emily, can't you do *anything* right? I told you this morning I needed it for tonight."

"I don't remember your mentioning it," Emily said in a small voice. She squeezed the napkins tightly between her hands.

"Your brain is like a sieve, that's why. You can't do anything right, can you? What do you need, a written list of chores every morning? Honestly!" He looked up to the ceiling, as if in search of a sympathetic ear there. "How long has the jacket been at the cleaner's?"

"Two weeks, I guess."

"Two weeks! They could have cleaned it fourteen times by now!"

"But we've been in Mexico—"

"So what!"

Tell him to go to the devil, Clare urged her sister silently, but Emily merely laid a hand on her husband's tense arm.

"I apologize, dear. I don't remember your mentioning anything about the jacket, and I'm really sorry you couldn't get through on the telephone." Emily's voice was soft with contrition.

"For Lord's sake, Emily, when a man can't even call his own home!"

"You could have left a message with the service. I check the service every hour, just as you told me to. I would have called you right back."

"You *know* I don't want any calls during the day. I can't be bothered with calls from home. 'Jonas, the dishwasher is leaking. Jonas, Kevin knocked out his front tooth, what shall I do?' " he mimicked in falsetto. "If I let you call me, I'd never get any work done."

"I never call you about trivial matters, or even serious ones," Emily said, offended. "I never call you at the office at all, you know that." Her eyes filled with tears.

"Get me a drink," he ordered. "A martini, straight up, and make it right, for a change. I've had a terrible day."

"I . . . I'm sorry, dear. I'll get you a drink right away." She raced back toward the dining room and the liquor cabinet.

Clare stood silently in the corner of the kitchen and watched Jonas remove his coat and toss it carelessly on a chair, although he stood only three feet from a closet. He knew, as did Clare, that Emily would return and hang up the coat. Just as soon as she had served him an ice-cold martini.

Clare went into the dining room. Emily was on her knees in front of the low cabinet that housed dozens of bottles of expensive whisky and liqueurs. "I can't find the gin," she whispered. "Oh, he'll kill me if we're out of gin." Her cheeks were wet with tears.

"Let me look." Clare moved two bottles of Napoleon brandy and found an unopened bottle of Tanqueray. "Here it is." She stood up and handed her sister the green bottle. "I won't be here for dinner, Emily. I put on a couple of pounds in Mexico with all that delicious food, so I think I'll just skip it, if you don't mind."

"Can't say I blame you," Emily said, trying hard, if unsuccessfully, for a smile. Her eyes slid to the door of the kitchen. They both heard Jonas tapping his keys impatiently on the table. Clare cringed inwardly, knowing how careful Emily was of the mirror finish on the oak table.

She gave her sister a quick hug. "I'm sorry. Will you be all right?"

"Oh, sure. I'll be fine. *He'll* be fine after his martini. It must have been a terrible day for Jonas." Emily wiped her eyes with one of the hopelessly wrinkled napkins.

No more than usual, Clare said to herself.

"TALK ABOUT COINCIDENCE," Emily said early the next morning when Clare arrived in the kitchen. Clare had waited until Jonas left the house at eight o'clock, knowing that on Tuesdays and Thursdays he went to work earlier than on the other days of the week.

"Who's talking about coincidence?" she asked dryly.

"Michael Duffy called you, even before I could call him about the dinner party. I would have come over to tell you, but it was snowing, so I told him you'd gone to bed early. I really should have a phone put in the guest house. I don't know why I never thought of it before."

"Don't do it on my account. I like the solitude, and besides, I'll be leaving soon."

"But now that men are starting to call— Leaving? When?" A look of alarm crossed Emily's face. "I don't want you to leave, Clare. I love having you here."

"I can't live off your charity forever, Emily. As nice as it is."

"It's not charity. You'd do the same for me, wouldn't you?"

"But I'm in no position to help you, Emily. You have everything."

"You're helping me now, Clare. I could never do the books without your help."

"Nevertheless, I plan to find a place to live soon. I *have* to, don't you see? Besides, Jonas won't suffer me forever." *And I can't suffer him forever, even if you can,* she added silently.

"I know you don't like Jonas. That's the real reason, isn't it?"

"I've never said I don't like him, Emily. He's *your* husband, not mine, so what does it matter how I feel about him?"

"But I want you to like him, Clare. He likes you, even if he doesn't show it. That's not Jonas's way."

Clare smiled blandly at her sister, swallowing an urge to speak.

Emily misconstrued the smile, jumping in immediately to defend her husband. "He has so many good qualities. He's generous, he's crazy about the twins—he'd die for them, believe me! He's a wonderful doctor. You have no idea how high his reputation is in the medical community. I mean, the things he can do with a scalpel, Clare. You should see some of the faces he has fixed—accident and burn victims, cleft palates. And he does lots of them for nothing—poor children from Harlem and Bridgeport, that type of thing."

"Hmm." Clare couldn't imagine Jonas in the role of humanitarian. He was a "society" doctor if ever she'd met one.

"Why don't you like him?" Emily burst out, causing Clare's self-control to snap.

"Because he's hateful to you, because his temper is out of control, because he's selfish, egotistical and overbearing!'' Clare pressed her lips together to silence herself. *Shame on me, I know better than to interfere in another person's marriage. What's the matter with me?* But she knew what was the matter. She thought Emily should leave Jonas, just as she had been forced to leave Teddy. Part of her wish stemmed from the fact that Jonas was a destructive man, but was there another part, a selfish side to Clare that wanted her sister to approve of what she herself had done? She hoped she was not as self-centered as the thought implied. Misery loved company, was that it? But she wasn't miserable; she loved not being married to Teddy. What she hated was the poverty, the loneliness, the horrible delay in starting her life anew that lack of money caused.

"You love Jonas, don't you?" she asked, her tone conciliatory. Between the miserable silences, between the times that Jonas erupted in anger at everyone within earshot, Clare had noticed the looks of tenderness that sometimes passed between the Hahns. Who was she, a woman who had failed at marriage, to criticize her sister?

"Yes, I love him. He's just going through a bad time in his life right now. I know that to you it must look as if we have everything, but Jonas seems to be searching for something else, something I can't give him, something even he doesn't understand. Everything will work out in the long run, you'll see." Emily smiled, a faint enigmatic grin that made Clare feel a twinge of envy, because it implied that Emily bore some wisdom that had eluded her younger sister.

Emily apparently decided to leave the topic of Jonas and the matter of Clare's moving unresolved, for she changed the subject immediately. "Don't you want to hear about Michael Duffy?"

"No, not particularly." Clare poured a cup of coffee and helped herself to a plump croissant from a box emblazoned with the name of an expensive bakery in

Darien. If Emily noticed that a croissant was hardly diet food, she declined to comment. Defiantly Clare added butter to the croissant, then heaped on a tablespoon of strawberry jam from the porcelain crock that said "Fortnum and Mason" in heavy black script across its front.

"Why not? He's a perfectly delightful man who is interested in you. It's about time you got yourself back in circulation. What do you have against him?"

Clare didn't reply.

"He said he'd called you several times, but that you had never called him back."

"I guess I didn't get the messages."

"Well, he'd like you to call him tonight. Here's his number in New Canaan." Emily handed Clare a sheet of paper.

"Is he coming to your dinner party?"

"Yes."

"Great." Clare decided she had better read one of Gene Janklow's books so she'd have something to discuss with him. That way she would be able to ignore Michael Duffy.

"Emily, I'll take the boys to nursery school if you tell me where it is. There's something I'd like to do with the car, but I'll be back right away so we can get started on the ledger." There had been an apartment—a room, really—listed in the paper, and Clare wanted to drive by to check out the neighborhood before she called the telephone number.

After dropping off the twins at their school, Clare, the newspaper folded on the leather seat beside her, drove slowly through an older residential section of Greenwich in search of the address listed in the classified advertisements. The houses were substantial, neither large nor new, built probably fifty or sixty years before, and set close together behind narrow front yards. The one she sought was on a quiet street, two blocks from a bus stop—good. And she would pass a grocery store on the walk from the bus to the house—even better.

Why go back to Emily's to call the number? Why not ring the bell and be done with it?

Clare left the station wagon, locked it and went up the walk to the front door of the house. Ignoring an electronic doorbell, she lifted a carefully polished brass knocker and let it fall, listening to its thud resound within.

"Yes?" The door was opened by a woman of sixty-five or so, wearing rather thick glasses and a rosy lipstick that did not quite follow the outline of her mouth.

"I saw your ad in the paper. I've come about the room—if it's still available, that is. My name is Clare Eckert."

The woman hesitated, blinked her eyes rapidly, and refrained from looking Clare up and down. "Won't you come in?"

Clare followed her into a hall paved with dark blue and white tiles upon which lay a silky-surfaced Persian rug. She relaxed noticeably, assured somehow that she and the landlady would like each other and that the room would be hers.

A half hour later, after two cups of tea and a friendly interview, Clare was shown the room at the top of the stairs. Even before she saw the double brass bed covered in a blue eiderdown comforter the same lovely hue as the tiny periwinkle flowers on the old-fashioned wallpaper, she knew that she would love living in Mrs. Alvina Sydney's house.

Clare sealed the bargain with a check for the first month's rent. Moving day was set for the Sunday following Emily's dinner party.

Chapter Six

A fixed smile frozen on her face, Clare accepted a third Campari-and-soda from a waiter hired for the occasion. She continued to pretend to listen to the ear, nose and throat specialist on her left, who was detailing the fine points of a new condominium office complex, located somewhere in the Carolinas, in which he and his partners had recently invested. Clare knew that all doctors were not like the one at her side. How had she allowed herself to be backed into a corner by him?

Clare didn't really want a third drink, but she found it awkward to stand around with her hands empty. She had already shredded two tiny cocktail napkins into a damp ball of confetti that was wadded in her left hand. Dinner was delayed while the guests awaited the arrival of an obstetrician who had been called to an early delivery. Clare's back ached from standing and her head from listening and feigning an interest she didn't feel. She longed to sit down on an empty sofa on the other side of the crowded room. No, what she longed to do was retreat to her apartment in the carriage house and finish packing for tomorrow's move, but her second choice would be to sit down. If she sat on the sofa, however, she would have to talk to Michael Duffy, who had been trying to catch her eye.

She wished she had worn a cooler dress. The paisley

wool challis, with its high collar and long sleeves, made her feel at once overheated and underdressed. The doctors' wives, Emily included, wore silk cocktail dresses that stressed cleavage, arms tanned from trips to Bermuda or Barbados or wherever doctors and their wives spent their winter vacations, and bodies toned to perfection by three-times-a-week attendance at aerobics classes. Clare envied the women their leisure time.

Michael Duffy was across the room, engaged in conversation with Myra Randolph, the antiques dealer. Clare hadn't spoken to him yet, but she was acutely aware of his presence. In a dark gray blazer, a light blue shirt with a white collar, and a black tie patterned with small red figures, he stood out from the other doctors. In fact, Clare realized, he didn't dress like a doctor at all.

She shrugged aside this thought and focused her attention on Myra. Although she knew Myra was in her late forties, the woman looked younger than Clare remembered from their previous meeting, and more petite. Her small head was tilted up in rapt interest in something Michael was telling her, one heavily ringed hand with perfectly painted nails wrapped around her cocktail glass. Clare shoved her own hand holding the shredded napkins into a pocket of her dress, thinking she should take better care of her fingernails. Myra had dark auburn hair shot with strands of gray, intricately wound and piled atop her head; her large eyes were deep-set beneath heavy lids. And she wasn't wearing silk, but a powder-blue suit of Ultrasuede. Myra looked sophisticated, interesting and more glamorous than all the other women present.

Clare was surprised to feel a sick lurch she refused to recognize as incipient jealousy in the pit of her stomach. She sighed with disgust at herself. So what if Michael Duffy had spent fifteen minutes engaged in rapt conversation with Myra Randolph?

"Excuse me, please," she said to the doctor at her side.

"I promised Emily I'd lend a hand in the kitchen." She made her way through the crowded living room, depositing her unwanted glass, still full, on an oversized hunt table beneath a large oil painting that looked to Clare as if one of her nephews had painted it.

She ducked into a powder room off the hall that led to the kitchen and examined her reflection in an ornate shell-framed mirror. Two red dots stood out on her cheeks, and her green eyes sparkled with an animation she knew she didn't feel. *It's the heat,* she told herself, certain that the thermostat registered at least eighty degrees. Maybe she was getting the flu. What better place to be diagnosed than in a house full of doctors representing just about every specialty except psychiatry?

Clare heard the bell announcing dinner, and she left the powder room. Outside in the hall, she almost ran into Gene Janklow.

"I've been looking for you, Clare. Will you go in with me?"

"Certainly, Gene. I'd be delighted." She took his proffered arm, which was covered in substantial heathery English tweed, as befitted an author-historian. So Emily had acceded to Clare's request to be paired with Janklow. Clare had been certain that her sister planned to seat her next to Michael, and she was surprised to feel a confusing mixture of relief and disappointment. Some perversity in her nature longed to be irritated anew by Michael Duffy. What was the matter with her? She was prepared for Gene, however, having read half of one of his books during the previous week.

As dinner progressed, she found Janklow a stimulating partner, a man who spoke knowledgeably about current events and a score of other topics that interested Clare.

Michael was seated on the opposite side of the table, down three people to Clare's left, and if she felt his eyes on her frequently during the meal, she tried to ignore him and to give her attention totally to Janklow.

Unsuccessfully.

Clare heard the guests complimenting Emily on her choice of caterer; she heard Emily give all the credit to Harriet, the cook; and she heard Jonas, at the head of the table, pontificating tediously on the backward economy of the Republic of Mexico. Throughout all of this, her awareness of Michael Duffy swelled until it was almost a throb in her breast, and she was furious with herself for entertaining the ripening attraction she felt for him.

"You don't like him much, do you?" Janklow asked, sotto voce.

"Who?" She had been wondering why Myra Randolph insisted on resting her ring-studded hand on Michael's sleeve with such frequency. Clare wasn't watching them—she swore she wasn't. Could she help it if her peripheral vision was sharp? An expression on her face must have betrayed her discomfort to Janklow, who had misread it.

"Hahn."

"Not much. But what's the difference how I feel? I'm not married to him."

"She's too good for him," Janklow said. He saw no need to use Emily's name.

"Probably." Clare did not want to discuss the uncomfortable subject of Emily's marriage with Gene Janklow. "Have you seen the new film at the revival theater in Norwalk?"

"What? Oh, yes. I love all those decadent Italian movies, don't you?" He began to analyze the film in a most intelligent way, and they found themselves arguing companionably about the film's message.

No wonder Emily thought him so interesting; Janklow was like a bright flower blooming in the desert of her existence. Too bad Emily hadn't met the historian years before Jonas had come into her life. Janklow was truly a gentleman, Clare thought. He had been immediately aware of her nuance of disapproval at his mention of Jonas and helpful in assisting her to change the subject.

"Shall we have coffee in the living room?" Emily stood up and began to lead her guests in that direction. Gene was right behind her.

Clare sensed, rather than saw, Michael approach her from her left. Across the artfully coiffed heads of several women, their eyes met for a brief instant. Clare lowered hers immediately and pretended that the bolt of electricity that had just jarred her legs to weakness had never happened. Again the heat of the house assailed her, and she touched a cool hand to her forehead, only to find it burning.

"Clare, wait," Michael called. The normal voice that she had strained to hear all during dinner was gone now, replaced by a sound that was intense, almost gravelly, and that made her heart turn over when he pronounced her name. With a sense of panic, she hurried to get through the door before he reached her. She didn't want to be alone with him.

Leaving the dining room, Clare stopped only to fill a small cup with strong espresso coffee flavored with the oil of a small piece of lemon peel. Then she hurried to the solarium, a large slate-floored greenhouse on the south side of the house. It was her favorite room in Emily's house, probably because it reminded her of California.

Clare found a private niche in the cool, dimly lit solarium. Hidden by a staghorn fern suspended from the ceiling and a four-foot schefflera, she sipped the pungent espresso coffee, closed her eyes and leaned back in the wrought-iron chair with a satisfied sigh. The ting of spoons against coffee cups and the volume of satisfied after-dinner conversation in the next room seemed far away.

She loved the earth-scented, humid solarium. Months before, Emily had sent Clare a copy of *House Beautiful* or

Architectural Digest, or some such magazine, in which the Hahns' house was featured in all its artistic, moneyed glory. While Clare recognized the prestige of being chosen to appear in the magazine, her sister's new house, which up to that time she had not yet seen, appeared cold and sterile to Clare. But she had liked the solarium, finding it the only room in the entire house that showed real character and warmth. She still felt the same way. It gave one an immediate feeling of peace, almost as if it were a secret glade in a thick forest.

She took advantage of her peaceful surroundings to think. Why was she afraid of Michael Duffy? He meant nothing to her, nothing. She *should* speak to him, she mused, if only to identify the strange sensations that had kept her off balance during the evening. She was certain he was not the cause of them, and again she wondered if she was getting a touch of the flu. But she never felt like this when he was not around.

Finish your coffee, she told herself. *Go in there and talk to him. He doesn't bite.* Avoiding him was rude, especially since Emily had invited Michael for Clare, even if he had spent the entire evening chatting up Myra Randolph.

Behind her, she heard the click of two pairs of high-heeled shoes on the green slate floor. As the footsteps approached the corner where she sat, Clare opened her eyes and sighed again. Why had she expected the peace and privacy to last? She should make her presence known—clear her throat, call out a welcome—but she thought that if she sat very still, they, whoever they were, might not see her and go away.

"I've got a juicy tidbit for you, Mimi," someone said in a hushed, confidential whisper just the other side of the luxuriant schefflera at Clare's back. "But you have to swear to God you won't pass it on. My husband would kill me if he knew I'd told anyone. He'd never tell me another thing, not as long as I live "

"Oh, do tell. Of course I promise!" Clare recognized the voice of Mimi McNamara, wife of an internist, good friend of Emily's and ace tennis player in her own right.

"Albie was in the city this morning looking at Porsches. He's been talking about buying one for the longest time, and he thought he could get a better deal in New York. Anyway, guess who he saw at the showroom—with a stunning redhead, he told me."

"Who?"

"Someone we know, someone buying a brand-new Porsche for his girl friend." The gossiper postponed her coming moment of triumph, savoring every hissed syllable, each second of delay.

"Who?" Mimi demanded impatiently. Clare sucked in her breath, a strong intuition sending off bells of warning in her breast. She knew the answer even before the whispered reply reached her straining ears.

"Jonas Hahn!"

Despite the premonition, Clare felt her stomach drop six inches, and the unwelcome memory of the chicken in spicy coconut sauce they had eaten for dinner came back to haunt her.

"His girl friend? He has a girl friend? Who?"

"That redhead who worked in his office last year. Don't you remember her? Emily had a fit when she saw her at the office once—said she was cheap and common and made Jonas fire her."

"Yes, I vaguely remember."

"So I guess he's still seeing her. More than seeing her, actually, if he's buying her a thirty-five-thousand-dollar car. Some severance pay!"

"Oh, poor Emily," Mimi said with a delicate groan. "Do you suppose she knows?"

"If she doesn't, she should, and you're the one to tell her, Mimi. You and she are good friends; you're her *best* friend."

"A good friend keeps her mouth shut. And I hope you will, too, Karen. Maybe Albie misinterpreted the situation. You've jumped to the conclusion the woman is his girl friend, but maybe Jonas just ran into her there and—"

Karen snorted her disbelief. "Maybe you're naive, Mimi. What's going on is as clear as the nose on your face, and I think Emily should be told."

"I disagree. Would you like to know if Albie was fooling around?"

"I certainly would! I'd have him in divorce court before he knew what hit him! He wouldn't even be able to afford to look at a Porsche in a magazine after I finished with him." Karen laughed.

"I don't think so. Would you like it if your friends were talking about your husband's affair behind your back?"

"No, not that. I see your point."

"But that's just what we're doing now. I hope you haven't told anyone else about this."

"Well . . . only one other person."

"That's too bad. If Emily wanted to divorce Jonas, she certainly wouldn't have to catch him cheating. He's hateful enough as he is. Obviously she wants to stay married to him. She's had plenty of opportunity to leave him—she even had a terrific man begging her to leave him—so it's not as if she'd be cast out on the street."

"She did? Who?"

"A good friend keeps her mouth shut," Mimi repeated, turning to leave. Clare heard the staccato of her heels on the slate. "It's too cold out here—let's get back to the party."

"Wait—I want to hear more about this mysterious man." Karen's shoes followed in haste.

"Not from me" came Mimi's voice from farther away. "You'll have to ask Emily."

Clare exhaled the breath she hadn't realized she was holding. She felt sick and burdened with an ugly knowledge she didn't want. She felt enraged—at Karen, at Jonas—but she had to admire Mimi McNamara, with whom she agreed wholeheartedly. Neither a friend nor a sister imparted to a wife the truths she refused to recognize on her own. Telling Emily about the redhead would do her no favor. Emily had a good friend in Mimi, that was certain. And a good sister in Clare, who vowed to keep her own mouth shut.

Abandoning the coffee cup and saucer on the floor beneath her chair, she decided suddenly to go to bed. The prolonged evening had exhausted her, and she still had packing to do before tomorrow. Once back in the living room, she realized immediately that Michael Duffy was gone, and so was Myra Randolph. Disgusting! The woman had to be at least ten years older than Michael, but if that was the type he preferred, so be it. The unexpected anger that swept over Clare propelled her through the social niceties of bidding everyone, even the malicious Karen, a good night.

She didn't bother to find her coat, deciding she could come back for it in the morning, and raced through the kitchen; the hired staff, under Harriet's noisy dictatorship, was busy washing pots and pans. Clare crossed the driveway with her arms wrapped around herself to ward off a stiff wind from the Sound. Her eyes were brimming with tears. *For Emily,* she told herself, but she knew they were tears for Clare—tears of loneliness and self-pity. How dare he go off with Myra Randolph! Michael Duffy infuriated her—probing into her personal life, ignoring a man who might have died on the plane, and now running off with a predatory female old enough to be his—

"Clare!"

She looked up. Her mouth fell open in surprise when, in the spotlight that illuminated the carriage house, she saw Michael seated on the third step of the stairs leading to her apartment. He didn't look happy. Not happy at all.

Chapter Seven

"Where the hell have you been?" Michael demanded, his voice gruff with anger. "I've been waiting here an age. I knew you couldn't stand much more of that party. Lord, what a bunch of phonies!" He grabbed her by the wrist, his sudden grasp almost, but not quite, painful. "You'll catch pneumonia out here with no coat on. Get inside."

Some doctor *he* was! she thought happily; everyone knew colds came from germs, not from the cold. He might look as if he were about to spit bullets, but at least he hadn't gone off with the antiques dealer. He pushed Clare up the stairs ahead of him, reaching in front of her to open the door, and propelling her into the sudden warmth and darkness of her apartment.

"How dare you push me around like this! Let go of me." Her voice vibrated with outrage, but she was secretly pleased, immensely pleased, that Michael Duffy was waiting for Clare Eckert and not squiring Myra Randolph to *her* door—or farther.

"We're going to have a talk," he said, continuing to hold her by the wrist. "Put on the light."

Silently she obeyed. The sudden yellow glow of the lamp made him grimace, and she noticed the laugh lines around his eyes. She liked the way he looked when he was angry, although she felt a thrill of fear at the temper that made the flecks in his eyes positively radiate. He *was* a handsome man, she decided finally, forgetting all the seesawing she had done about his looks in the past. In the small confines of her apartment, she liked the way he loomed imposingly and the way his light brown hair was a bit unruly, seeming to defy his efforts to keep it in place. She would bet he didn't know how often he pushed the hair back from his forehead, a gesture that gave him an endearing earnestness.

"I'm freezing. Got any brandy?" He doffed his overcoat and tossed it on a club chair.

"Yes, in the kitchen," she replied.

"Well?" he glowered.

"Oh, yes." She'd been almost hypnotized by her appraisal of him. She headed toward the small kitchen and took two brandy snifters from a shelf. Turning around, she crashed into Michael, who had followed her silently into the narrow room. Clare dropped one snifter on the brick floor, where it shattered into a hundred glinting pieces.

"I'm so sorry," he said, reaching behind her for a paper towel from the roll that hung near the sink. He stood so close that she could feel the warmth of his body and smell the sharp, clean scent of the cold night air on his skin and hair.

"Don't worry," she answered, her voice nearly a whisper. "I have another." She half turned in search of it.

His arms went around her waist, the broken glass forgotten. Even though she remembered that his body was lean and wiry, the hardness of his muscles surprised and delighted her anew.

A fleeting thought to rebuff his advances was gone as it raced through her mind. Why should she? she asked herself. He was extremely attractive, this bad penny of hers, self-contained and dynamic. She relaxed her body into his, lifting her chin to meet the gaze of his penetrating blue eyes, and felt the warmth of his breath just before he

kissed her. Clare closed her eyes, the better to inhale slowly
the echoes of the white wine they had drunk with dinner
and the traces of that distinctive scent he exuded. His
hands were like ice, even through the wool of her dress; the
skin of his face was cold, too. She wondered how long he
had waited outside for her in the subfreezing air.

What she did not anticipate was the electric thrill that
shot through her limbs at the touch of his lips on hers. A
new and heady fullness, almost a raw ache of desire, shook
her, and she wrapped her arms around his neck and pulled
his mouth against hers with an urgency that shocked her.
Her lips opened under the pressure of his, and she allowed
his tongue to enter and tease the soft inner skin gently, to
probe the secret recesses of her mouth. She was not an in-
experienced woman—there had been Teddy, after all—
but she had never before felt such an overwhelming desire
spring full-blown, and in but a moment's time.

They kissed for a long minute in the small kitchen before
another emotion rippled through her body. She recognized the cold grip of fear. Losing control of the situation;
she was losing control. Clare had promised herself that
would never happen again.

"Michael, this is wrong," she said finally, and with a
great effort of will.

"Why? Why is it wrong? I'm a very direct man," he said
into the skin of her neck. "And I want you. You made me
furious, ignoring me tonight, refusing even to look at me,
flirting with that pompous writer all during dinner and
then slipping away before I could talk to you. What the
hell's the matter with you, Clare?"

Pleased that his jealousy had matched hers, she cut
short his litany without resorting to the mention of Myra,
to whom he had paid at least as much attention as she had
to Gene. "But really, we hardly know each other."

"That's not true, and you know it! Even if it were, what
difference would it make? Where it counts—the way we

want each other—is all we need to know for now." His voice was low and soothing, seductive with its gruff notes of passion; between the words, his lips were trailing small kisses across her jaw and onto the lobe of one ear. Each touch left a warm tingle in its wake.

Clare inhaled raggedly, attempting to fill her lungs with an oxygen that was suddenly too thin and too fragile to satisfy her need.

"Am I wrong?" he persisted. "I can't believe I've misread you."

"No. Yes. No." She exhaled a long sigh. "No, you're not wrong."

Clare ran her fingers through his hair, aware of its resiliency against her skin as though all her senses had recently burst into life. She saw that her hand trembled as her fingertips combed the strands. "I find you extremely attractive," she told him. "But it's too fast. I wasn't expecting... I had no idea... You surprised me, that's all." *Can't you see that I'm not ready,* she asked him silently.

Kisses that were trailing across the bodice of her dress stopped. Although she had pulled back first, Clare felt a distinct loss as Michael stood erect and looked directly into her green eyes with a piercing gaze that seemed to shoot down to her toes. She tried to read his face, searching vainly for remnants of his previous anger in the now cloudy depths of his eyes.

"You're afraid of me," he said at last, surprised at the discovery.

"No," she assured him. "Yes," she admitted, after a moment's hesitation. "Not really of you, Michael. Just afraid."

"I think I understand." He dropped his hands, then lifted them to adjust the knot of his tie. *Fleurs-de-lis,* she noted idly. A black tie with sedate *fleurs-de-lis* peppering its surface.

"Are you offended?" she asked him. "Don't be—"

"No, I'd say disappointed is more the word. Let down, to make an extremely bad pun. But I have hopes for the future." He smiled slowly, the blue eyes again compassionate, but knowing. *Yes, knowing,* she thought. *Eyes without dreams.*

Clare laughed nervously. "What about the brandy? I'll put on some coffee, too. Did you like espresso? I could make some more." Although her breathing was slowly returning to normal, she felt as gangly and awkward as a schoolgirl in his presence.

"No coffee, but I would love a brandy," he replied. His voice betrayed no anger and was friendly, if slightly impersonal. After they cleaned up the mess on the floor, Clare poured brandy into two balloon snifters, an inch more of the amber liquid into his glass than she allowed herself. She set the snifters and the bottle on a tray, which she carried to a table in front of a love seat.

"You're moving?" he asked, inclining his head in the direction of two boxes that stood in the corner, already sealed and ready to go to Mrs. Sydney's house the next day.

"Yes, I took a room in a house on Keeler Street. I'm moving in the morning."

He sat on the love seat at her side, not touching her, but excruciatingly close. She felt the warmth from the length of his muscular thigh where it flanked hers on the wide-wale corduroy upholstery.

"What are you afraid of, Clare?" he asked her suddenly, placing his arm behind her on the back of the love seat.

"I . . ."

"Hurt badly by the breakup of your marriage?"

"Oh, well. . ." She tried to dismiss the subject with a casual toss of her head. "Maybe you're right," she admitted. Why did she allow him to ask her such personal questions? She had never discussed her feelings about Teddy, about the loss of her former life, with anyone, not even with Emily. Michael, however, with one or two questions, made her want to open up more quickly than anyone she had ever known. He was easy to talk with, and he demanded honesty. "I . . . my marriage . . . well, it was terrible. I lost everything, as I told you before. I never want to be caught up in things I don't understand. Secrets, betrayals . . ."

"What you need is to be courted in a leisurely manner, lovingly, by a man who respects you. That way, you'll learn to trust again." His mouth was very close to her ear. She liked the sound of his voice, liked it very much. Even more, she liked the sense of his words. She stared at a point on his knee.

"I don't miss the comforts so much, although I admit life is more difficult without them, but the calmness of having an ordered life—that's what I miss. I feel cheated of all my hopes, can you understand that? I worked hard to assure us, my husband and me, a good future together, and I'm still getting used to the idea that my life has changed totally. What hurts is the way it happened—no explanations, no cross words, just . . . nothing! One day he didn't come home from work, and then the roof fell in." Not really the truth, she realized as she spoke. Although at the time the end seemed to come that quickly, things between Clare and Teddy had been bad for a long time. Even so, she had never dreamed he would simply walk out on her.

"So what's the explanation?" Michael's hand had dropped from the back of the love seat to rest on her shoulder. She felt his fingers on her skin through the wool challis of her dress as if there were no fabric at all between his hand and her bare back.

"Things weren't perfect between us, not from the beginning. But why did he just up and leave? I don't know," she answered, genuinely perplexed.

"And what are you planning to do with the rest of your life?"

"I don't know that, either. I'm looking for a job right now. Why are you so interested?" She turned to Michael and searched his face. She wanted to kiss him again, more slowly and tenderly; wanted to go on kissing him endlessly, to the point of oblivion. Twin thrills of desire and fear alternately warmed and chilled her.

"Everything about you interests me, Clare. Everything. It's been that way from the very beginning. You've been fighting it, but I know you feel as strongly as I do."

"You're right," she admitted.

"I won't rush you, Clare. That I promise. But beginning tomorrow, I will be your suitor."

Suitor—what a charming word! She smiled shyly at him. Yes, that was exactly what she wanted, a suitor.

Michael stood up suddenly and reached across to the club chair for his overcoat. Clare didn't want him to leave, but she couldn't make herself say the words that would allow him to stay.

"You'll need help moving," he said. "What time do you want to go in the morning?" He put on the coat and buttoned it.

"Is t-ten o'clock all right?" Clare felt a sense of loss already, although he stood but two feet from her.

He extended an arm to help her up from the love seat, and when she fell into his arms, he held her close before he raised his hands and laid them, one on each cheek. Holding her face tenderly, he spoke in a low voice. "You won't have anything to fear from me. What is the most important thing to you?"

"Honesty," she said immediately. "Honesty is what I want from you." Lies brought heartache and suffering. Lies brought the betrayal of that vital but fragile marital trust that, once weakened, could never be regained. Teddy had lied, Jonas was lying. At the thought of Jonas, Clare shuddered involuntarily. Yes, honesty was the most important thing a man and woman could share.

"Honesty," he repeated, as if it were a new idea to him. He shook his head almost imperceptibly. Then he kissed her again, slowly and tenderly, just as she wanted him to. Now he tasted of brandy and a bit of her lipstick.

"I'll see you in the morning," he said.

"EMILY, IT'S TIME we had a talk," Jonas said out of the blue at breakfast the next day. Clare felt her heart fly to her throat, but she knew the accompanying cold stab in the pit of her stomach was merely a pale imitation of what her sister, seated across the table, was probably feeling.

"Not now, Jonas," Emily said after a brief hesitation. Her green eyes flicked to Clare's, then down to the half-eaten meal in front of her. A talk meant that Jonas did the talking, his voice escalating until a full-blown scene ensued.

Immediately one of the twins—Clare thought it was Kevin, but it might have been Ian—began to whimper. He left his chair and made his way around the table to his mother, where he stood at her knee with outstretched arms. Emily took him into her lap, pushing back her chair to do so. "Not in front of Clare," she added quietly.

"Clare's family. She won't mind—will you, Clare?"

Clare was silent, refusing to meet Jonas's eyes. She buttered a piece of toast, methodically drawing the knife back and forth, so that it made a harsh, grating sound in the quiet room. *I wish I'd never said yes to this breakfast invitation.*

"Where's Harriet? This meal isn't fit to eat," he said.

"She went home. Her husband was sick. We were lucky she stayed last night, in fact."

"Lord, she's never around when you need her! And last night's dinner was rotten, simply rotten. I want you to find a new cook right away."

"But, Jonas," Emily said slowly, "I thought the dinner was a great success. Harriet is very reliable *and* a marvelous cook. Besides, the boys love her."

"She spoils the boys, just like you do. Put Kevin down immediately! You're turning him into a sissy. It's not right to pick him up every time he makes a peep. And dressing them alike, especially in those short pants they wear—they look ridiculous! For God's sake, Emily, get those boys haircuts!"

Kevin threw his arms around his mother's neck and buried his face beneath her long hair. At the other end of the table, Ian began to cry softly.

"They're only three years old, Jonas," Emily said reasonably. "Children need to be held and shown that you love them."

"Well, don't blame *me* if we have to spend a fortune on psychiatrists when they're older." He crossed his arms over his chest in triumph.

"Jonas, please. Can't we have a nice breakfast for once? Clare's leaving in a little while. We don't want her to think we're—"

"I don't give a hang *what* Clare thinks of us. She has nothing to say about it anyway. She's a guest here, and she has to take potluck."

Clare had finished buttering the toast, but she was no longer hungry, although the baked eggs on spinach under a velvety hollandaise sauce that only Emily could prepare to such perfection had tasted wonderful two minutes before Jonas's outburst.

"I think I'd better be going along," Clare said. Terrible bands were tightening inside her head. "I've a bit more to do before—" She half rose from her chair.

"Sit down, Clare," Jonas ordered, yanking roughly at her sleeve until she fell back into the seat. "I want you to hear this. Emily, we've been home from Mexico for more than two weeks, we're well into the month of March, and I feel there are things that I, as the husband and provider around here, have every right to demand, to expect, and that you, as my wife, have a duty to do."

"W-what?" Emily spoke from pale lips.

"The suitcases. You haven't even unpacked the suitcases yet."

Emily was silent for a few seconds. "But they're not in your way," she pointed out quietly, without a trace of argumentation. "They're in one of the back bedrooms. You never even go in there."

"That's not the point, old girl. The point is the sloppiness of your mind. What would happen to us if I ran my practice the way you run this household? How can you expect to lead an orderly life if your mind is in such a mess? The suitcases are symptomatic of your lack of organization."

"Jonas—"

"Don't Jonas *me*," he exploded, giving Emily a look glimmering with warning. "I'm talking!"

As Ian began to sob in earnest, Clare pushed her chair back with a noisy scrape on the brick floor. "I'll be running along now, Jonas."

"Why? Can't you stand the heat in the kitchen, Clare? Are you just like your sister? Is that why your husband walked out on you?"

Clare sucked in her breath in disbelief. *Oh, he went for the jugular.*

"Jonas!" a shocked Emily cried.

"It's not the heat in the kitchen," Clare said through clenched teeth. "It's you I can't stand. You're a hateful excuse for a man, for a father and for a husband! You're a pretentious, money-hungry, deceitful snob, and Emily is much too good for you! Why she stays married to you is beyond me."

"You ingrate!" Jonas retorted, rising from his chair so precipitously that it fell to the floor with a crash, causing Kevin to wail in fear. "Don't bother to come back to my house, because you won't be welcome!"

"Don't worry—I'll never step foot in here again!"

Clare went out the back door, slamming it savagely. She heard Emily call her name once, twice, but she ran across the yard and raced up the steps, two at a time, to the carriage house.

She was finished with Jonas, having said all the ugly thoughts she'd carried around in her heart for the past three months. He was an unbelievable man, cruel and malicious, a man without minimum consideration for others. Clare wasn't hurt so much for herself as she was for Emily. She didn't care to avail herself of Jonas's hospitality for another minute, but to be cut off from her sister and her nephews. . . No, she wouldn't allow Jonas to separate her from her family; she would confine her visits to his frequent absences.

She was glad she'd said the words, though, very glad. She only wished she'd been able to say them to Teddy, too. She realized her situation with Teddy differed only slightly from Emily's with Jonas. The details varied, but the men were exceedingly similar in the bad points—all the insults she'd shouted at Jonas. If Jonas had another woman somewhere, a woman for whom he'd purchased an expensive foreign sports car, he was acting in a most immoral way. In Clare's eyes, that made him a bad man and a bad husband. Teddy had been a bad husband, a man who spent their money foolishly and kept his crazy investments secret, a man too weak, or cruel or careless to face Clare with the truth. She wondered what skewered event in their past had made Emily and her choose such lousy husbands.

She was still brooding when Michael Duffy arrived at the door of the apartment.

"Are you angry with me again?" he asked immediately, the blue eyes cutting through her like a knife. He did have an uncanny ability to see right into Clare. She eyed his gray corduroys and dark red parka and, finding no sign of a designer label anywhere, she smiled with approval. Thank goodness Michael was different, like a breath of fresh air.

"No, not with you," she said with a wry laugh, trying, fairly successfully, to shake off the bad taste that remained from the breakfast confrontation. "It's that jerk Jonas, of course. I'm so glad you came early. I'm dying to get out of here."

"I couldn't wait to see you," he said, giving her hand a squeeze that warmed her.

Michael carried the boxes down the narrow stairs, managing somehow to stow them in his tiny car. Clare had to wait for him to open the door on the passenger side. She thought no men did that anymore, not since the advent of women's liberation.

No one was there to say good-bye when they left the driveway in the Volkswagen.

"It's just a room, my new apartment," she told Michael as they neared Mrs. Sydney's house on Keeler Street.

"But it's yours."

"Yes, that's the point," she replied, pleased that he understood.

"HOW ABOUT DINNER at Cobb's Mill Inn?"

"I'd like that. I've heard of it, of course, but I've never been there." They were sitting alone over empty teacups in Mrs. Sydney's kitchen, and Clare was studying the way the hairs grew on the back of Michael's left hand, which lay alongside hers on the oak table. Mrs. Sydney had gone to visit a niece in Pelham, some miles down the turnpike.

Michael had good hands, Clare decided—big, strong, long-fingered, always dry and usually warm. The minute one of them was touching Clare, as one was now, she felt anchored and less alone. A doctor's hands, clean and capable. Reassuring.

"Put on your party clothes." He stood and stretched, his muscles tight against the oxford-cloth shirt he was wearing beneath a black sweater he had removed sometime before. She was tempted to rest an open palm on his torso, to wrap her arms around his waist, but she did nothing. "I'll wait for you here. Then, if you don't mind, you'll have to wait for me while I change."

"No, I don't mind at all." She wanted to see where he lived. She wanted, in fact, to know much more about him. She ran upstairs and changed into a dark green wool skirt and a silky beige shirt that tied at the neck with a flattering bow. Over the separates, she put on a loosely woven coordinating jacket of a muted beige and olive-green plaid.

Michael's apartment was nothing like what she had expected. Located on a busy street that bisected New Canaan, it had that impersonal, furnished air common to many rentals. Her own single room at Mrs. Sydney's was a hundred times homier than Michael's one-bedroom, third-floor flat overlooking a pond behind the apartment complex. Clare was surprised, and she said so.

"I haven't been here long," he explained. "And I've been too busy to look for a more permanent place."

She knew there was a story somewhere behind his explanation. The apartment had the antiseptic atmosphere she had seen in places on which the occupant had no desire to put his own stamp. If Michael hadn't told her he was a lifelong bachelor, she would have assumed that he was newly divorced and making a single life for himself in the no-man's-land of the suburbs, where an unattached person was just that—rootless and out of place. She congratulated herself for having found Mrs. Sydney. What she was forced to forgo in privacy would be balanced by the warmth that came from living in a real home.

Three hours later they sat over an after-dinner drink at Cobb's Mill Inn. Michael was drinking Kahlua, and Clare, Sabra, a chocolate liqueur from Israel that he had urged her to try. Clare was sleepy and content after a dinner of roast duckling in a sauce of dark cherries, and she gazed out a window to her right that overlooked a rushing waterfall. On the far side of the narrow river that ran right next to the restaurant, a dense forest of trees stood bare in the coming March twilight.

"Will you come back to my place, Clare?" he asked.

She was silent.

He looked at her for a long moment. "It's not what you think," he said at last, "although if you change your mind, I'm willing." He smiled at her, attempting unsuccessfully to leer.

They had eaten in the late afternoon, and it was still early. What awaited her at Mrs. Sydney's? An empty room. She had nothing to read, nothing to do except arrange her clothes in the tall dresser of the single room. To be with Michael for a little longer was more appealing than the thought of spending the rest of the evening alone in her room. A hundred times more appealing.

"All right."

They drove back to New Canaan on a different route, taking country roads where antique houses were built so close to the road that Clare wondered aloud at the inconvenience of their location.

"It's because in the old days the roads were narrow, and everyone wanted his house next to the road," Michael explained. "No winding private driveways for those farmers who had to work for every square foot of clear land. See all those picturesque stone walls? They came from clearing the fields, not because the settlers thought to create a cozy effect for you and me to admire three hundred years later. In Pennsylvania our farmhouses are often made of stone like these walls, and some of them are quite beautiful. I'd like you to see them sometime, Clare. I've often wondered why people didn't build stone houses here in Connecticut, too. I suppose they had so many trees it didn't matter. Wood is probably easier to work with."

The headlamps of the Volkswagen picked out the walls of which Michael spoke. Clare thought of his parents, who hadn't wanted him to study medicine, and she realized she knew little more than that detail about Michael, while she had confided much more of her own life to him. She wondered if he meant to introduce her to his family—if that was what he had meant when he spoke of courting her. She was willing. She hoped he would invite her on a trip to Pennsylvania. She had never been there, and she would like to see the state. In fact, she grew warm when she thought of going away with him for a weekend.

"How far is it to Berwick? Isn't that the name of your hometown?"

"Yes, that's right," he answered, glancing her way, clearly pleased that she had remembered. "About two hours from here, I guess."

"Do you go home often?" No, he couldn't, or he would know how far Berwick was from New Canaan.

"Not much. We don't have a lot in common anymore, my family and I. How about you?"

"I used to go once a year or so, but I haven't in the past two years because of . . . of things. My parents don't really understand what happened to me. They thought the sun rose and set on Teddy. Besides, they're totally opposed to divorce, so I gave up trying to explain myself to them a long time ago." Clare bit her lip in exasperation; Michael again had turned the conversation back to her. He had a trick of doing that.

"That's too bad," he said, "but I can certainly empathize."

Here was the opening to ask him a personal question, but he was already pulling the Volkswagen into the driveway of his apartment complex, and so she let the moment pass.

Upstairs in his apartment, he helped Clare with her coat and jacket, both of which he hung in the hall closet. He offered her a drink, which she declined, and a cup of coffee, which she accepted. She waited in the living room while he started the coffee, then followed him into the utilitarian kitchen to watch him prepare it. Like Emily, he began with beans that he ground, then carefully he concocted the brew. She imagined that a single man his age could be extremely fussy in his living habits, yet Michael Duffy didn't seem that way.

"Why is your apartment so...so cold?" she asked. "There's nothing personal here at all. It's like a hotel."

"I guess for me it *is* a hotel," he agreed. "I'm just here on a temporary assignment from the home office. I'll be going back in a month or two."

Going back! Clare's heart sank. "How long have you been in Connecticut?"

"Six weeks, on and off."

"So where do you usually live?"

"I live in Virginia. A place called Fairfax."

"I've never heard of it."

"Fairfax is a suburb of Washington."

"Are you often sent around to different offices? Or is 'labs' the right word?"

"Yes, and yes," he answered, handing her a cup of strong black coffee. "Do you want to watch television?"

"Sure."

"The only problem is—the television's in the bedroom. Want to chance it?"

"Sure." And she did, she realized. She followed him into the bedroom and watched him fluff up some pillows and lean them against the headboard of a double bed. Clare sat on one side of the bed, extending her legs in front of her on the spread and resting her back against a pillow. Michael turned on the television, found a station he liked, then sat down on the opposite side of the bed and kicked off his shoes. The volume was adjusted so low that she could hear nothing, and she watched silent figures mouth the script. She had seen the movie already, she realized, but she wasn't here to watch television.

She said nothing when he shut off the lamp on the table

next to the bed. The room was plunged in semidarkness, the only light coming from the flickering image on the television screen and from a shaft slanting in through the open door.

"In Virginia, do you live in a house or an apartment?" Virginia, to Clare, meant rolling green fields with white fences that protected thoroughbred horses. Virginia was Southern mansions, perhaps with Spanish moss hanging from trees surrounding them. She had never been there or anywhere else in the South, but she wanted to fix an image of Michael's true environment in her mind. He did not belong in this nice, but cold, apartment. He was too warm and open. "Do you have horses?"

"Horses, no!" he replied with a laugh. "Fairfax is a suburb of Washington, and I couldn't possibly afford enough land to keep horses in Fairfax. Come to think of it, I don't know if zoning would allow you to keep horses in town. I live in a house. It's brick, it's built on a hill, it has three small bedrooms and a garden in the back, and it's not yet paid for. I don't grow anything special in the garden, since I'm away so much. Someone comes in and cuts the grass for me in the summer. The house isn't too new or too big or too anything, but it's home and, for that, I'm fond of it. I travel a lot, so it's nice to have a place to go back to. I'd like to cut down on my travelling, actually. At first I liked my job a lot because I got a chance to see different parts of the country and spend time in each one—really get to know the people. But after a while, it all began to mix together, one place looking pretty much like another, and I started to appreciate the old adage, 'There's no place like home.'"

He'd seldom said so much about himself, she realized; and yet, what had he told her? Almost nothing. "Why don't you open your own practice, Michael?"

"You asked me that before." He stretched out on the bed and closed his eyes, ignoring his coffee, which sat untouched on a night table. Clare held her mug in her right hand, her left hand resting on the spread. Her hand was no closer than six inches from his leg, but she was aware of the warmth that radiated from his body. Or was it the warmth of hers? She felt dazed and slightly feverish, and she wondered if the after-dinner drink had been too much after the bottle of wine they had shared at dinner. No, she hadn't even finished her final glass of wine, she recalled, realizing with a start of surprise that she was intoxicated merely by the nearness of Michael himself. She hadn't been this close to a man, certainly not in bed—or, more accurately, *on* a bed—for a long, long time.

In silence he lifted her hand and touched it to his lips, and she felt a tingle snake up her arm.

"Put down your coffee," he said in a low, hoarse tone.

She obeyed.

"Stop me if you feel scared," he whispered, pulling her down on the bed beside him. Willingly she moved into the crook of his arm and settled against him, feeling the length of his body next to hers.

"I'm not afraid of *you*, Michael."

"Yes, I know," he whispered. His lips moved to an earlobe and kissed her, causing the nipples of her breasts to contract suddenly. She slipped an arm around him, while he allowed his other arm to enfold her and his hand to rest on her back, where it began to draw lazy circles on the silky beige blouse.

"Really, I'm not. I'd...I'd like to make love with you." There, it was out, and she knew the words were true. Somehow the fact that he had promised her time was enough to allow her to admit that she wanted him. This was on her own terms, she told herself. She hadn't been forced to come back to his apartment. He hadn't coerced her to lie on his bed and pretend to watch a television film that didn't interest either one of them. She knew why she was here, and she was willing. She was more than willing.

"And I'd like to make love with you," he answered, his voice husky with emotion.

Her fingers glided through his hair, her mouth soft and parted and only half an inch from his. They lay close together, but she wanted more. As he began to move his lips back and forth on hers, slowly and gently, she opened fully to admit his tongue, longing for the taste and touch of him. His taste was of honey to her lips, and the unexpected sweetness of the sensation held her still against him for the long moment of the kiss as his mouth opened to hers with determination, his tongue probing hungrily.

He broke off the kiss to begin a pattern of increasingly warm kisses down the line of her throat. His hand found the tie of her beige blouse, loosening it with one quick pull, and he began to open, slowly and deliberately, the tiny pearl buttons at the front of the blouse, slipping his hand inside to cover the surface of one small breast.

Clare inhaled with pleasure at the touch of his warm palm on her breast, and a shiver coursed through her. She felt his skin burning into hers, and she whispered his name.

The hand left her breast, left it feeling cold without him, and traveled to the zipper of her skirt. In the quiet room there was only the rustle of Clare's removing of her skirt with Michael's help and the uneven flicker of the ignored image on the television screen.

She was wearing a dark rose half-slip trimmed with three inches of lace at the hem, and no bra. He gazed at her breasts and sighed his pleasure and approval, lowering his head to bury his face in them, resting his cheek against her so she could feel the moist exhalations of his breath across her skin. Within her swelled the familiar but long-forgotten pleasurable ache of desire. She felt warm and safe and cherished. She felt she was important to Michael's happiness, and that he wanted her desperately. Even in the half-light, she could see how much his body yearned for hers; she could see his blue eyes, intense with a longing that matched what she felt within herself. Yes, she wanted him. She trusted him. She longed for him to make love to her.

By tacit agreement, he left her and stood to remove his own clothes, tossing them haphazardly on the carpet. While he was occupied, she took off her stockings and the slip, sliding them both down her legs and pushing them to the bottom of the bed.

Then he was back at her side, his naked body stretched the length of hers, and she felt his desire full against her thighs. The hard, uncompromisingly aroused touch of him sent a tremor racing through Clare's limbs. He ran his hands, the skin of his palms a little rough, up and down the length of her spine, allowing the fingers to slide teasingly into the curve of her buttocks. She trembled once more.

"You're certain?" he asked.

"I think it's too late to change my mind," Clare whispered. "Not that I care to." Her hands slid down to the tight muscles of his hips and she drew him to her, then over her, turning to fall on her back and open her thighs for him.

She was ready. She was more than ready, she was impatient for him. Finally he was inside her with a slow, deep thrust, and he was moving against her, moving with her, taking the lead, allowing her to have the lead. As they moved apart and then together, apart and together, she felt the tension, already nearly unbearable within her, grow to impossible bounds. She arched her back, and her body shook with release a long moment before his. He hesitated, holding himself still as she trembled uncontrollably, and then he, too, shattered, collapsing breathlessly on her breast, the stubble of his beard rough and lovely against her skin.

She wrapped her arms around him, allowing herself to doze.

How weak I am, she mused. *I feared making love with*

this man because he would bring me comfort and security, not because he wouldn't. One short evening with him and I'm back where I began—leaning on a man for strength.

But his strength was what she wanted, she realized, what she had sought when she came to his apartment after dinner. She must finally put away the fears born of her past. Just because she was once betrayed, why should she suspect Michael Duffy would do the same? In Michael's strong arms, she felt safe and trusting, like a child come home to a loving house. For the first time in months, her body relaxed completely, and she nestled herself into the crook of his well-muscled arm.

As she dozed, she felt him cover her gently with a fleecy blanket. One finger played with a strand of her dark hair that lay across the pillow. She was aware that he was awake. She heard him speak her name softly in the darkness, but she didn't answer because a response seemed unnecessary. He seemed to want to say the word, no more.

Half-asleep, fully content, she smiled lazily as his hand stroked her dark hair. She had no reason to believe that Michael felt emotions substantially different from hers, nor that he had reason to lie on his back, tense and sleepless, his eyes wide open and staring at the grayish light that flickered on the ceiling above the bed.

They lay that way for hours.

Chapter Eight

"Tell me about your past, Clare," Michael said at dinner the following evening. They knelt on tatami mats before a low table in a small private dining room of a Japanese restaurant in Westport that Clare had been wanting to try. As he spoke, he poured a thimbleful of warm sake for her.

"I've already told you," she replied, tasting the wine.

"I know, but I want to hear more."

His eyes told her why. Now that they had made love, every time he looked at her, his blue eyes seemed to say, "Come closer to me. Catch me up on everything that has ever happened to you. We've been too many years apart." Michael's eyes were the most expressive Clare had ever seen. He was a quiet man, so quiet, except for his eyes. In them she read depths of tenderness he seemed incapable of expressing verbally.

"Well, my life was somewhat like Emily's, although we didn't have the kind of money the Hahns do. After three years of marriage, I stopped working and became a provisional member of the Junior League. I volunteered one day a week at a nearby hospital and spent a lot of time decorating our house. It was a nice house, not too far from the ocean, too big for just the two of us, but I expected to fill it with children one day." This last brought a stab of regret to Clare's heart, but she pushed it away, knowing that, in practical terms, her lack of children was fortuitous. What if she had been saddled with twin three-year-olds like her sister's? Remaking her life would have been immeasurably more difficult. "Those were pretty shallow days, now that I look back on them."

"Didn't you want to continue working?"

"Teddy—my ex-husband—didn't want me to," she explained. "He had certain ideas about how the wife of a future partner of Byington, Wilson and Ruthfield should behave, and he wanted me involved in those activities. The partners' wives filled their days that way, you see."

"So you did what he asked. Did you always?"

Clare thought for a moment. "Yes, pretty much. After all, it was for the good of our mutual future. I could see the reason in what he requested of me." Those were the days they both had so much hope. In due course, Teddy would have become a partner. Even before that long-awaited day, as soon as he gave the okay, Clare would have started their family of two children. She closed her eyes and waited for the pain to hit again, but to her surprise, none came. She wondered if she was really getting over the disappointment of it all.

"But you told me you put him through law school. What were you doing then?"

Michael's hand reached out to cover hers. His skin was so warm she felt as if an electric current had jumped between them, uniting their bodies in an unbreakable grip. His eyes told her he felt the same magnetic bond.

"I was a bookkeeper at a small company that made parts for the aerospace industry. And at night I took courses in accounting at UCLA." Clare was pensive, thinking back on those hectic days. "After Teddy got his job at the law firm, I quit mine and went to school full-time for two semesters. But then he told me to stop that and get involved in charity work."

"So you did whatever he asked," Michael repeated.

"Much to my regret."

"Why?"

"I was such a fool, Michael. If Teddy told me to jump, I'd ask where, when and how high. If he said, 'Sign here,' I signed, and I never questioned what I was signing. That's one of the reasons we got into such trouble."

"What do you mean? What kind of trouble?"

"Well, clearly I have some understanding of numbers or I wouldn't be interested in accounting, and if I had really examined what he was getting us into, I never would have let him invest our money in the crazy schemes he did. He was trying to be a big shot, trying to keep up with the partners and with the friends he made. He invested in real estate—condos, a miniature golf course, land in Nevada, shares in a marina—crazy investments, really. Those are the ones I know about now, but there were probably more I never heard of. He seemed to have a deadly touch, since just about everything he got us into went bust.

"Then one day he disappeared. He came home, told me he wanted a divorce, packed a bag and left." Clare spoke dispassionately. For the first time, she was able to tell the story without recalling the terrible fear and desolation she had felt at his announcement. "Naturally I assumed he was somewhere nearby, but he must have left town. Later I discovered he'd been fired from Byington, Wilson and Ruthfield for doing something shady and that he hadn't worked in a couple of months. When the roof caved in, I didn't have any answers for anyone, but my name was on all sorts of things—loans from the bank and finance companies; the mortgage, of course; a second mortgage; personal notes; joint tax returns, all underpaid. I had to make good, at least on my half. I don't know what Teddy did or is doing about his half. He never showed up at court, so I divorced him by default. By law, they could only charge me for half of our debts. The house went first, of course." At the thought of the house, she felt another twinge of regret, but it was more the memory of pain and nothing like the horror she had experienced when she realized she was being thrown out on the street.

"Clare, how could you have been so...so..." Michael waved a hand in the air, and a frown furrowed the skin between his brows. Now the blue eyes turned hard and steely, as if he wished to chastise her.

"Stupid," she finished for him. "You're very polite, but I'm not afraid to say the word. It's incredible, isn't it? And me an almost-accountant. I can't believe it myself, and yet my attorney told me she saw women like me all the time, women who loved and trusted their husbands and simply signed away their rights. I don't know why I was such a fool."

A waitress, kimono-clad, entered the room and bowed. Kneeling, she set earthenware dishes of pickled vegetables before Clare and Michael, then departed. Clare picked up a pair of wooden chopsticks and adroitly began to eat.

Michael watched her with fascination. "How can you eat with those things?"

"Everyone in California knows how," she answered with a laugh. "Well, not everyone, but Japanese food is very popular out there. Why don't you ask for a fork?"

"Never!"

"Here, let me show you." She held up one stick. "Rest one like this on your fingers, then move only the top one." Reaching across the table, she plucked a vegetable from Michael's dish and fed it to him. "Now, you practice."

"I'm coming over to your side of the table," he said, making good on his word and settling himself next to Clare. "That way, if I can't use the chopsticks, you can feed me. Besides, the food tastes better when you feed me." His thigh was next to hers, and in the small room the scents of their skin mingled.

"It's just an excuse to get closer," she said with a giggle. "You're already handling the chopsticks like a pro."

"You're very astute, madam." His eyes twinkled as he

lifted a pickled radish from Clare's plate and offered it to her. While she chewed the crunchy radish, he whispered in her ear, "How could we possibly get closer than we've been?"

Clare flushed, thinking back on the previous evening, but the red color high on her cheeks wasn't visible in the dim light of the room.

"You're very beautiful, Clare," he said in a low voice. "Very." He laid his lips on her neck, just below the ear. She felt his tongue on her skin, and a thrill like a bolt of lightning shot through her. This time she blushed in earnest.

"How could anyone have treated you that way? He really victimized you, didn't he?"

So lost was she in the sensation of his touch, Clare had to ask Michael to repeat the question. When he did, she tried to change the subject. She was tired of talking about Teddy and trouble and her own stupidity. She wanted Michael to whisper sweet nothings into her crimson ear forever.

"But it's so boring, Michael. Who cares about the past anymore? All that matters is right now, right here!" She smiled up at him, inhaling his essence, noting every rise and fall of his chest as he breathed in and out.

"I care. I want to know."

Clare sighed in exasperation. "All right. Was I a victim? Isn't that what you asked?"

He nodded.

"It would be very easy for me to agree with you. I'd like to, of course, but the truth is I am a competent adult and I'm responsible for my own actions. I should have realized what was going on." Something made her think of her sister, and Clare realized for the first time how similar Emily's blind trust in Jonas was to her former trust in Teddy. "I was a lot like Emily is now."

"What makes you think that?"

"Emily has no idea how their finances are. Jonas gives her a wad of cash every so often and she spends it. I wonder how she'd cope if she were ever on her own. She doesn't really have the slightest idea of how much it costs them to live."

"Plenty, I bet. How do you know he gives her cash?"

"She told me. I helped her do the household books for their accountant. Jonas gives her a couple of thousand every two weeks. The Hahns live well, don't they?"

This elicited a dry laugh from Michael. "Considering that Jonas works only three days a week, they live very well indeed." His movements were more awkward than Clare's, but Michael had mastered the chopsticks and ate with gusto as she spoke.

"Three days a week? What makes you say that? No, I'm certain you're wrong, Michael. Jonas goes to his office every day. Even on Saturdays he goes in for a few hours in the morning."

"He told me himself," Michael replied, concentrating on his food. "He told me he doesn't work on Tuesdays and Thursdays." Clare could almost feel the tension in his body as he emphasized his point.

"But he leaves the house even earlier on those days. As I recall, he goes in much earlier then, while the rest of the week he doesn't go in until nine-thirty."

"He's never in his office on Tuesdays and Thursdays," Michael insisted. "He told me so himself."

"Then where does he go?"

"To see a Porsche dealer, perhaps?"

"You know about that?" She opened her eyes wide and pulled back to stare into his. "How did you find out?"

He lifted his shoulders in a small shrug. "I saw you go into the solarium. When I followed you, I overheard those two women—"

"Mimi and Karen."

"Yes."

"Did you hear everything?"

"That wasn't enough? Was there more?"

Clare shook her head. "Oh, poor Emily. I suppose the entire town knows. I'd really like to see her dump that man and start a new life for herself. He's nasty, someone who should be brought down a peg or two. Not that it's any of my business," she added, although she felt it was her business to save Emily the heartache she herself knew so intimately.

"Why don't you do something about him?" Michael asked, his voice low and suggestive.

"Me? What could I do?" Clare raised her eyebrows.

"Blow the whistle on him," Michael said softly, his voice fading to a whisper.

"Blow the whistle on him," Clare repeated in an equally small voice. "Why? What is he doing wrong? Is there some law against verbally abusing your wife and kids? Against buying a Porsche for somebody who's not your wife? I don't think adultery is even against the law anymore."

Michael rolled his eyes. "Boy, you *are* naive! No wonder your husband stuck you with all those bills."

"What do you mean, Michael?" She paused as the waitress returned to remove their salad plates and leave steaming bowls of bean soup at their places. "Why am I so naive?" she asked when the woman had left them alone again.

"Anybody who throws cash around like Jonas Hahn does... Well, what does that type of behavior imply to you?"

"He's a show-off?"

"Yes, but aside from showing off. He throws his money around like water, but it's always cash money." He waited for a frowning Clare to make the connection that was clearly elemental to Michael, but which eluded her entirely. She shook her head in bewilderment.

"He likes cash," she said weakly, her voice rising in question as she realized from the look on his face that she had failed the test of his logic. "He doesn't like to pay interest on credit cards. I can't say I blame him."

"He wants no record," Michael corrected. "He wants no record of what he spends—or what he earns. In cash."

"Why?"

"So he doesn't have to pay income tax on it, of course."

"What makes you think so?" The slight frown became a definite scowl. Although she had often considered the Hahns' use of cash impractical, if not downright eccentric, it had never occurred to Clare to question the reason behind their behavior. Every family ran its finances in an individual manner, and how the Hahns ran theirs was none of her business.

"Look, Clare, Jonas has got to be in the very top income-tax bracket, wouldn't you agree? Even by Greenwich, Connecticut, standards, the Hahns live like kings. Waterfront property, a live-in housekeeper, fancy cars. Two Mercedes, isn't it?"

"And an old station wagon—a Ford, I think—that they use for heavy things, like taking the dogs to the vet or when the gardener buys shrubs or wood chips."

"A gardener, too." Michael nodded. "Tell me, does the housekeeper get paid in cash?"

"Y-yes."

"Then we can assume it's cash to the gardener, as well."

"Right."

"What else is cash? Entertainment? The trip to Mexico?"

"Yes."

"Clothing?"

"Some," she said. "Most, actually. I know Emily paid cash for a lynx jacket she bought in the fall. I was with her when she bought it." Clare remembered that the jacket had cost nearly six thousand dollars. "I'll take it out of the egg money," Emily had said with a laugh while she counted out a stack of one-hundred-dollar bills for the furrier. Emily often made jokes about her incredibly elastic egg money.

"So there," Michael said triumphantly, arms folded across his chest, all pretense of eating abandoned as his soup cooled.

"Your theory doesn't make any sense, Michael," Clare said decisively. She rested her elbow on the table, her chin on one hand. What was he trying to prove? Everyone knew insurance paid for at least part of everything that went on in a medical office. "Doctors don't get paid in cash these days. Everything is Blue Cross, Blue Shield. And everyone is insured, except for the indigent, whose bills are paid by the government—and never in cash. You can't live without insurance. I should know. I have my own individual policy, even though it costs me a fortune to maintain, but I wouldn't dare be uninsured. Only people in the underground economy get paid in cash—street vendors, people like that."

"Not everything medical is insured, Clare. Elective surgery, for instance, is rarely covered."

"Elective surgery?"

"Nose bobs, breast augmentation, face-lifts."

"But Jonas does more than just that type of work. Emily told me he performs a lot of restorative surgery—burn victims, cleft palates. She said he does quite a bit for free, too."

"A great humanitarian, our Dr. Hahn. Like Caesar's wife," Michael said with a cynical laugh. "Above reproach. How about some more sake?"

Clare laughed, too. "I'll admit it doesn't sound like Jonas. Yes, I'd love some more." She watched him pour. "If what you imply is true, how would Jonas do it?"

"I don't know, but I can imagine. Two sets of books, one for insured patients, one for cash transactions. Give a discount to patients who pay cash."

Who keeps the second set of records, Clare wondered immediately. She couldn't imagine Jonas bothering with paperwork. Would he share such skulduggery with his accountant? She had her doubts. Too risky.

"That's illegal, isn't it?"

"So is not paying your income tax. But people like Jonas usually get caught, you know."

"The IRS investigates people like him?"

"Of course, Clare! Why do you think so many doctors get into tax trouble? If the IRS suspected Jonas of evasion, they would send in a ringer for a consultation, have the agent—probably in Jonas's case, a woman—pay cash, and then look for the name in the bookkeeping records. If it wasn't there, well..."

"I hate the IRS. They auctioned off my house." She saw Michael wince at her words and was grateful for his compassion.

He looked at her steadily for a long moment, the clear brilliance of his blue eyes dazzling, even in the dimly lit room. "A lot of people do. But why should you and I pay taxes to subsidize Jonas Hahn's life-style?"

"A good point," Clare agreed, taking another sip of sake. "A very good point. However, what he does is none of *my* business. I'd just as soon forget he existed." She was tired of talking about Jonas.

"Tell me about you and your sister as children," Michael suggested, understanding her mood and changing the subject rapidly. "I'll bet you were a gorgeous baby."

"Not so gorgeous," Clare said with a laugh. "Skinny."

They finished their dinner trading childhood experiences.

There was no more talk of Jonas Hahn, but Michael's suspicions played on Clare's mind, and she vowed that the next day, when she finished up Emily's household accounts, she would look more carefully for evidence that Jonas was cheating on his income tax.

On Tuesday morning she took a bus to Emily's street. Having first determined that Jonas's Mercedes sports coupe was not in the driveway, she entered the house by the kitchen door. There, at the round oak table, a cup of coffee cold and abandoned before her, sat Emily in tears. Before the large double window above the sink, Harriet was noisily rinsing the breakfast dishes and loading them into an open dishwasher. On the floor in front of a washer and drier located in a corridor that led to the office, summer clothes lay sorted by color. It seemed that Emily, with Harriet's help, had finally unpacked the family's bags from the trip to Mexico.

"Let's go into the office," Clare suggested. Emily followed her as Clare stepped over the mounds of soiled clothing in the hall. Almost immediately Harriet appeared at the door with a tray in her hands and offered them both fresh coffee. There was a heavy silence while Harriet, cheerful as usual, bustled around, setting their cups before them and pretending to straighten the small room, which was already immaculate.

"What's the matter?" Clare asked the minute Harriet had left the office, a wastebasket in one hand, the empty tray in another.

"Nothing," Emily replied. The desolate look on her face was contradictory to her weakly voiced denial.

"Jonas again?"

"Really, Clare, it's nothing." Emily suddenly began to cry in earnest, reaching into the pocket of her wool skirt for a tissue, only to find one wadded into a useless ball. "Oh, he's so cruel to me sometimes. I do everything to make his life run smoothly, but whatever I do is never enough! Someday he'll be sorry."

It was the first crack in Emily's facade that Clare had ever heard, but when she pressed for details, her sister confided no more. Clare wondered if somehow Emily had heard about the woman with the new Porsche, yet there was no way to ask without revealing her own knowledge. She passed Emily a tissue from a package she carried in her purse. Half of Clare was offended that Emily would not confide in her; the other half understood that Emily wanted to spare her own dignity.

Clare posed some innocuous questions about the household accounts and bent her head to study the ledger she had nearly completed, hoping to give Emily an opportunity to compose herself. Outwardly Clare was the picture of calm, but inside she seethed with anger at her brother-in-law. Here, among these neatly added numbers, lay a possible means of making Jonas sorry. Did she dare mention Michael's suspicions to her sister? Did she have the right? She studied the numbers.

Yet, as she had suspected, there was nothing concrete in the dry columns of figures that she herself had entered in the leather-bound book. When Clare asked for a look at the previous year's ledger, Emily said it was in the safe in her bedroom. She left the room and returned five minutes later, her red and swollen eyes revealing that she had continued to cry during her absence.

Emily requested another tissue and blew her nose audibly. She made a valiant effort to stem her tears, pressing yet another tissue hard against her eyes. She drew in a shaky breath and said for the third time, "Oh, I'm so silly. Crying about nothing. I'm just blue, that's all."

Clare hated to see Emily unhappy, Emily who had everything—a beautiful home, two adorable sons, every material luxury imaginable. It seemed ironic that Clare, who had nothing, had begun to feel happy again, while her sister carried a heartbreak she wouldn't, or couldn't, discuss with anyone. Clare would give up some of that newfound happiness to comfort Emily, who had been so kind to her. She opened her mouth to speak, then closed it just as quickly.

After paging through last year's ledger, she found it as

uninformative as that of the current year. No, Clare thought, she had no right at all to intervene. Besides, not a shred of evidence existed to prove that Jonas was involved in anything illegal. If she decided to say anything to Emily, she would need proof, concrete proof.

With a life of its own, a plan began to form in her mind.

"Tell me Jonas's schedule so I don't run into him accidentally," she said casually to Emily.

"Monday, Wednesday and Friday he leaves for the office at nine-thirty." Emily sniffled once or twice, but having found a safe topic, her voice gained strength as she went on. "Tuesdays and Thursdays he leaves around eight. He's almost always home for dinner by six-thirty unless he gets delayed at the hospital, in which case he calls me. On Saturdays he works from nine until one or two."

"He works a long week!" Clare exclaimed. "I thought doctors kept bankers' hours and that none of them worked on Wednesdays."

"He works only three-and-a-half days a week. On Tuesdays and Thursdays he teaches a course at Columbia, and afterward he goes to his club in the city for lunch. Then he visits museums or libraries or something. I don't know what he really does—Jonas hates it if I pry. He thinks everyone should have privacy."

I bet, Clare thought. Jonas had two full days for his private life. Two-and-a-half, if she counted Saturdays. Wasn't Saturday the day he had been seen at the car showroom in Manhattan? Clare wondered what he *really* did on his free afternoons. He couldn't buy Porsches every week.

"Is it likely that he'll come home early and catch me here on a Tuesday or a Thursday?"

"Oh, no. Jonas's schedule is as regular as clockwork."

CLARE DWELT ON EMILY'S RECITAL of her husband's schedule, and her mind continued to come back to what Michael Duffy had suggested. The more she thought of the inconsistencies of what she had learned, the more convinced she became that Jonas's life was not what it seemed. Without mentioning the subject to Michael, she vowed to find out what Jonas was really doing on Tuesdays and Thursdays.

On Wednesday night, Clare told Michael she was tired and couldn't see him, although he had invited her to go to the movies. She called a taxi and took it to an agency that specialized in renting old cars, the only kind she could afford. There she leased a five-year-old Plymouth. She returned to Mrs. Sydney's house and left the car overnight on Keeler Street.

At seven forty-five the next morning, she was parked at the end of Jonas and Emily's quiet street, feeling nervous and silly in a pair of wide sunglasses. In her hands she held a copy of the previous day's *New York Post*, which she had found on the floor of the Plymouth, and pretended to read the screaming headlines of the tabloid newspaper while watching for Jonas's dark brown Mercedes sports coupe in the rearview mirror. At exactly eight o'clock she saw the car rounding a curve behind her, and she started the engine of her rental car. Jonas drove past without giving Clare a glance, stopped at the sign on the corner, and turned to his right. His sports coupe still emitted clouds of steam from the tailpipe, proof that the morning was as cold as the weather forecast on the radio said it would be.

Clare followed Jonas to the Connecticut Turnpike, where she expected him to continue on to New York City. She didn't know where Columbia was located or whether Emily had meant the hospital or the university, but she had a vague idea that Columbia was on Manhattan's Upper West Side. Consequently she was in the wrong lane when Jonas swerved off to the left, following a sign that said "Throgs Neck Bridge, Airports, Long Island."

Cutting across two lanes without heed for the heavy morning traffic or the blare of outraged horns that greeted her maneuver, Clare caught up with the brown Mercedes and quickly dropped three car lengths behind. She lagged in her new position to watch Jonas, in the exact-change lane, toss a token into the hopper for the bridge toll. Luckily, she was prepared for tolls, having laid a pile of coins on the dashboard for just such a contingency.

The traffic thinned out in the eastbound lanes when they reached the Long Island Expressway. Although Clare was a newcomer to the New York area, she knew that Columbia was not on Long Island.

Cautiously, she stayed in the middle lane, afraid Jonas would again make a move that would leave her stranded on the expressway. He was a careful driver, however, and seemed unaware that he was being followed. She thought he was prudent about his driving because the sports car's obvious value could attract the attention of police patrolling the highway, and also because he took great pride in the brown Mercedes itself. Clare was not impressed. Mercedes coupes were a common sight in southern California; and anyway, status cars had never been a weakness of hers.

Despite the small size of Jonas's car, Clare was able to keep it in sight with ease. She was grateful for the sunglasses she had tucked into her purse at the last minute that morning. The day was deceptively clear and bright, contradicting the icy temperature outside, which was still in the low teens.

The Mercedes turned off at the town of Mineola, made two right turns in quick succession, and pulled into the parking area of a one-story brick office building on a commercial street. Clare drove by slowly and saw Jonas lock his car, pocket his keys, and enter an unmarked side door of the building. A patch of bright red drew Clare's eyes to her right. At the extreme end of the lot, parked diagonally across two spaces for protection from careless drivers who might open their doors and bang its pristine paint job, sat a shiny new red Porsche.

It was nine-thirty. She backed the rented car into an empty space in the lot, as far from Jonas's as possible. After watching the building for a minute, she noted a small bronze plaque at one side of the main entrance door, too far away for her to make out the words written there. Cautiously she left the Plymouth and approached the door.

"Rejuvenation Clinic," the plaque read.

She had heard of the clinic before, but she couldn't remember when or where. Had she heard the name on the radio? Seen it on television on one of those high-pressure ads that interrupted late movies? Something nagged at the back of Clare's mind.

At a diner across the busy street, she found a seat at a window table and ordered the breakfast special. A waitress brought her two fresh eggs, a thick slab of toasted homemade bread and a cup of steaming black coffee, all for ninety-nine cents. With the *Post* open before her on the table, she ate slowly, stretching the meal to twenty minutes and peering out the window every so often. The parking lot across the street was becoming crowded with cars. She ordered another cup of coffee and curiously read a sensational serialized autobiography of a Hollywood star that the *Post* was featuring that week, turning the page slowly as she reached the end of a column.

Clare's heart jolted with a shock of recognition as the words "Rejuvenation Clinic" leaped from the newspaper. A muddy reproduction of the armless Venus de Milo took up a third of the quarter-page ad on the right side of the page. "Specialists in plastic surgery," a text in black script read. "Come in for a free consultation. Privacy assured. Four specialists." An address and telephone number followed.

And here she was, on the very street in Mineola where the Rejuvenation Clinic was located. "Teaching at Columbia, indeed!" she muttered beneath her breath.

Clare dug around in her purse for the small calendar she carried and flipped to the blank memo pages at the back. She began to count and make note of the women who went through the main entrance of the clinic, filling in the time of their arrivals and departures. A cheerful waitress refilled her cup, but she ignored the coffee, allowing it to cool as she watched the building across the way.

Finally, she had no excuse to occupy the window table any longer. She paid her bill and left, tipping generously.

Back in the car, she kept the engine running until the Plymouth grew warm. She decided to stay until noon at the latest, switching the engine on again only when she began to feel numb.

Between the time she had spotted the ad—about ten, she thought—and noon, she had counted thirty women entering and leaving the clinic.

Clare had already steered the Plymouth out of its parking space and was heading toward the street when she heard the growl of an engine and realized that someone had started the ignition of the Porsche. In the rearview mirror she saw the red car nose in behind hers, and she decided immediately to follow it. Left or right? If she turned in the wrong direction, the Porsche would get away. There was too much traffic to negotiate a reversal. Praying she was correct, Clare turned to the left and was gratified to see the Porsche do the same. She slowed, allowing the sports car to pass her, and saw a black-haired woman of about thirty at the wheel. Too much lipstick, hair clearly dyed, and a nicely sculptured nose, probably one of Jonas's doing.

The Porsche didn't go far, pulling into the lot of a small shopping complex four blocks to the east. The woman, dressed in shiny black boots and a bright red wool coat the exact shade of the car, entered a delicatessen. Clare was right behind her. Courteously, the woman held the door for Clare, giving her adequate opportunity to study the heavily made-up face.

Yes, thirty, Clare thought, but a thirty that had lived a hard life. The skin was youthful, but there was a hard set to the mouth and a resigned look to the eyes. That the woman was pretty there was no doubt, but hers was a studied, artificial dazzle, and Clare was certain that the slightly tilted, slightly too-perfect nose was not the one she had been born with.

"What's it going to be today, Angel?" a man behind the counter asked.

Was that a name? Or was it an endearment, like "honey" or "sweetie"? How would Clare determine this woman's name?

"Two tuna fish on white bread, one pastrami on rye, no mustard, two diet sodas and a Doctor Pepper." The harsh sounds of a regional accent grated on Clare's ears as she listened while Angel—if that was her given name—and the counterman made friendly conversation. The woman was obviously a regular at the deli. Clare watched her, growing more convinced that Angel was indeed her name. After she had paid, Clare ordered a coffee and an English muffin and waited while the man packed them in a brown paper bag. He didn't call Clare "Angel"; he didn't call her anything at all. Instead, he gave her a broad smile and squeezed her fingers flirtatiously when he handed her a few coins of change.

The Porsche was just turning to the right, in the direction of the clinic, as Clare emerged. She discarded her package in a trash bin outside the deli and, on an impulse, went back in through the glass door.

"Do you have a public telephone?" she asked.

A nod of the counterman's head confirmed there was a telephone in the corner.

Clare paged through a dog-eared Mineola telephone book that hung suspended by a chain from the steel shelf beneath the telephone. She dialed the number of the Rejuvenation Clinic, then turned her back to the counter so she wouldn't be overhead. "Is Dr. Hahn in?" she asked the woman who answered.

"He's with a patient at the moment. Can someone else help you?"

Clare ignored the question and asked another. "Is Angel there?"

"Mrs. Chetnik is out to lunch right now. She'll be back in a little while. Would you care to leave a message?"

"No. I'll try later. What time do you close?"

"We close at five o'clock. We're open every day from ten to five."

"I'll try Mrs. Chetnik later," Clare said, repeating the name in order to commit it to memory. "Thank you." She replaced the receiver.

Every day from ten to five. That means Jonas wasn't working alone at the clinic. If he were, the office would be open only on the days he was available there. No, she knew that already, she realized; the newspaper had advertised four specialists. The Rejuvenation Clinic was a good-sized operation, then. Four doctors, a woman who answered the telephone, the curvaceous Angel... how many more behind those doors? Did they actually perform surgery there? Or were the patients sent to an affiliated hospital? How could she find out?

She stood at the telephone for a long minute, her hand still on the black receiver. Why should she want to find out the details of the Rejuvenation Clinic? What did all she had discovered matter? She could never betray Jonas, because Jonas's life was Emily's life. To hurt Jonas was to hurt her sister.

She filed away what she had learned, planning to do nothing with it, but feeling immensely satisfied that she had discovered Jonas's secret, which even his wife did not know.

Or did she?

Clare returned to Greenwich and parked the Plymouth in Emily's driveway, careful to leave a clear path of exit for a dark gray Peugeot sedan that was already there. Without a firm idea of what, if anything, she would say to her sister, she supposed she wanted to sound her out to determine if Emily knew of the clinic's existence. Since she had no excuse for this unannounced visit, Clare planned to say that she wanted to take the two ledgers home with her for one last check before turning everything over to the accountant. It was a good plan anyway; this year's ledger had to conform with that of the previous year, and she had not spent that much time studying the book Emily had taken from the bedroom safe.

After closing the car door, she walked along the path that led to the kitchen. As she turned a corner of the house, she came upon Emily and a man standing just outside the kitchen door. Clare pulled herself up short. Her sister was coatless, and her hair blew becomingly around her shoulders. But the man... Although his back was to her, Clare immediately recognized the tweed jacket he wore.

The couple's hands were at their sides, firmly locked together, and they were kissing intently, totally oblivious to Clare's arrival. Emily's face was turned to Clare, her eyes closed in rapture and a becoming pink flush on her one visible cheek.

Clare was mute with shock at the sight of them.

Chapter Nine

If it had been possible, Clare would have disappeared into the frozen ground beneath her feet. She thought of backing away silently, returning to the car and making a hasty exit, but there was no escape. Emily's eyes opened, and Clare was caught.

"Clare!" Emily tore her hands from Gene Janklow's and fastened them to her hair, smoothing it nervously. Janklow stepped away from her side just as Emily's face blushed crimson. "It's not what you think, Clare," she said, her voice quavering with the shock of being discovered.

"I'll come back later," Clare said. "I'm . . I'm sorry." The roar in her ears made her realize she was probably as pink as her sister.

"There's nothing to be sorry about," Janklow interjected calmly. "I was just leaving, so don't let me inconvenience you." As he spoke, he buttoned his jacket, straightened the tie he wore and, in an unconscious echo of Emily, smoothed his hair with one hand. Then he drew a handkerchief from his pocket and wiped traces of Emily's lipstick from his mouth. "I'll give you a call, Emily."

Emily's mouth worked in confusion. "Good bye, Gene," she said finally. As he walked down the driveway toward his car, Emily opened the kitchen door, holding it for Clare, who ran up the two steps and went past Emily, feeling as she did so a warmth emanating from her sister. "I can explain, Clare."

"Where's Harriet?" The house was strangely quiet.

"I gave her some time off to look for another job. I had to give her two week's notice."

"Why? Wasn't she working out?"

"She was working out perfectly. She cooks like a dream, she adores Kevin and Ian, and this house has never been so spotless. Not only that, I've never met a more cheerful woman in my entire life. Do you know how hard it is to find help that willing, that good?"

"Then what happened?"

"You were here when Jonas told me to get rid of her. That's what happened. If I don't, he'll just make her life miserable, and mine as well. You know how he can be when he gets a bee in his bonnet, and for some reason he doesn't care for Harriet. Oh, Clare, I don't know what the twins will do when she's gone. The three of them are so close you'd think she had raised them from birth."

"And the boys? Where are they?"

"They're at their play group. It meets twice a week. We—the mothers—take turns." Emily ran a hand through her blond hair. "Why are we discussing all these inanities? Clare, please let me tell you what happened. Let me explain."

"You don't owe me any explanations, believe me. I just stopped by to pick up the household ledger. I want to go over it one more time before it goes to the accountant, but I should have called first."

"No, I want to explain," Emily continued nervously. She went to the refrigerator and took out a tomato, which she washed quickly and began to eat as if it were an apple. "Want one?" She held the tomato out to Clare, who wrinkled her nose in distaste at its pale, gas-ripened color. After living so many years in California, Clare couldn't accustom herself to the tasteless red cotton that passed for tomatoes on the East Coast during the endless winter.

"No, thanks." Clare took off her coat and sat at the table. Emily sank into a chair opposite her, spreading a paper napkin to protect the polished oak surface of the table. She set the half-eaten tomato on the napkin.

"Gene wants me to sleep with him."

If you haven't already, Clare thought. She had been so interested in the revelation that Jonas had a mistress, she had neglected to put any significance on the definite interest that existed between Emily and Janklow. Thinking back, Clare knew the signs had all been there—Janklow's ultimately unexplained visit about the faulty heat in his rented house, his obvious disappointment in having mistaken Clare for Emily, his seeking out Emily's company at the dinner party. On Emily's part, there had been her out-of-character fascination with Janklow's books, her warm words about the historian and her initial reluctance to pair him off with Clare. *Nothing's ever what it seems,* Clare told herself. *I constantly make the same mistake.*

"But I could never do that," Emily continued, "although I find him immensely attractive. Immensely. In fact, sometimes I think I'm in love with him, but then I tell myself it's only a fantasy I entertain because I'm lonely and he's always so considerate. Look, he brought me these books to read. He respects my mind, you see, and he doesn't want me to be shallow, as he says so many of my friends are." Emily wiped her hands on the napkin and reached across the table to push a stack of books toward Clare.

Clare glanced at their spines: a book of Civil War history, a new literary novel that had been well reviewed the week before, a classic on raising children to be independent. Janklow's tastes were certainly eclectic, she mused.

"Really, Emily, you don't owe me any explanations at

all, and frankly, I couldn't blame you for having an affair with Gene Janklow. How could I? I mean, Jonas can be such a tyrant!'' Clare didn't really mean what she said. After all, married was married, and just because Jonas seemed to be cheating on Emily, Clare wasn't certain she approved of Emily's cheating on Jonas.

"A tyrant, indeed! That's just it, Clare. I wouldn't dare be untrue to Jonas.''

"Why not?''

"Two reasons. Primarily because marriage is sacred. We married for better or for worse, and if things are currently worse, well...that still doesn't give me the right to be unfaithful.''

Emily's forthright sincerity convinced Clare that her sister believed just what she said. "And what's the second reason?'' she asked.

"If I ever did anything like that, Jonas would take the boys away from me. He's already told me so, and I believe him.''

"So do I,'' Clare said.

"He has the money, the power and the temper to do it. He knows my weaknesses, he knows I'd simply die without my babies, and if Jonas got angry enough, he'd do his best to hurt me in the cruelest way he knows how—through the boys.'' Emily picked up the tomato and took another bite.

"Do you love Jonas?''

There was a long moment of quiet as Emily thought over the question. "Yes, you know I do,'' she finally said. "I fell in love with him the first time I met him. Certainly I still love him.''

I don't believe you, Clare thought. "But love isn't really eternal, Emily. Love can change. Love that isn't nurtured dies. Love that's betrayed dies. You don't think, for instance, that I still love Teddy, do you? How can you still love Jonas, considering the way he treats you? I know his problem—he thinks you'll love him no matter what. I can't see anything Jonas is doing to contribute to the so-called sanctity of your marriage."

"Oh, it'll pass. I'm sure things will get better."

"How?"

"Someday he'll come to terms with all this newfound affluence." She waved a hand to encompass the modern kitchen, the spacious waterfront house, the entire life-style of the Hahns. "And the old Jonas will come back. Then he'll be the man I fell in love with so long ago."

"Hogwash, Emily! Jonas is living exactly the way he wants to live. It's you who are unhappy here. Why don't you just leave him?"

"That's what Gene is always saying. He wants to...to marry me," Emily confessed shyly. "What do you think of that?"

Clare was shocked. She had no idea Janklow and Emily had proceeded so far in their...their... What was it? Not an affair, if Emily was to be believed. And yet the word "friendship" hardly seemed to fit the circumstance. Clare decided to consider their involvement a "flirtation." Yes, Emily was having a flirtation with Gene Janklow.

He'd probably make you a good husband is what Clare thought. "How flattering" is what she said aloud, however. If Emily knew what Jonas was *really* up to, she'd probably accept Gene Janklow's proposal. But Clare determined immediately that she wasn't going to share her newly discovered knowledge with her sister. Acutely sensitive to her sibling, Clare saw that Emily didn't really know what she wanted. If she did, she wouldn't be asking Clare's opinion; instead, she would be giving her a hundred reasons why she planned to leave Jonas. If this were not a flirtation, if Emily truly wanted an excuse to jump out of her marriage, she would already be aware of Angel Chetnik and her red Porsche, and probably of the Rejuvenation Clinic as well.

"Where's Jonas now?" Clare asked.

"He's in Manhattan. He called about half an hour ago and said he'd be home late tonight because of a faculty meeting at the medical school. He forgot to tell me about it earlier. I have an idea—do you want to have dinner here?"

"No, I can't. I have a date with Michael Duffy," Clare lied. "I must run, Emily. I should be at the computer software business in fifteen minutes." Another lie, but she had to return the rented car before going to her job. Clare stood up and pulled on her coat.

"Let me give you a lift." Emily stood up, too.

"No," Clare said quickly. "No, thanks. I have a borrowed car."

"You're not angry with me, are you, Clare?"

"Me? Never, Emily! I'm on your side, no matter what. Always have been, always will be—ever since we were kids." She hugged her sister tightly.

"I know that, Clare. I can count on you. Well, if you can't stay, maybe I'll call Gene and see if he's free—if I can get a sitter, that is. It's so inconvenient without Harriet around."

Be careful, Emily. But Clare said nothing. "The ledger?" she reminded her sister, recalling her excuse for having come by at such an inopportune moment.

"Oh, yes, come into the bedroom with me while I get it for you."

Emily led the way through the quiet house until they reached a master bedroom suite that overlooked the Sound from a window wall in the back of the house. The room was thickly carpeted with an off-white Berber rug that Emily had told Clare had been custom-woven for the Hahns in Tunisia. In the center of the room stood a large king-size bed on a raised platform, also carpeted, with an ultramodern chrome four-poster headboard that glinted dully in the flat afternoon light. The room was as neat as a photograph in a high-style decorating magazine, sterile and cool in atmosphere, almost entirely white. Its only color came from two bright oil paintings in primary hues that hung on opposite walls beneath directional lights, now extinguished. Emily went to the painting farthest from the bed and removed it, lowering it gently to the rug and revealing a large wall safe set into the wall.

She twiddled the dial and opened the safe. Inside there was a row of ledgers, half of them blue, the remainder red. At the front of the safe were two stacks of cash neatly bound in thick rubber bands. Emily pulled out a red book that sat to the extreme right. "This is the one, I think," she said.

"What are the others?" Clare asked.

"From the office," Emily replied.

Clare took the ledger and watched while Emily closed the safe, twirled the combination dial and replaced the painting.

CLARE RETURNED THE CAR to the rental agency and took a bus to the computer software company's downtown Greenwich office. She spent her usual three hours there completing the firm's weekly bookkeeping, which consisted mostly of balancing the checkbook and writing out checks for incoming bills that would be signed and mailed by the owner the next morning. Her mind was not on her work. Her thoughts kept going back to Jonas and Angel and the clinic in Mineola, and to Emily and Gene and their clandestine meeting that afternoon.

Clare was almost totally convinced that Emily was faithful to her husband, but what about her sister's role in the Rejuvenation Clinic? Did Emily know where Jonas actually spent his Tuesdays and Thursdays? What about in the summer? Did Jonas pretend to conduct classes at Columbia all summer, too? Or did he say he was at the country club that figured so prominently in the Hahns' social life? Could Emily really be so naive?

There were many ways to cheat, she realized—cheat on

taxes, cheat on spouses, even cheat the inexorable passage of time with an artful face-lift.

Lies. Clare hated lies.

She put on her coat, bade the owner good night and went down the stairs to the street. Despite how clear and sunny the morning had been, the weather had changed again in one of those quick about-faces that characterized a New England winter, and another wet snowstorm had blown up in the late afternoon. Did winter never end here in the East? Clare was happy to have left her old life behind, but she couldn't help longing for the predictable beauty of the weather in southern California.

She put up her collar and ran for the shelter of a bus stop two blocks away. Before she had reached the corner, a vintage Volkswagen pulled up to the curb, blocking her way.

"Ride, lady?" Michael grinned at her from the driver's seat.

"Anywhere!" she exclaimed. He reached across the small front seat and opened the door, and Clare happily fell into the Volkswagen, which was warm and dry and smelled of Michael. "I've got to get myself a car. You wouldn't want to sell this old heap, would you? A car like this gives the medicine business a bad name, Michael. A doctor is supposed to drive a BMW at the very least! And a Rolls when things are going well."

"I know. I've never been a man for fancy cars. Are you hungry? I was in the area and I remembered that you work down here on Thursday afternoons. I thought I'd take a chance on finding you."

"Thank goodness you did. Look at the bus stop." A line of wet commuters, their backs to the wind-driven snow, was huddled in misery as the Volkswagen rolled past. "This will be the night the bus is an hour late."

"Come back to my place for dinner," he suggested. "I've got a steak."

"I'd like to. Michael, I have so much to tell you!" She

was bursting with her newfound information, bursting to share it with him. "I would have called you at the lab this afternoon, but there wasn't any time. Anyway, I don't have your number there."

"I'm nearly impossible to get hold of at the lab," he said in a matter-of-fact tone. "Best you call me at home." Her excitement was not at all infectious, she realized, because Michael didn't seem the slightest bit surprised at her enthusiasm. If she didn't know better, Clare would have thought he already knew what she was going to say.

"Where have you been all day?" he asked. "I called Mrs. Sydney's half a dozen times, but there was no answer."

"Mrs. Sydney is down at her niece's house, and I've been on Long Island."

"Long Island?"

"Sleuthing," she said mysteriously. "I'll tell you all about it at dinner."

MICHAEL TOPPED OFF Clare's glass, then poured a second glass of red wine for himself.

"So, Nancy Drew, where have you been all day?"

"At the Rejuvenation Clinic. Ever hear of it?"

"I don't think so."

"I'll show you." She left the table and went to a chair in the entrance hall on which she had left her purse. As she returned to the dining ell, a telephone in the kitchen rang.

"Want me to answer that?" Clare asked. "I'm already up."

"Sure, go ahead," he replied.

Clare picked up the telephone. "Michael Duffy's residence."

"Who is this speaking?" asked a woman whose melodious voice was almost, but not quite, familiar.

"This is Clare Eckert."

"Oh." There was a brief hesitation; then the woman asked to speak to Michael.

Clare returned to the table while Michael went to the kitchen to take his call. Trying not to listen, Clare cut a piece of steak and chewed it thoughtfully. Michael was speaking in such a deliberately lowered voice she could barely hear him, the sense of his words totally lost to her.

He wasn't gone long, two minutes at most, but when he returned to his seat at the table, his face had a closed and furtive look, very much like Teddy's used to be after he'd negotiated business on the telephone behind the locked door of his study. The change in atmosphere gave Clare a sense of disquiet.

"If you're seeing someone else, I'd like to know about her," she said suddenly, surprising herself with her forthrightness. She was aware that these days people were free until they publicly declared otherwise, but the thought that Michael was dating, and perhaps even sleeping with, another woman appalled her.

"I'm not seeing anyone else," he answered emphatically. "She's a woman from work, a woman who is involved in an ongoing project at the. . .the lab. Once in a while she calls me at home to ask one or two things about some of the experiments."

"You seem so secretive," Clare said, despising the tone she heard in her own voice. How she hated to demonstrate what she recognized was jealousy, which she considered the most destructive of emotions, as painful for the object to witness as it was for the doubter to experience. And yet she couldn't help herself. She was unable to remember ever having felt jealousy before meeting Michael. With a start, she understood for the first time that she had become very emotionally involved with him. The realization renewed some of the fear she had felt when they first met.

Michael tossed his napkin on the table, stood up and came around behind Clare, slipping his arms around her rib cage, just below her breasts. She felt his breath warm and moist on her neck. "I'm not seeing anyone else, Clare.

You're enough woman for any man. I'm not the kind of guy who runs around with just anyone.''

"You're a bachelor with no commitments," she said in a quiet voice. "I know you have the right to do whatever you like. It's only that. . . only that I would find it very hurtful. I believe in one man–one woman, which is kind of old-fashioned, I guess, but that's how I am." She tried to laugh, but the sound was a sad one.

"So do I," he said, kissing her neck. "So do I. What were you going to show me?" he added, straightening and returning to his seat.

With a sense of immediate relief, she got up and retrieved her purse, which now sat on the couch behind her. Crossing to Michael, she pulled out the advertisement for the clinic, which earlier she had torn from the *Post*, and laid it on the table in front of Michael, smoothing it with her hand. She believed him, and the feeling warmed her. It was not only that she wanted to believe him, which she did, but that his simple words had been sincere and honest. She thought of him as an honest man, a man whose emotions were easy to read on his face—a quality she liked very much.

"This is where Jonas spends his Tuesdays and Thursdays," she said. "Noses, breasts and faces, just as you suspected." She sat down and took a sip of the wine.

Michael picked up the piece of newsprint, studied it in silence, then whistled softly. "I can't say I'm really surprised," he told her. "It's the only thing that makes sense. How did you find out?"

"I rented a car and followed him this morning. He went into this clinic at nine-thirty and was still there when I left at noon." She told him about the Porsche and Angel Chetnik, whose name made Michael grin broadly. "So clearly he's up to no good," Clare concluded.

"In what way? This ad doesn't prove a thing." Michael pushed the clipping away and cut a piece of steak, which he popped into his mouth.

"Why not?" Clare was disappointed in his reaction. "He could have been inside having his ears fixed."

"His ears are perfectly fine. Besides, I called the clinic and asked for Dr. Hahn, and the receptionist told me he was with a patient."

"So he works there. What does that prove?"

"Emily thinks he's teaching a course at Columbia."

"Are you sure?" This elicited slightly more attention, but Michael kept his head down and continued to eat. "Delicious salad," he said.

"I'm positive. I asked her before I followed him, and again afterward. Right this minute she thinks he's at a faculty meeting in New York."

"That's a bit more to the point, but on the other hand, maybe he's ashamed. Maybe he doesn't want his wife aware of what he really does for a living. Maybe he doesn't want his friends to know he's involved in nose bobs because he wants to be thought of as the great humanitarian who specializes in charity cases. However, I don't see anything illegal in what he's doing. I can't even make a case for immoral, although I've always assumed that husbands and wives who are honest with each other have better marriages than those who are not."

"Well, what do *you* think he's up to?"

"Tax evasion. I've always thought so."

"Then why are you making all these objections?"

"I like to play the devil's advocate," he said with a smile. "That's the entire structure of research. And now that you suspect Jonas's big secret, what do you plan to do about it?"

"Do? Nothing. What could I do?"

"Prove it."

"How could I prove it, and why would I want do?"

"Why? For your own satisfaction and to protect your sister, especially since Jonas is involved with another woman. As to how—I'm certain you could find a way, if you really wanted to."

"Sure," she said with a laugh. "If I wanted to. But I don't."

ALTHOUGH CLARE HAD DISMISSED his suggestion lightly, Michael's words kept her awake that night. She had been left without protection when Teddy walked out on her, and she wondered if Emily was aware of how vulnerable *she* was. But if Emily knew the details of Jonas's double life, she would have leverage in case Jonas decided to leave her to be with Angel Chetnik. Just thinking of Angel made Clare shake her head in wonder. There was no accounting for taste, she mused, especially where attraction to the opposite sex was concerned. Tasteful or not, Angel was a threat to Emily's position.

A plan began to form in Clare's mind.

She called Michael at seven the next morning. "Can I borrow your car?"

"Certainly. When?"

"Now. I'll take you to work, and I'll pick you up afterward. I won't inconvenience you at all."

"Uh. . . All right. I'll come by for you about eight."

Clare was ready, waiting just inside the door of Mrs. Sydney's house and watching for Michael's battered Volkswagen long before it pulled up. Her stomach nervous, her hands cold, she asked herself if she really had the nerve to go through with her plan. Although there was fresh snow on the sidewalks and lawns, the sun was already out, and a promise of spring was in the air. She knew the snow would melt by noon and the day would be lovely.

When Michael arrived, she locked the front door, raced down the steps and jumped into the car. He smelled of soap and a light cologne as she kissed him on the lips.

"What are you up to?" he asked. "You have the most devilish look on your face."

"I'm going to the clinic," she announced.

Michael frowned and gave her a quick look of surprise. Immediately she regretted her words, convinced that he would try to stop her. He was the protective type, always taking her arm, holding doors open for her, never allowing her to lift a thing.

He surprised her, however. "What for?"

"Just to see how it operates," she answered.

"What are you going to do?" he asked slowly.

Here it comes, she thought. She was certain he wouldn't let her have the car now. Well, it didn't matter. She could rent another one from the rental agency, although the expense would strain her already threadbare budget.

"Nothing much. Have a consultation, I guess."

"What if you run into Jonas? What will you tell him?"

"I won't run into him. Today is Friday, and he's always in Greenwich. It's perfectly safe, Michael, and I don't want you to worry. They're not going to take me prisoner like in some scene from *Revenge of Frankenstein.*"

He laughed. "Of course not! Actually, I think it's a marvelous idea. In fact, I'd like to go with you, but I can't today. How do you plan to pay?"

"I don't know. A check, I guess. I never thought about it."

"Pay cash. That way Jonas will never know you were there."

"What do you think it will cost?"

"A hundred should see you through."

"I don't have enough with me. I'll have to wait for the banks to open."

"Here, take it out of my wallet." He pushed his coat aside and reached awkwardly into a back pocket to pull out a brown leather wallet. "There should be a hundred in there."

Clare took the wallet and opened it. Inside were three crisp fifty-dollar bills and two twenties. She took two bills. "I'll write you a check," she said.

"There's no hurry. In fact, forget it. Consider it a present, a variation on the flowers-and-candy routine. I can't stand to be trite," he said lightly.

She smiled. "No, I couldn't. I'll pay you back as soon as I can." She laid the wallet in her lap and opened her purse to put the money inside. As she did, she caught sight of Michael's Virginia driver's license and another laminated identification card. She pulled the license from its slot and studied his photograph. "Nice likeness," she commented. "I like your hair longer." Indeed, in the photograph his hair was quite long, almost covering his ears; the style made him look years younger, although the license was barely a year old.

He reached over and picked up the wallet, closing it quickly.

"You forgot your driver's license," Clare said. "I'll put it back for you." She held out a hand for him to return the wallet.

"Give it to me," he demanded tersely. His mouth was set in a grim line, and he was looking straight ahead, deftly maneuvering the car in the heavy morning traffic.

"I'm sorry," she said, stung by his coolness. She handed him the driver's license. "I didn't mean to pry."

"That's all right."

He turned on the radio, and she listened in silence to the news. Clare was confused and edgy, not knowing exactly what she had done to cause so abrupt a change between them, but aware that she had committed a definite faux pas. They did not speak as he turned into a winding driveway that cut through an industrial park and up to the imposing entrance of the drug firm. He got out of the car, after giving Clare a quick kiss on the cheek, then strode rapidly to the plate-glass doors without looking back.

With some difficulty, she climbed across to the driver's seat, then realized she didn't know when to come for him. Leaning back toward the passenger side, she hurriedly rolled down the window and called after him. "What time do you want me to pick you up?" But Michael didn't hear her because he was already passing through a revolving glass door. "Michael!"

She would have to go after him, she realized. She opened the door of the car and had one foot on the wet pavement when a security guard approached her.

"No stopping here, miss," he said.

"But I'll only be a minute," Clare argued. "I forgot to—"

"You can't leave the car here. Put it over in the visitors' parking area."

Clare followed his pointing finger and realized immediately that by the time she parked and locked the car, Michael would be long gone. She decided to telephone him instead. On the telephone she could tell him she was sorry for offending him, whereas in a busy office there would be no opportunity to apologize. Besides, she was anxious to get on the road to the clinic.

Chapter Ten

Seated in the waiting room at the Rejuvenation Clinic, Clare couldn't keep the butterflies at bay. Her hands were cold, her stomach clutched with tension, and she had a terrific desire to pick at a troublesome hangnail. Without seeing a thing, she paged through the high-fashion pages of *Vogue*, stopping only when she came upon an article on plastic surgery.

She tried to read the article, but her eyes were drawn repeatedly toward Angel Chetnik's back. The woman sat not ten feet away behind a chest-high Formica partition, wedged between a copying machine and a telephone that rang frequently. Her head was down, her concentration given totally to the work she was doing. Clare had twice made an excuse to approach the receptionist, asking fabricated questions, in order to see what Angel actually did in the office. She had decided finally, from the look of ledgers and papers spread before Angel on a desk, that the woman was the bookkeeper.

Without an appointment, Clare had been forced to wait while the doctor, or doctors—she did not know how many were present—saw other patients. Finally, at eleven-thirty, there was no one else left in the waiting room. She was ushered into the office of a tall, thin man who stood up at her entry.

She looked around her. The room was ordinary and

not in the least sinister, reminding her of a dozen other medical offices she had seen in her lifetime. On one wall there were bookshelves loaded with medical tomes; above them hung several framed degrees that were too far away for her to read. On the opposite wall there was a very fine framed reproduction of a French Impressionist painting. Behind the doctor's desk, venetian blinds were closed, shutting off the view of the parking lot.

"Well, Miss. . ." The doctor looked down at a piece of paper on his desk to remind himself of her name. Clare noticed there was a slight tremor in his hand. "Well, Miss Donald, what exactly can we do for you today?" Donald was the maiden name of Clare and Emily's mother, and the first name that had popped into her mind when the receptionist had interviewed her. "I can see you're not here to talk about your nose, which is perfect, or wrinkles around your eyes, for you have none. So what's troubling you?"

Clare had been planning to discuss nose surgery—or rhinoplasty, as it was called, something she had just learned from the *Vogue* article—and the doctor's abrupt words left her speechless. Yes, her nose was just fine, perfectly proportioned to her face. How had she thought she could get away with using her nose for an excuse to get inside?

"I. . ." Clare couldn't speak. Her mind went blank. What did she think she was doing, snooping around Jonas in this way? She must have been out of her head when she came to the clinic. She eyed the door apprehensively.

The doctor, whose name she had not heard, came around to the front of the desk, where he perched casually two feet from where she sat stiffly in a fake leather chair. He was tall, sandy-haired and distinctly round-shouldered. He was probably ten years older than Jonas, and his once-handsome face, fairly wrinkled, had only the hint of a double chin. Under his eyes, however, were darkened pouches, and the whites of the eyes themselves were bloodshot. Again she noticed that his hands trembled slightly.

"Now, now," he said. "I know you're nervous. Many women are when they first come in here. You have nothing to be ashamed of, nothing at all. Thousands of women, women from all walks of life, have had the operation you are contemplating, and the one thing they have in common is their recognition that they have a right to the most beautiful bodies surgery can give them."

"They do?"

"Yes, Miss Dunlop, they do. Here, let me show you some before-and-after photographs. They'll ease your mind, and also help you choose the shape you want." He went over to the bookshelves, from which he removed a black vinyl album, then flipped through several pages before laying the book in Clare's lap. "Just keep in mind that bigger isn't always better. Everything should be done in proportion to the body. That's the trick to making the change seem natural. No one will ever know—well, only your husband or your boyfriend. There will be small scars, of course, but they fade with time. We have a wonderful vitamin E cream to be used after surgery. The scars disappear like magic."

Clare looked down at the album. Four naked breasts stared back at her.

"Breasts," she whispered.

"That's what you're here for, isn't it? You are, if I may say so, a bit on the flat-chested side."

"Yes, of course," she murmured. On that score Clare definitely qualified. How could she get out of here? She eyed the door again.

"This particular model, number twelve-A, is the one I'd suggest for you. They aren't too big, a perfect C-cup, actually. You're a thin woman, and anything larger would overpower your body. Unless you're in show business—'' He looked at her for a denial, which was forthcoming when Clare gave a quick shake of her head.

"Yes, of course," she replied, dry-mouthed. "Twelve-A looks fine to me."

"Take your time, please. This is an important decision. Why don't you take the book into the examining room and look at the photos while you're waiting for me? I'll be there in just a moment. Have to make a phone call first." He ushered a mute Clare, who carried the album, to the door of an adjoining room and pushed her gently inside. "Look at the 'before' pictures as well; you'll be really impressed with what we can do here at Rejuvenation. Take off everything above the waist, Miss Donnelly. There's a gown on the table to your left." He closed the door behind him. Within seconds Clare heard him on the telephone, ordering his stockbroker to sell a hundred shares of real estate trust.

She sat in a chair for a minute. Could she run out the door? Should she? She had already paid for the consultation, so she might as well go through with the examination. To leave early would be truly suspicious behavior, although it crossed her mind that more than one woman probably had lost her nerve at the Rejuvenation Clinic upon meeting the trembling doctor. Maybe not; maybe anyone else who came here was so highly motivated to begin with, she stayed no matter what.

"I'll go through with it," Clare mumbled aloud, realizing that she had lost sight of her own motivation, which was to gather information for Emily's sake. A quick examination, and everything would be over. What had she learned so far? Exactly nothing. She hated to think she had wasted the morning and Michael's eighty-five dollars, the amount the receptionist had collected in advance. She would ask the doctor to check for lumps while he was at it. Perhaps the visit wouldn't be a total loss.

She stripped off her sweater and her blouse. She didn't wear a bra. As the doctor had noticed, she was hardly in need of support. Covered by a paper gown, she was lying supine on the examination table when the doctor returned. With him was a young nurse who stuck her head in the door, then left immediately.

He actually rubbed his hands together before he began to palpate her left breast. "What did you think of the sample book?"

"Very nice," she said. "You do wonderful work."

"It's not all mine," he admitted. "I have three associates, but I'll operate on you if you prefer."

"Yes, of course," she replied. *I'd prefer to be drawn and quartered instead.*

"Did you pick a shape you like?"

"Mmm."

He moved to the other breast, and she realized his hands actually did tremble; she shrank inwardly at the touch of his skin. She wondered what his problem was—a stroke? Some type of palsy? Love of martinis?

"You're perfectly healthy," he said "When would you like the surgery to take place?" There hadn't been a single question about her medical history, about the incidence of breast cancer in her family, about her reasons for wanting breast surgery in the first place—questions that the *Vogue* article had pointed out as important information to consider.

"Oh, soon," she said vaguely. "But I really need to talk about the cost. You see, I can't afford surgery if it's too expensive."

"It's six thousand if your insurance covers."

"It doesn't."

"Forty-five hundred, then. Cash, of course," he said mechanically. "I can operate immediately."

"Well..."

"I mean right now. We've just had a cancellation for this afternoon."

Clare's heart leaped, and she shivered involuntarily. She had no idea she'd be faced with such an offer. She had intended to skulk away after the breast examination, never to be seen on Long Island again. "Oh, I couldn't possibly—"

"If you take it, I'll do the surgery for three thousand. You can't beat that, Miss Donovan."

"But I can't stay today, doctor. I have to get home. Besides, I didn't bring that kind of money with me. Do you actually operate right here?"

"Right here," he assured her. "We have all the finest facilities."

The very thought made Clare shiver again. What provisions were made for emergencies? Did they use general anesthesia? Was there a certified anesthesiologist at the clinic? She knew people died unexpectedly from an unforeseen reaction to anesthesia, and she wondered what would happen here in such a circumstance. On the other hand, she couldn't imagine anyone undergoing breast augmentation while still conscious. The idea appalled her.

"I *will* take a check," the doctor added, "although my associates don't like to."

"No, not today."

"Then when?" he asked, clearly disappointed.

"Do you have a day free next week?"

"You'll have to ask the receptionist. But next week the cost is forty-five hundred. You did understand that the lower price was only for this afternoon."

"Yes, I understand." Clare sat up as he left the examining room. A shudder ran through her. She dressed quickly and returned to the waiting room. No one was at the desk.

"The receptionist is out to lunch," said the young nurse whom Clare had seen fleetingly in the examining room. She was wearing a dark blue coat, which she was buttoning in preparation to leave the office. "Do you need another appointment?"

"I'll telephone later," Clare said. "When will she be back?"

"Oh, there's a party today. I'm just on my way myself. We don't usually close at lunch, but the doctor is letting us take some time off because things are slow right now. One of the girls is getting married, you see, and we're giving her a shower, so if I were you, I wouldn't call before two. Do you mind if I run along? I'm going to be late."

"No, of course not."

"Just make certain the door is latched behind you. It locks automatically."

"That's fine," Clare said. The nurse went out, leaving Clare alone in the waiting room; it was so quiet she could hear only the hum of an air-purifying machine that sat on a magazine-strewn table in one corner. She looked at her watch, which read ten minutes after twelve. Was there only one doctor in the clinic that day? She thought so, from what the young nurse had said. But where was he now, she wondered, slowly drawing on her coat and tying her scarf absentmindedly. Did he go out for lunch? Or did he drink it at his desk? Was there another exit? There had to be, but she had no way of knowing if he had already used it.

She eyed Angel's desk, moving two or three steps closer, only to stop and stand indecisively in the middle of the room. *Why not? This is my only chance.* Throwing caution to the winds, she approached the area where Angel had been working. After a momentary fumble with icy fingers, she was able to open the latch of the half door that led to the small space behind the receptionist's desk.

The ledgers and papers were still there, almost exactly as Clare had seen them before her appointment with the doctor. On top lay a blue ledger like the ones she had noticed in Jonas and Emily's wall safe. She opened the book to the last page, which was marked with a long satin ribbon. Without particular comprehension, she read the most recent entries. There were no patients' names, only transaction numbers, followed by the date of service rendered and money collected. There was a column marked "FOP," which Clare knew meant "form of payment," but the entire column was blank. She closed the ledger and picked up another, this one bound in black leather. Again opening to the last page, she saw what she had expected to find: patient's names, insurance numbers and balances due.

There was a distinct noise from the inner office. Clare, caught with the black ledger in her hand, stood paralyzed as she realized that footsteps approached the interior door of the waiting room.

Knowing there was no way to explain her presence in the office, let alone her position behind the Formica barrier, Clare threw herself on the floor and crawled hastily into the knee hole of the receptionist's desk, pulling the rolling chair close behind her. The chair was still moving when she heard the door open. She bunched her loden coat around bent knees, hastily stuffing the offending material down in the crack between her and the chair.

She held her breath.

Someone came into the waiting room, clearing his throat. The doctor! Was he passing through, on his way out to lunch? Or would he come into the office area?

Into the office! She heard the latch of the half door open, and he entered the small office, his highly polished black loafers coming to a halt not four inches from her own brown boot. Her worst fears realized, she was certain he had seen her. The dark green coat she wore contrasted starkly with the white Formica of the desk. Her face was level with the hem of his camel hair coat. Clare closed her eyes in misery, her lungs nearly bursting. Her legs, folded tightly beneath her, cramped painfully.

She had to breathe; there was no recourse. Slowly she exhaled, exercising massive control over the sound of exhalation. She was beginning to inhale gratefully just as he picked up the telephone on the desk surface above her. He tapped out a number, asked for a man and waited, humming tunelessly until the party came on the line. Apparently his car was in need of fine-tuning, and he was attempting to cajole the service department of his car dealer into allowing him to bring it in that afternoon. Clare's legs went numb.

Say yes, tell him to bring it over right away, please say yes, she prayed. Her legs were now totally numb, and her neck ached from the angle at which her head was tucked beneath the desk.

"Fine," the doctor said. "I'll be right over, say, in ten, fifteen minutes. Can someone give me a lift back to my office?" Reassured, he hung up the phone, and the black loafers disappeared. Clare heard him go out the office door, which latched audibly behind him. Although he was gone, she did not move, fearing he might have forgotten something and would return. A moment later, she heard the sound of an engine start.

With one toe, she pushed away the rolling chair, stretching out her legs until circulation of the blood was restored. Her hands trembled visibly, and she thought she might be sick to her stomach. She stood on painful, shaking legs.

"After all that, I'm not leaving without something for my trouble," she said aloud to the empty room. She returned to Angel's books and papers. In front of the ledgers rested two stacks of invoices that she paged through hurriedly until she found her own on the very bottom of the second pile. The invoice seemed perfectly normal, made of the varicolored self-carbon paper that all doctors seemed to use these days—one for the patient, one for the insurance company and one for the office.

She realized she had not been given the patient's copy, so she removed it from the invoice and pocketed it.

A wastebasket beneath the desk caught her eye because it seemed full of the pink, white and yellow invoices, something Clare, as a bookkeeper, knew was highly out of the ordinary. No one discarded invoices, no one. She scooped up the flimsy papers, hurriedly straightening them into an orderly stack, and stuffed them into her purse.

Quickly she returned to the ledgers, opening them to the last entries. She took the first and bent back its covers to isolate one page, which she laid in the copying machine next to Angel's work station and waited as it flashed, hummed and spat out a copy. She repeated the process with the second book. Although she was fairly certain the ledgers held no information of significance, she thought she would show them to Michael for his opinion. They did, after all, back up what he had suggested—two sets of books. Clare was astute enough to realize that the existence of two records was far from questionable, nor was it necessarily conclusive of anything. She had no idea how the office organized its bookkeeping, and it was certainly possible that the clinic separated its cash and insured transactions for simplicity.

When she had finished, she noticed that the spines of the ledgers showed the effects of the bending necessary to fit a single page into the copying machine. She hoped no one would be aware they had been tampered with. After all, if one were not suspicious, one was not likely to see the obvious.

Like her sister Emily, she thought sadly.

Clare stuffed the duplicated papers into her purse. Cautiously, she let herself out of the silent office. It was nearly twelve-thirty.

Chapter Eleven

Because the plane was half-empty, Michael Duffy had been able to select a window seat. In the chaos of a busy morning, he had missed lunch, but he was not hungry. He stared morosely out at the ever-clogged traffic arteries of Washington as the twelve o'clock shuttle circled again, awaiting permission to land at National Airport. With a sigh, he thought back on Harriet Alpert's second unexpected telephone call, which he had received that morning. The last thing he needed now was to be called home for an emergency conference at headquarters. Not only that, Clare had his Volkswagen, and there had been no way to get in touch with her before he left for La Guardia Airport.

He was browbeating himself for the gross errors he had made that morning. First, allowing Clare to see the wallet that contained his government identification card—how could he have been so careless? Although Clare had said nothing about the card to him, commenting only on the long hair she had noticed on his driver's license picture, it was more than likely she had seen the telltale card and chosen to remain silent.

And then, most stupid of all, letting her get away without making a date for the end of the day. He was certain she would call Schoenfeld-Loewe in search of him, even though he had deliberately discouraged her from calling him at work. And then what? She would discover that he was unknown there, that no Dr. Michael Duffy was on the payroll now, nor had he ever been. He squeezed shut his eyes, then opened them at the gentle lurch the plane gave as it angled into yet another circle.

When Clare confronted him with her discovery that Dr. Michael Duffy did not exist, there was a distinct chance that the investigation would be blown. Clare would tell her sister, and Emily would tip off Jonas. All the time and effort he and his team had concentrated on Jonas Hahn would skitter away like so many leaves in the wind.

Did he care anymore?

Yes, he cared, but not for the investigation. About that he didn't give a damn. He'd trade anything he owned, he thought, not to be involved in this particular case. But then, he wouldn't have met Clare.

The investigation had begun like so many others. A young agent in the Stamford office, an ambitious comer, had spotted an article peppered with lush color photographs in an extremely prestigious magazine that specialized in the self-aggrandizing display of homes of the rich. With an eye to enhancing his career in the Service, and since the owners of the featured home, Jonas and Emily Hahn, lived in his tax district, the agent had pulled the couple's federal income-tax records. In them he discovered that Hahn, a high-profile taxpayer like many other physicians, had been routinely audited by the government three years running. His books had come up perfect every time. It was noted, in fact, that Hahn had *overpaid* his income tax and was due a refund for one of the years.

But the agent, rightly, had persisted. A quantity of original art had been featured in the photo spread; it was not difficult to research the cost of the modern canvases, such information being a matter of public record. There were also various pieces of antique furniture scattered throughout the Hahn mansion, distinctive items acquired, according to the copy, at Sotheby Parke Bernet and Christie's, the two largest auction houses in New York. Their prices, too, were a matter of public record.

In the photographs, the agent had spotted sensors of an expensive and sophisticated built-in alarm system high up on the walls of the living room, the master bedroom and the luxurious kitchen. Adding one thing to another—the price of two acres of prime real estate on Long Island Sound; the tax assessment of the Hahns' rambling beach-front house; the cost of two Mercedes-Benz automobiles, a thirty-two-foot sailing sloop and an undistinguished American station wagon, all of which were evaluated and taxed by the state of Connecticut in documents available to both the federal government and the general public— the agent had concluded that the Hahns lived far above their reported means.

It took the young man six weeks to put together his report, but every detail on the ten-page memo held the punch of a hand grenade. A blue-bound copy was waiting on Michael Duffy's desk when he returned from his vacation at the end of the Christmas holiday.

The official Internal Revenue Service investigation commenced.

Michael Duffy kept a dog-eared copy of the magazine on his desk in Washington. It never ceased to amaze him how carefully a tax evader hid his income by means of crack accountants specializing in labyrinthine schemes, only to blow it all in a flamboyant gesture designed to stroke an insecure ego. Jonas Hahn wasn't the first rich man the IRS had plucked from the pages of magazines like *Architectural Digest*, *House Beautiful* or *Town & Country*. He wouldn't be the last.

Michael's first order of business as Special Agent in Criminal Investigation was to ascertain where Jonas and Emily banked, a simple matter of a few telephone calls made from his desk in Washington. A quick visit to the bank manager, the flash of an identification badge, and a delegated agent in Stamford knew the balance of the Hahns' checking account and the absence of savings or investment accounts. Another few questions, and he determined that the Hahns did not maintain a safe-deposit box. If they had, the agent would have asked the bank to open it. The bank would have complied without question. The Internal Revenue Service did not bother with court orders; there was no need. Commercial banks, savings banks, brokerage houses—all quietly cooperated with the department as a matter of course. Cooperation saved them the pain of a special audit of their own records.

From the information that came from Stamford, Michael deduced that Jonas Hahn had a safe-deposit box, but one that was private, located either in his home or in one of those new twenty-four-hour safe-deposit repositories that had sprung up lately. A check of the Connecticut companies and those in nearby Westchester County, New York, came up blank.

So the safe was in his home.

Michael needed to put someone inside the house. Thanks to the temper of Dr. Hahn, it was only a short time until Emily called a prestigious domestic employment service, a small business easily bullied into cooperation by dogged tax agents. Harriet Alpert, with whom Michael had worked several times, was the obvious choice for housekeeper.

Michael also realized immediately that he would have to become a physician. He had played the role before, and he actually knew a surprising amount about medicine, having studied intensely before his first foray into undercover investigation nearly ten years before. He had also been, in his various guises, a minister, a newspaper reporter, a lawyer and a psychiatrist. He specialized in assuming other identities.

The first thing Michael did as Dr. Duffy was to join

Jonas's two clubs—a country club in Darien and a men's club in New York City. There he watched Jonas from afar. Although money never visibly changed hands at these clubs, Michael became aware of the plastic surgeon's reputation as a man who preferred to deal in cash, a fact the Service had already discovered about Emily.

Michael also befriended other physicians, played squash and backgammon—golf being out of the question in the winter—and listened, listened, listened, until he heard, among other things, that the Hahns planned a winter vacation in Mexico.

He made a quick trip to Guadalajara, familiarizing himself with the layout of the city and researching the university where Jonas had gone to medical school. His Spanish was already adequate, thanks to a summer he had spent in Spain as the guest of a college roommate, but he practiced the Mexican accent carefully, mildly surprised that two countries could vary so completely in their use of the same language. He returned to Guadalajara on the same plane the Hahn family used and checked into the Hotel El Tapatio ten minutes before they did.

When he saw the Hahn party for the first time, Michael wasn't certain which woman was Emily, because the two women resembled each other so strongly. One blonde, one brunette, both quiet, both seemingly very unhappy. But after prolonged observation, he determined that it was the brunette who might be helpful to him. No wedding ring, no visible attachment. He knew that meeting her, becoming friendly with her, would further the course of the investigation.

Michael had never had a problem with the Service's methods before. He took for granted the means employed: paid informer, court harassment, threat of jail, assessment of interest and penalties.

And the employment of undercover investigators like himself.

Michael Duffy had always done his job without question, believing he was on a team of white-hatted good guys who spent their very secure government careers going after the bad guys. To pay one's taxes was patriotic; not to pay was un-American. Michael had always felt secure in his moral position.

Until now.

What in hell had happened to him? One look into Clare's serious eyes... No, it hadn't been quite that fast, he realized. He hadn't begun to fall under her spell until sometime during their first dance.

What amazed him was that Clare, an amateur, had discovered the source of Jonas Hahn's other income when no one else had been able to do so. It was an oversight on the part of the Internal Revenue Service; eventually someone would have come up with the idea. He excused their joint stupidity by rationalizing that the Service did not go in for Grade-B movie ploys, such as following the subject of an investigation. He excused them all, but the fact remained that Clare, unknowingly, had led them to the Rejuvenation Clinic, giving them the break they needed. Tuesday morning a team of Internal Revenue agents planned to descend upon the clinic with a subpoena for all its books. In less than two hours, the time Michael estimated the examination would take, it would become clear how Jonas and Emily Hahn managed to live in such splendor on a reported income that barely matched that of a blue-collar working couple.

After all the months of investigation, to be so close to breaking the case should have elated Michael. This stage of an investigation had always given him a powerful feeling of impending satisfaction mixed with the heady scent of his quarry dead ahead. He searched himself for his usual emotions, but was forced to admit they were missing. He felt instead an unexplained depression Uncharacteristically, he lacked the sense of warm camaraderie he had always shared with his fellow agents.

Worst of all, for the first time in his life, he thought of himself as smarmy and deceitful. For the first time in his life, he wanted to run away from the entire investigation.

He knew his reaction had to do with his deceiving Clare. Clare, the innocent bystander, the victim. He had lied to her about everything: his profession, his schooling, his reason for meeting her in the first place. The little time they had shared together, hours of pleasure and peace, would prove to be no more than a castle built on sand. There was no doubt in his mind that the truth would destroy him forever with Clare.

He knew what his boss, Marcone, would say. Michael had broken the cardinal rule of a professional. He had become involved.

Michael had not meant to become involved. He had always been a loner. Some of what he had told Clare about his past was the truth. He had done everything in his power to escape Berwick, Pennsylvania; to get away from a cold, uneducated family that wanted him to go down in the mines or work a dead-end job on a dying railroad. Before the short time he had known Clare, he felt he had nothing in common with the world. For some unfathomable reason, he had never met a person he could love.

There had been one woman once, about five years before. He thought he was in love at the time and had spent nearly a year in her comfortable company. But ultimately it had come to nothing. He was ambitious, on the road all the time; she was ambitious, absorbed in her Washington career. There had never been enough between them to impel either to sacrifice a part of life's business for the sake of the other person. He was sent on a job to Birmingham, Alabama. He thought he'd be home in three weeks, but closer to three months passed before he returned to Washington. And when he did, she was dating someone else. They parted amicably. He was even a guest at her wedding.

Since that time, he had yet to be involved in more than a short-lived affair—three months at the most—with any woman. He had known affection, yes, and plenty of sex.

Sex. Never in his twelve years in the Service had he slept with a woman in the line of duty, nor did he consider what had taken place between him and Clare as part of the investigation.

For what had happened he had no explanation, never having experienced the rush of conflicting emotions that Clare set off in him—a desire to protect her, an overwhelming physical need of her, a recurring obsession to wreak some sort of revenge on the bastard who had been her husband. Michael had the means, too; he could be certain that, with one word to the right person, Teddy Eckert would be audited every year until the day he died. It would have given Michael a sense of immense satisfaction to set those wheels to grinding. To hell with the moral implications.

But what good would the satisfaction do him if he lost Clare?

What he would not tell Marcone was that he was *more* than involved. He was in love.

Michael started at the sudden bump of wheels touching tarmac, followed by the roar of engines thrust into reverse. As the jet taxied to a stop at the shuttle terminal, Michael stood with the rest of the passengers and moved up the aisle, lost in thought. He could try Clare's telephone number, he supposed, but it was surely too early for her to have returned from Long Island. What would he tell her? How could he explain this sudden trip to Washington, especially if she had seen the identification card in his wallet?

He decided to work on the problem and call her after the meeting broke up. It wasn't due to start until three, a bad omen for a Friday afternoon. He hoped it wouldn't be one of those marathons that went on and on until the wee hours of the morning.

"ARE YOU ABSOLUTELY *certain* there is no Michael Duffy in your directory?" Clare stood at the wall phone in Mrs. Sydney's neat kitchen, her fingers tangled in the spiraling cord that connected the handset to the receiver, her forehead puckered with a confused frown. "Could you ring the laboratory? That's where he would be."

"We have no laboratories here, madam. This is a business office only."

"Of course you have labs there," Clare snapped, bristling from the tone of the woman's tinny voice. Hadn't Michael told her he was in research medicine? Where else did researchers work if not in labs? She heard her own voice rising and made a massive effort to control her temper. "Dr. Duffy is on temporary assignment from the main office in Washington," Clare explained in an even voice, despite her clenched teeth. "He's only been at the lab a few months. Maybe you have a new listing or something. . . ."

"The main office is in Geneva, Switzerland," the woman retorted. "And we have no labs here, none at all. Are you sure you have the right company? This is Schoenfeld-Loewe."

Clare slammed down the telephone in annoyance, hoping that Mrs. Sydney, who had returned home earlier that afternoon, hadn't heard her small tantrum with the operator from the drug company. She was furious with that stupid woman! She would have to go back to the firm and simply browbeat someone there until he or she found Michael for her.

"What's the problem, Clare?" Alvina Sydney came into the kitchen and smiled. She crossed to the sink to fill a kettle with water and placed the kettle on the stove in a quick, practiced movement. Clare had noticed that the landlady's remedy for life's every upset was a cup of hot tea. After the infuriating telephone conversation, Clare felt more like demanding a dry martini and knocking it down in a single gulp before a shocked Mrs. Sydney.

"Oh, it's an operator at Schoenfeld-Whatever," she said, trembling with anger. "She's trying to tell me their headquarters are in Switzerland, when I know it's a Washington company. Honestly, the ignorance of some people!"

"But it is."

"It is what?"

"Schoenfeld-Loewe is a Swiss company with headquarters in Geneva. I know because I own two hundred shares of the corporation."

"It is?" Clare frowned again. "But—"

"Yes, my husband gave me two hundred shares for Christmas once. The stock certificate is in two languages, French and German, and there's an engraving of a dancing bear at the top of it. You know, of course, that the bear is a Swiss symbol, although I personally believe it's the symbol of Bern and not of Geneva.

"It's after four o'clock, my dear. How about a nice cup of hot tea?" She opened a cabinet and pulled out two ornately painted teacups and their matching saucers.

"No . . . I have to go out now."

"Drive carefully, Clare." Mrs. Sydney was too much of a lady to allow any disappointment to show on her wrinkled face. Clare, who knew the woman longed for adult company after spending a few days with teenagers in Pelham, felt a stab of guilt as she pulled on her loden coat and rushed out the door.

There was a mistake, she reasoned. Even if Schoenfeld-Loewe was Swiss, even if there were no labs in Stamford, she had seen Michael go into the building that morning—which meant he was still there and waiting for Clare to pick him up from work. She would simply go there and find someone to help her locate Michael. And if no one would, or could, she would stand in the lobby until he eventually came out of his office.

She waited until six o'clock, when the departing employees had slowed from a trickle to none. She had searched every single face leaving the building, and not one of them belonged to Michael Duffy. One guard, who started out to be kindly, turned suspicious as the hour grew later. He finally ejected her and locked the revolving glass doors.

Her thoughts confused and wary, she took stock. She did not want to distrust Michael, but the evidence seemed clear. He did not work for Schoenfeld-Loewe. So where did he work? And why had he lied to her? Oh, how she hated lies!

He will find me, she thought. *I have his car, so he has to come back. And when he does, I'll get the answers to all my questions.*

Clare returned to the house on Keeler Street, had a quick dinner with Mrs. Sydney, and sat with her while the older woman watched her favorite Friday-night television shows. By eleven, when the news began, the telephone hadn't rung once. Clare retired to her room and tried to sleep.

SHE AWOKE EARLY on Saturday morning and began to call Michael's apartment in New Canaan. She telephoned every hour until two o'clock in the afternoon. Finally she left the house, telling Mrs. Sydney that she was going to the Town Center in Stamford, a large shopping complex in the middle of downtown. After all, she had a car at her disposal. Although she could hardly afford to buy anything in the expensive stores like Abercrombie & Fitch or Jaeger's, at least an afternoon of healthy window shopping would get her mind on something else beside Michael and the mystery that surrounded his odd behavior.

After an hour of wandering through the stores, Clare sat on an upholstered bench at one side of a large fountain and watched the Saturday afternoon crowds mill about the multistory complex. From where she sat, she had a view of the three stories beneath her, and as she gazed down, she thought she recognized someone in the crowd on an escalator. When the man passed quite close to her, she was certain. Gene Janklow's head was down, and he seemed intent on his destination. Clare did not call out to him, although her first thought was that it might have been pleasant to spend thirty minutes over a cup of coffee with the historian. No, she amended hastily; Gene, like Emily, would try to explain their friendship. Clare felt she was better off in ignorance.

Within seconds she saw another familiar face. Jonas Hahn was rushing off the same escalator that Gene had just vacated. Like Gene, he was in a hurry and passed so close to Clare that she could have tripped him. In fact, she thought of doing just that, imagining the satisfaction of seeing her brother-in-law sprawled on the industrial carpet of the Town Center. Jonas was dressed in his country-gentleman weekend uniform—a thigh-length sheepskin jacket open to show loud lime-green pants and a pastel sweater in lime and shocking pink stripes. He looked like an ice-cream cone with fur around it.

She rose from her seat and followed him. He seemed to be following Gene, since Gene had just ducked into a Williams-Sonoma store, with Jonas twenty feet behind him. The store was crowded, as it always was on Saturdays, so Clare was able to stand undetected in one corner and watch the two men. Gene did not know he was being followed by Jonas, who, in turn, did not know Clare was following him.

Ten minutes and one purchase later, Gene went out of the store, up another escalator and into a dark restaurant. Jonas was right behind him, but lagging back so as to remain invisible. Clare lost interest at that point, knowing she did not want to enter the restaurant, too. She would probably be seen if she did, and she would certainly be forced to spend money she didn't have to waste on cloak-and-dagger schemes. She returned to the Volkswagen and drove home, intending to call Emily immediately to apprise her of the incredible behavior of her husband.

"Hello, Mrs. Sydney, I'm home," she called, entering the front door of the quiet house. Automatically Clare walked back to the kitchen, expecting to find the older woman preparing dinner. Instead, the kitchen was empty and dark, the tea kettle cold. On the table there was a note for Clare, written in Mrs. Sydney's precise, if cramped, hand.

"Michael telephoned from Virginia," it read. "He was called home because of a problem at his house and will be back tonight. He will contact you from the airport when he arrives in New York. Speaking of airports, my niece is on call this month and has an emergency trip to Puerto Rico tonight, so I have had to return to Pelham until tomorrow night. You will find a pork roast in the refrigerator. It is tasty both hot and cold, so I hope you will eat it. Fondly, Alvina Sydney."

Clare dialed Emily's number from memory. The phone rang six times before it was answered by a young girl who identified herself as the baby-sitter. She told Clare that Emily was not expected home until after six, and she would leave a message for her to call her sister.

Clare ate some of the pork roast and went to the movies. Although Mrs. Sydney's message hadn't said when Michael was returning, she knew she would probably miss his telephone call. But if he couldn't have bothered to tell Clare he was leaving town, she felt no compulsion to remain in an empty house to wait for him.

CLARE PAID HER ENTRANCE to the theater and bought the smallest container of popcorn available. She had to settle for a seat in the middle of a row much too close to the screen for her taste.

Saturday night in Connecticut, just as in the town where she had lived in southern California, was by far the most popular night to go to the movies. Looking around, she realized she was probably the only single person in the place. Now that Michael had become part of her life, she was spoiled by a man's companionship again.

Alone in the movie house, she felt an ache of solitude replace the anger she had been nurturing against Michael for apparently having lied to her about Schoenfeld-Loewe and then running off to Virginia without another word.

If he had asked her, she would have accompanied him on his weekend trip. Why hadn't he? She didn't like the way he kept his other life secret from her. Clare was an open book to him, answering whatever questions he posed. And he asked plenty of them. But what about him? What did she know about Michael Duffy, anyway? A few stories from his childhood, the fact that his family had been opposed to his medical studies, a vague description of his house.

She also knew how the hard strength of his body felt against hers; how his breath, scented with desire, felt on the skin of her neck; how his hands—strong and capable hands, gentle and tender hands—made her body sing when he touched her.

Yes, she was lonely for him. For one thing, popcorn eaten alone was not as tasty as popcorn shared. She placed the waxed container, its buttered kernels barely touched, on the floor behind her feet.

She knew he was polite. The way he treated her with courtly deference pleased Clare, although she was trying hard to prove that she was perfectly capable of taking care of herself.

She knew he was capable of expressing his emotions. Hadn't he told her that he needed and wanted her? Sometimes he said little, but his feelings were there to be read in his brilliant blue eyes. Yes, she was certain she read him well.

That's what love is all about. That's how it should be between a man and a woman, she thought, nodding to no one in the dark theater. During her unhappy marriage with Teddy she had never been able to read him, although she watched out for him at all times, seeking his approval, courting his affection. All in vain. With Michael, however...

Clare wondered again why Michael held some of himself back from her. It made a lie of his actions. What about the way he stared at her when he thought she wasn't watching? What about the first time they had made love? He'd held her in his arms for hours, stroking her hair, murmuring her name without even knowing he had spoken.

Most of all, she knew that she and Michael had found something to cherish in each other. Something that, left to grow and flourish, might become permanent. Was that love? Did she love Michael Duffy?

Clare sighed, causing the woman on her right to turn to her with a look of query. There was apparently nothing in the film, a complicated espionage thriller set somewhere in the Middle East, to elicit sighs from the audience. An embarrassed Clare, who hardly knew what events flickered across the screen before her, became aware that her sigh had been inappropriate. She shifted in her seat, settling down to a more comfortable position.

But what about that lie?

He probably hadn't lied at all, she reasoned. One of those typical bureaucratic snafus had taken place. An uncooperative switchboard operator, most likely suffering from a headache or a hangover, had simply looked on the wrong list and concluded that Michael Duffy did not exist.

Somewhere behind the glass walls of Schoenfeld-Loewe, Michael Duffy worked, temporarily assigned from headquarters in Washington.

Hadn't he told her Washington? No, he had said "headquarters," and Clare had assumed Washington, knowing that Fairfax, where he lived, was a suburb of the capital. But what about Mrs. Sydney's assurance that Schoenfeld-Loewe was a Swiss company?

Oh, it was all crazy! He owed her an explanation, just as soon as he arrived back in Connecticut. She slid down in her seat and tried to concentrate on the film, but she had lost the thread of the story long before. In addition, she had begun to worry that Michael might call to request that she pick him up from the limousine, or even from the airport itself. After all, she had his car. And she couldn't wait to demand some answers.

Clare climbed over four pairs of legs and left the theater. The movie was hardly compelling. She hadn't followed one single element of the plot.

"CLARE, I'VE BEEN WAITING here for hours!"

Clare slammed the door of the Volkswagen and ran to the front steps of Mrs. Sydney's house. "Emily, what's wrong?"

Her sister sat slouched in the shadow of the rhododendron bushes in front of the darkened house. Emily's normally rosy face was ashen, her hair shaggy and disheveled, her eyes anguished and red-rimmed from crying.

Clare grabbed her sister's hand, which was as cold as ice, and pulled her to her feet. "Come in the house. You're freezing!"

"I've been sitting here waiting for you," Emily said in a small voice.

Looking around, Clare saw that the Mercedes station wagon was parked illegally in front of a fire hydrant across the street. "Why didn't you wait in your car?"

"I...I don't know. It never occurred to me. Oh, Clare..." Emily burst into fresh tears.

"Come on, Emily, let's get inside." She opened the door and switched on the light in the front hall, dropping her keys and purse on a small table that stood against one wall. "I should have left some lights on. I should have given you a key in case you ever needed to come here. Come into the kitchen and let me make you a cup of hot tea." *Lord, I sound just like Mrs. Sydney.*

"I'd rather have a stiff drink, I think." Emily sniffled in an attempt to control herself. With a moan, she began to cry again.

"I've got some brandy upstairs in a packing box. Wait a second, I'll get it. Just sit down—sit near the radiator and get warm. I'll be right back." Clare took the stairs two at a time and found the still-packed box in the back of her closet. She pulled out the bottle and hurried down to the kitchen.

Emily was perched stiffly on a straight-backed chair she had pulled close to the old-fashioned radiator. In the down vest she wore over faded jeans and a designer sweatshirt, she looked shrunken and defeated and very, very young. She reminded Clare of a lost child.

Clare, a worried frown on her face, poured a generous portion of brandy into a juice glass she found on the drainboard next to the sink. Her face set with concern, she watched as Emily drank the brandy in three quick gulps and then held the glass out to her.

"You want some more?"

"Please."

"Are you certain?" Emily wasn't much of a drinker, a fact that Clare knew from years past. Two drinks and she would either dance on the kitchen table or, more likely, find a quiet corner and fall asleep.

"I'm certain."

Clare poured again, this time more judiciously. "What happened? You look as if you just saw a ghost."

"It's worse, Clare, a lot worse. Oh, Clare, it's my worst nightmare come true! Jonas has kidnapped the twins!"

Chapter Twelve

"Kidnapped the twins? I don't understand. What do you mean, he's kidnapped the twins? Where did he take them?" Clare sank into a chair at the table, found she had the brandy bottle still in her hand, and reached across to the sink for a coffee cup. She poured another serving, this time for herself.

"I don't know. They're gone, all three of them," Emily said in a rush, tripping over her words as she explained. "Jonas was f-furious, screaming and yelling and cursing at me. I was out shopping, and when I got home I saw the baby-sitter—her name is Ginny—standing on the street, crying. She was waiting for her father to come and pick her up. She said that Jonas came storming into the house, threw ten dollars at her and shouted for her to get out. Then he raced upstairs to where the boys were. Oh, Clare, what am I going to do? It's all my fault."

"I'm sure there's some explanation, Emily."

"They're gone forever. I know they are."

"No, they're not. I'm certain there's a perfectly logical explanation." There had to be one. No one, not even Jonas, acted like a crazy man without reason, not unless he had experienced some sort of mental breakdown.

Emily couldn't speak for a moment. She inhaled roughly and wiped her eyes on the sleeve of her sweatshirt. Finally, when she had taken another sip of her brandy and composed herself, she went on. "Yes, there's an explanation. I went shopping this afternoon."

"Yes, you already told me that," Clare said gently. "But surely a little shopping trip—"

"But I wasn't really shopping, you see," Emily interrupted. "I...I went to meet Gene for a drink." She looked away, guilt written all over her pale face.

"Oh." *The plot thickens, and I know what's coming.* "In the Town Center?"

Emily turned her eyes back to Clare. "Yes. How did you know?"

"I saw Gene there, but he didn't see me."

"Well, Jonas saw him, too. Apparently he followed Gene around all afternoon until we met. Oh, was he proud of himself! Acting like Sherlock Holmes or somebody, skulking around Greenwich and Stamford, watching Gene do his Saturday errands! He's been suspicious, and he was intent on catching me. He—Jonas, that is—has been acting very funny lately, asking me all sorts of questions about how I spend my afternoons and making strange little comments about Gene and his books. I never saw any connection, never saw the point he was trying to make, but I knew something was up. As a rule, Jonas doesn't pay the slightest attention to what I do with my time."

No wonder Jonas had been running around the shopping mall with murder on his face. The nerve of the man! Clare fumed inwardly. Everyone in town except Mrs. Jonas Hahn knew he was keeping that trampy Angel Chetnik, but Jonas had the arrogance to make a fuss about Emily's meeting a friend for a drink. Clare was disgusted with the duplicity, with the silent conspiracy, of Emily's society. Nevertheless, she couldn't stop herself from asking the obvious question. "Why did you go to meet Gene if you knew—"

"I don't know," Emily exploded, with agony in her voice. "Oh, I was such a fool to go, but Gene said he had to see me! I swore to Jonas, I swore on the heads of my sons, that Gene and I weren't lovers, but he didn't believe me. He has Ian and Kevin, Clare. What am I going to do?''

"He can't keep them, Emily. That's ridiculous!"

"He kicked me out of the house. He got two plastic garbage bags from the kitchen and threw them at me. He said I could have anything I could fit into them and that he'd give me ten thousand dollars, but he never wants to see me again. And I can't ever see the boys again. Never. He's going to divorce me." Emily put her hands to her face and began to sob. "My little boys, my babies..."

Clare crossed to her sister, crouched down and put her arms awkwardly around Emily. "Jonas can't steal the boys, sweetie. Jonas thinks he's a big shot, but no matter how puffed up his king-sized ego is, he doesn't make the laws of the land, Emily. Only a judge can decide who gets the children. I can't imagine any judge in his right mind awarding Jonas custody of Ian and Kevin. On Monday you can call a lawyer and have everything taken care of. Now stop worrying, okay?"

"But, Clare, he can do whatever he wants. He's got all the money in the world—well, not that much, but a lot. He can have those boys on a plane to Seattle or Paris or Rio de Janeiro, and who would stop him? I'll never seem them again!"

Although Clare secretly agreed that Jonas was angry and foolish enough to do just such a thing, she kept her voice calm. "You're hysterical, Emily. Jonas has a medical practice here. He can't just pick up and leave. He'd never do anything so foolish."

"You don't know him. He always gets what he wants, most especially when his temper is up. I've never seen him as furious as he was tonight. Never!"

"Yes, I do know what he's like. He's an incredible bully, that's all. Look, Emily, where do you think he is now? At a hotel?"

"Maybe. Maybe they're already on a plane to some-where."

"What about his mother? Jonas won't want to care for two little toddlers all by himself. He has neither the pa-tience nor the expertise."

"I think I told you that his mother had a minor stroke last year, so she can't care for the boys. Just being around them makes her nervous. She'd have another stroke if he showed up with Ian and Kevin. Besides, Jonas is still afraid of his mother. I can't picture him explaining to her that he'd kidnapped the boys."

"Let me think," Clare said, returning to her chair and taking another sip of brandy. As far as she could tell, Jonas didn't even like his children. He was using them as a weapon, no more, against Emily. Given a few days to come to his senses, Jonas would return the boys to Emily, if only because he wouldn't want to be saddled with their care. As for actually stealing them away and hiding, as one heard happened in bitter custody fights... No, Jonas would never do such a heinous thing. If he disappeared, he would leave behind his lucrative practice—practices, she amended—his gorgeous house and all the artwork he and Emily had collected over the years. If there was anything Jonas held dear, it was his material possessions. Clare was certain Jonas would return to Greenwich.

But when he did, when Jonas divorced her, Emily need-ed to protect herself.

"You have to go home, Emily," Clare said decisively.

"Can't I stay here? I don't want to be alone in the house. He gave me an hour to get out—I came here as soon as he and the boys had gone. There's no telling what he'd do if he came back and found me there."

"Certainly you can stay here. That's not what I meant, not at all. But you have to go back and gather some things for yourself."

"Can't you lend me a few things? I didn't bring my. . .

my garbage bags. I didn't bring a thing with me." Emily tried to joke, but her eyes filled with tears instead.

"You have to go into the safe, Emily. Take whatever cash is there, if Jonas left any, and all those ledgers."

"Why?"

"First of all, what are you going to live on? You don't even have a purse with you, let alone clothes or anything. And to protect yourself, don't you see? If Jonas really divorces you, if he thinks he can prove you've been having an affair with Gene—"

"But I'm not," Emily insisted. "I swear I'm not."

"I know that, and so do you, but a good lawyer can make you look like mincemeat in court. What happens in divorce court has absolutely nothing to do with the truth. It all depends on who can afford the best lawyer. You've seen some of your friends tossed out into the cold with nothing to show for their years of faithful 'service' to their rich husbands, haven't you?"

Emily nodded. "Y-yes. But Clare, what can I do to protect myself?"

"I told you. Go back home and get every one of the ledgers in the safe. Every one of them."

"I can't do it, Clare. Besides, what good will the ledgers do me?"

"Are you kidding, Emily? Those ledgers are Jonas's lifeblood. If you have them, Jonas will give you a fair shake in court. You'll see."

"Why?"

"Why are the ledgers in your safe in the first place? Why aren't they in the office where they belong?"

"Some of them are our household accounts. As for the others, I don't know why we keep them at home. I suppose for privacy's sake. Jonas doesn't like anyone to nose around in our business."

"Listen to me. I'm a bookkeeper, and I know what I'm talking about." There was no need to go into her suspicions with Emily, not now, when her sister was so upset about the twins. Later Clare could explain about the Rejuvenation Clinic and its two sets of books. She remembered vividly having seen red and blue books in the bedroom safe—red for household, blue for cash accounts at the clinic. The last thing in the world Jonas Hahn wanted was someone in a position to make his secret books public. No finer weapon existed. "Take my word, Emily. He'll do anything to get those ledgers back. Anything—including returning Ian and Kevin. Don't drink any more." Clare stood up and grabbed the juice glass from Emily's fingers. "You have to have your wits about you."

"But Clare, I can't go home, I can't," Emily wailed, biting her pale lower lip until it throbbed an angry red. "The dogs are loose. They'd kill me."

MICHAEL DUFFY HUNG UP the telephone in exasperation. There had been no answer at Clare's when he called from National Airport, hoping he could talk her into coming to La Guardia to meet his plane. Nor was there any answer now, after the shuttle's arrival in New York. He went to a courtesy telephone on the wall of the shuttle terminal and waited for someone to pick up the phone at the Connecticut Limousine Service. During his years of work-related travel, Michael had learned that Saturday night was the worst night of the week to arrive at any airport. Most ground services were cut in half, all airports being geared for the Monday-to-Friday business traveler.

At last a sleepy voice responded and told him that he would have to wait thirty-five minutes for a car. Michael went in search of an open coffee shop. He had to walk to the next terminal before he found one, and then it was merely a stand-up affair. He bought a cup of coffee from an attendant and a bologna sandwich from an automatic dispensing machine.

Friday's meeting had gone on until after eleven in the

evening, too late to call Clare at Mrs. Sydney's and explain his absence. Marcone had reconvened the agents at eight on Saturday, too early to disturb her. Anyway, Michael had prepared no plausible story for Clare, not until late in the afternoon when the meeting had finally adjourned and he had been able to speak to Mrs. Sydney. Then it had occurred to him that he could claim his basement had flooded.

That happened occasionally in the spring at his house in Fairfax, which was built against a steep, rocky hill that allowed ground water to seep up through the floor of the cellar. Cleaning up a mess like that was a time-consuming process, and the excuse would hold water, Michael thought, inwardly groaning at his miserable play on words.

The Criminal Division of the Service was in good shape. They had their court orders—one to raid the Rejuvenation Clinic, another for a search-and-seizure operation at Angel Chetnik's Queens apartment, where Michael surmised other incriminating records might exist. Even without knowledge of an individual's Social Security number, the Service could find just about any taxpayer in the United States through its immense resources and determine his or her occupation. But a woman with a name as unusual as Angel's, especially a woman who had kindly listed her name in the Borough of Queens telephone book—well, child's play. Angel Chetnik was a bookkeeper, and Angel now drove a brand-new Porsche, all of which fitted a profile with which Michael was familiar: physician plus bookkeeper-lover sometimes equaled collusion for tax fraud.

The Service had in hand a third order, one to search the Greenwich house and boat of Dr. Jonas Hahn. If the incriminating records could not be found at any of those four locations, Michael might be forced to conclude that there were no incriminating books.

He refused even to consider the possibility that the books might not exist. He smelled the putrid odor of tax fraud, and his nose was seldom wrong. Not only would he grab Hahn, he'd get the other doctors involved with the clinic, too. That would make a nice catch for a few months of investigation, a nice catch indeed.

It had taken time to secure all the court orders because it was a weekend, and because they had been forced to deal with the personnel of three separate legal jurisdictions. But the Service eventually got everything it wanted. The Service always did.

His stomach upset, he threw away the second half of the stale bologna sandwich. Too little sleep, he told himself. And too much strong black coffee in the past two days. He patted his pockets for the roll of antacids he had purchased at National Airport, found it and chewed one of the chalky tablets with a grimace of distaste.

The sandwich might taste of cardboard, the coffee might be too strong, but Michael knew it was the prospect of seeing Clare that had upset his stomach. Within two days, everything would be over between them. Nowhere in his vocabulary existed words adequate enough to explain that he loved her despite the low deception he had practiced since the night they first met. *I'm not a doctor,* he imagined himself saying. *I'm an Internal Revenue agent assigned to criminal investigation who purposely struck up a friendship with you in order to spy on your brother-in-law and your sister. I never intended to bed you, and most of all, to fall in love with you. That's not how I operate, Clare. Can you forgive me? Can you understand that I was only doing my job? That what sprang forth between us was an accident, unplanned, unprecedented, unfair—especially to you?*

Doing my job. What a trite, disgusting excuse, overused by so many bureaucrats, by anyone who refused to accept responsibility for his actions. How could he say those hackneyed words to the woman he loved, to Clare? There was no doubt in Michael's mind, no doubt at all, that Clare would never forgive him after Tuesday's raids.

And why should she?

It was with a sad heart that he returned to the Eastern Airlines shuttle terminal and waited next to a sliding glass door for the arrival of a distinctive blue-and-white stretch Chrysler from the Connecticut Limousine Service.

STARING UP AT THE CEILING, Emily lay meekly and allowed Clare to tuck her into bed. The brandy, quickly imbibed and as rapidly assimilated into the bloodstream, had done its work. But first, Emily had written down and helped Clare memorize the combination of the wall safe in her bedroom.

She looked up from her cocoon under the blue comforter and watched Clare remove a black wool turtleneck from the top drawer of a tall dresser. Clare shucked a red cotton shirt and replaced it with the turtleneck, which she pulled down with rough jerks, tucking it into the waistband of her blue jeans. The wool scratched her skin, but in her haste she ignored the irritation. She banged the drawer shut. Picking up a brush on the dresser, she yanked it through her hair three times and then pulled the hair back, swiftly wrapping a rubber band around the thick mass.

"You're sure you'll be all right?" Emily asked in a sleepy voice. "I know you're not afraid of the dogs, but what if they start to bark? What if someone comes?"

"They won't bother me, Emily. I get along fine with them. Even if they bark, as soon as they smell me, they'll calm down. Dogs know, don't worry."

"And you haven't forgotten how to turn off the alarm?"

"The alarm is on? I can't believe you put on the alarm." Clare had imagined Emily rushing from the house in hysteria, and the fact that she remembered to set the alarm surprised her.

"I always put on the alarm," Emily said. "Jonas would kill me if I ever forgot. The combination is my birthday and the twins'. Ten-five, plus three-nineteen. If you make a mistake, don't panic. All you have to do is enter the numbers again. You have forty seconds after violation before the audible alarm goes off and before the phone dials the police."

"I know, Emily. I took care of the house when you were in Mexico, remember? Everything is going to be all right. I'll be back in a minute."

Clare ran down to the kitchen and grabbed the brandy bottle and a box of wooden matches that Mrs. Sydney kept next to the gas stove. She returned to her room and saw Emily covered to her chin with the blue comforter. Emily had neglected to remove her shoes, which rose in a large lump at the bottom of the bed.

"Take off your shoes, Emily, and go to sleep. I'll be back before you know it."

"I'd forgotten my shoes." Emily sat up and grinned sheepishly. "I should never drink," she said with a giggle as she fumbled under the comforter and removed her Top-siders. "It's a good thing you're going, instead of me. With my luck, I'd probably end up in jail, even if it is my own house. Oh, Clare, the safe. . .the safe is behind the reddish painting on your left as you come into the bedroom. Not the other one. The other painting is a Rothko, and it's permanently protected. There's a wire attached to the wall, separate from the main-house alarm system, so if you lift the Rothko—bang!—a siren goes off. Be careful." She lay back down again and stared at Clare. "What are you doing?"

"I'm burning the cork from the brandy bottle. Isn't that how you make stuff to blacken your face?"

"I-I guess so." Emily watched, fascinated, as Clare darkened first her forehead, then her cheeks, then the skin of her neck where it showed above the high-collared sweater. "Clare, you think of everything! You're so imaginative. Really, I had no idea. Only the whites of her eyes... All you need is an aqualung, and you'd be James Bond."

"For heaven's sake, go to sleep."

"I think I will. I'm feeling pretty looped, as a matter of fact. I took a sedative before you got home, nothing too strong, but the combination is making my head swim. Doctor's-soon-to-be-ex-wife mixes dangerous drugs dangerously. Oh, my." Another giggle erupted from her throat. Then, at last, she closed her eyes and fell quiet. Clare thought her sister had gone to sleep, but she was wrong. Just as Clare, dressed in black and dark blue denim, her face grimy with burned cork, turned off the lamp on the bedside table, Emily opened her eyes once more.

"Take the Mercedes. It will look suspicious if you park that junk heap you're driving in our driveway." She fumbled under the covers in search of the keys. "I left the keys in my down vest. It's behind you on the chair."

"You're not that looped," Clare said with a smile. "Good thinking, Emily." She bent and gave her a quick kiss on the forehead. Grabbing the keys, Clare went out the door, leaving it open behind her and turning on the light in the upstairs hall in case Emily needed to find the bathroom.

In the front hall, she picked up her purse and hesitated. Did she really need to carry it along? It was against Clare's sense of civil obedience to drive without her operator's license, but she actually laughed aloud as she dropped the Volkswagen's keys inside. They rested atop the folded invoices and photocopies from the Rejuvenation Clinic that she had neglected to remove the day before.

I'm about to burgle Jonas's house, and I'm worried about a driver's license! She replaced the purse on the polished mahogany table and left the house.

In less than ten minutes, Clare had pulled the station wagon up to the Hahns' gates. The house was quiet and dark. From where she sat, the closed garage doors of the attached garage were visible. The gates were also shut, which Clare knew was done to keep the Dobermans confined to the property at night, when they were free to roam the two acres. It surprised her that a confused and nearly hysterical Emily had remembered to shut the gates behind her. As far as Clare recalled, they were never locked; but even if they were, she assumed the key would be on Emily's gold key ring, which dangled from the ignition.

Clare opened the door on the driver's side, which not only turned on the interior light but set a discreet bell tinkling. Quickly she latched the door to stop the noise and crossed to the gates, which opened at her touch. Then she nosed the car into the property and immediately closed the gates. The last thing she wanted was two trained attack dogs roaming around the neighborhood.

She considered putting the Mercedes in the garage so it wouldn't be seen by passersby, most especially by the town police who patrolled the quiet neighborhood regularly, thanks to its residents' extreme generosity to the Police Benevolent Fund and other various charities. But the Mercedes, as Emily had pointed out, belonged to the Hahns and would not look strange parked in their own driveway late at night.

She drove the car into a small turnaround, backed it so its nose was facing the street, and looked in the glove compartment for a small, matte black flashlight Emily had told her would be there.

It was.

Clare left the station wagon unlocked, its keys in the ignition, as she made her way to the kitchen door. The night was black, there was no moon, but Clare was familiar with the path that continued to the rear of the property where the guest house stood. Halfway to the kitchen door, she heard the clink of the dogs' choke collars, and she went down on one knee to await their approach.

When she thought she saw their blurred forms coming around the back of the house, she called out their names. "Heidi, Rolf, it's me, it's Clare. Good girl, Heidi," she said in a quiet voice, not bothering to whisper, but careful to keep her tone low. The Dobermans rushed upon Clare, then began to lick at her face and hands. She heard only the rasp of their rapid breathing and the thump of one of their tails as it hit the other's flank. She could barely see them—the dogs were as black as the night—but she felt their bodies quiver as their tails wagged ebulliently in recognition of her scent. She rubbed Heidi's neck and scratched Rolf behind his ears. "It's okay," she soothed. "I'm just here for a quick visit. You be good little children and go back to your patrolling, or whatever you do all night. Good dogs, good dogs." They followed Clare to the kitchen door. "Shoo! Go on," she whispered. They sat, both heads cocked to the right, and watched her as she unlocked the door.

Immediately she heard the barely audible high-pitched whine of the digital panel that controlled the alarm system. Although the panel's lights would indicate that violation of the premises had taken place, Clare had forty seconds to enter the personalized code that would deactivate a raucous siren mounted under the eaves of the guest house. And, most important, the silent signal that went through the telephone lines to the police station.

Switching on the flashlight, she crossed the dark kitchen to the wall where the panel was located. She shone the light on the panel. One small red light signaled that the back door had been opened. There were other, still-extinguished red dots that would light if another exterior door had been opened or if the sensors had detected smoke, excessive heat or cold, or the sound of breaking glass. In addition, the system consisted of a series of interior light beams across strategic corridors—from where she stood, Clare could see the glow of one in the hall that led to the dining room. Under four different rugs throughout the house, sensor mats waited to catch the unwary burglar. The cellar door, if opened from the inside, was wired as well. If the electric power failed, by accident or through the machinations of a burglar's hand, the system switched automatically to an auxiliary battery. If the phone lines were cut, an alarm went automatically to the police station. The entire house, if empty of inhabitants, could be protected, and there existed the option of setting the system for exterior violation only, to give its owners peace of mind while sleeping.

All in all, a sophisticated, nearly foolproof and very expensive system, guaranteed to protect one's physical safety and possessions. Clare had a fleeting thought that the burden of ownership was a heavy one. She herself no longer owned anything worth stealing, and she realized for the first time how free she felt without material property.

She punched Emily's birthday, then the twins', into the panel.

Immediately the whine ceased.

The night sounds of the house were unfamiliar to her. She stopped every five feet to listen and accustom herself to their rhythm. As she made her way through the dining room and living room, en route to the master-bedroom suite, she kept the small beam of the flashlight aimed at the floor.

Clare considered herself a basically honest person, but in the short space of two days she had found herself going into forbidden places, pawing through the possessions of others and sticking her nose in where she knew she didn't belong. She wondered what had come over her. Yet she felt a security in her moral position that overwhelmed the dishonesty of her actions. Emily deserved more from life than the unfair shake Clare had gotten from Teddy, and Clare knew she would go to almost any lengths to protect her sister from the heartache she herself had been through.

She was in the hall leading to the bedroom now. First she passed Jonas's dressing room on the left and, next to it, the enormous master bath with its sunken round tub surrounded with endless dials that roiled up the water at the bather's whim. The room smacked of Jonas's nouveau riche taste, not of Emily's quiet refinement.

On her right was Emily's dressing room, its door open. Clare flashed the light in her hand over the racks of neatly hung clothes, all sorted by color compatibility, and over the plastic boxes of shoes carefully stacked on the wall-to-wall carpet. The light reflected back at Clare from a mirror above a dressing table covered with jars of cream and perfume bottles. How was Emily going to accustom herself to life after divorce? No matter how much the court awarded Emily, her standard of living would fall. Not as far as Clare's, perhaps, but substantially.

At last she was in the bedroom itself. On her right was the large raised bed, unmade; she could see the outline of its rumpled surface in the dark. Clare, who knew Emily's house was usually in perfect order, was surprised. But then she remembered that the housekeeper had been fired. Emily had probably let things slide. Women whose children had just been kidnapped did not stop to make beds.

On her left hung the oil painting, Clare's objective. She turned off the small flashlight and stuck it in a back pocket of her jeans. Lifting the painting awkwardly to reveal the wall safe, she set it down on the carpeting. Its wooden stretcher hit the wall behind with a muffled thud that made a flash of sweat break out under Clare's sweater. She rubbed the palm of one hand in a circle on her chest, feeling as she did so the thump of her heart beneath the irritating wool. For a long moment she stood still and listened to the sounds of the house. Then she sighed, retrieved the flashlight and, from her front left pocket, the combination of the safe. She thought she knew the combination by heart, but why take a chance when the numbers were written there for her to follow?

Around twice. . . She mouthed the directions silently. *Seventeen left. . . around once to the right, stopping at seven. . . thirty-two left.* How did Emily remember all the numbers, the combinations and the keys in her life? The dial made the smallest whispered whirr as it twirled, but each time it reached a number written on the paper in Clare's hand, there was another distinctive click that signaled accuracy. She realized she was biting down hard on the skin of her cheeks within her mouth, and afraid her teeth would break the skin, she made a conscious effort to relax herself.

Silent on its oiled hinges, the safe door swung open. She shone the light inside. Everything lay exactly as she remembered: two stacks of money neatly placed in front of a row of ledgers, both red and blue. Should she take every one of the leather-bound books? To do so would necessitate at least two trips back and forth between the bedroom and the car. But she had time, didn't she? She had lots of time.

First the currency, two neat piles held together by wide red rubber bands, the top bill of each a twenty. Unable to estimate the total, Clare knew she had never actually handled so much cash in her life, and she exhaled a noiseless whistle as she lifted one bundle. Laying the flashlight down within the safe, she pulled the black turtleneck sweater loose from the waistband of her jeans and stuffed the bills under the sweater. When she tucked in the wool once more, the money rested against the skin of her stomach, just under her breasts. *That's appropriate,* she thought with an inward laugh. *From breasts to breasts.* She wondered how many secret operations the cash represented.

Now the ledgers. She removed the four most recent red and blue books, stacking them at her feet. Should she take them all out, close the safe, then carry them to the car? Or should she take what she could carry now and leave the balance in the safe? She opted for the latter and tiptoed quietly from the bedroom, her arms laden with ledgers. Even though Clare knew the house was empty, something impelled her to silence. Slowly, and without benefit of flashlight, she retraced her steps to the kitchen, where she deposited her cargo just at the back door, rather than deal with the dogs while her arms were full. She left the money under her sweater.

Back in the bedroom, back at the gaping safe, Clare pulled out the balance of the books. She was in the act of turning to lay them on the floor when a distinctly male voice cried, "Don't do it!"

Clare's heart stopped, her body frozen in a half-crouch. An explosion of raw fear shot through her limbs, paralyzing her in the awkward position.

Chapter Thirteen

Michael Duffy permitted himself the faintest of smiles. How foolish he had been to worry that Clare was not at home. The thought had obsessed him, returning again and again to his tired brain.

As the taxi entered Keeler Street, he emitted a sigh of relief, feeling the muscles in the back of his neck relax for the first time in more than two hours. His Volkswagen, battered and disreputable, sat in the driveway of Mrs. Sydney's house. He really should buy a new car, he thought, not just because driving the eight-year-old jalopy was hardly appropriate to his cover as a doctor, as Clare had mentioned more than once, but because he was beginning to feel, very strongly, that it was time for a change in his life.

What if the car hadn't been there, he asked himself. What if Clare had been out when he arrived? During the two hours that had passed since he had last called her from La Guardia Airport, he realized how anxious he was to see her.

Before meeting Clare, he had never felt that way about a woman. It was her air of gravity that Michael had first noticed, the way she acted with him—diffident, slightly reluctant, but attracted to him nonetheless. Despite her prudence, he had recognized Clare as a victim of the same jolt of heady electricity that shook him whenever he looked at her. Sometimes he studied a Clare unaware of his scrutiny, and he recalled the way the skin of her smooth back felt beneath his palm the first time he had touched her—delicate, silken, exotic in its difference from the skin of all others.

He tried to imagine himself living with her, awakening at her side each morning, sleeping close to her silky skin each night, his body curved around hers. He tried to picture how Clare would weather the inexorable process of growing old; perhaps the lines of worry that were only now beginning at the sides of her mouth and across her almost smooth forehead would deepen. But Clare was one of those women whose appearance, like the body of a fine wine, would improve with age.

When he attempted to imagine beyond those things, his mind drew a blank, and a heavy sadness he was unable to shake off filled his heart. Michael was a realist; he knew there was no future for him with Clare.

How stupid, he thought, how unprofessional. He had a job to do, a job at which he had never before failed. He must not allow his personal feelings to interfere.

The house was not dark. While not exactly ablaze with lights, various windows glowed on both the first and second floors, confirming to him that Clare was awake and waiting for him. He hoped Mrs. Sydney was fast asleep, however. He wanted to be alone with Clare. It was too soon to tell her the truth about his actual role in her life, but perhaps, just perhaps, he might sow the seeds for a rapprochement that night. Was there the remotest possibility that his relationship with Clare could be salvaged?

No, he knew none existed.

Michael emerged from the taxi, then paid and dismissed the driver. He looked at the house for a long moment, a frown of concentration on his brow. The story about a flooded basement would hold, he decided. It would have to, for the time being.

He went up the steps to the entrance. Ignoring the door-bell and the heavy brass knocker, he rapped softly on the door. If Clare was on the first floor, she would hear him, and he wouldn't disturb a sleeping Mrs. Sydney. He waited, listening to the night sounds on the street—trees dripping moisture, the hum of traffic on a main artery two or three blocks away—and then he knocked again, more loudly.

Damn! He'd have to ring. There wasn't a peep from the quiet house. A small window in the front door sat too high for Michael to see through, but he stepped back and gazed through a crack in a curtain that protected the living room from the gaze of a passerby. Within the house, nothing moved.

Michael tapped the doorbell. In response he heard two short bursts from a bell in the kitchen. He waited, then tapped it again.

Finally the door opened, and he stared agape at a sleepy and shoeless Emily, the sweatshirt she wore askew, a mix-ture of confusion and fear on her face. Clearly the bell had awakened her.

"What are you doing here?" they both said at the same moment. She smiled, but her eyes slipped away from his, only to study the floor.

"Where's Clare?" he asked. "Is she here?" Had he suc-cessfully suppressed the stab of disappointment that im-paled him at seeing Emily instead of her sister? Michael was reluctant to demonstrate his anxiety to Emily, especially since, within three short days, he would be responsible for a cataclysmic change in the woman's life.

After an awkward hesitation, Emily finally said, "She's out, but she'll be back soon."

Evasive, definitely evasive, he thought. A second con-strained silence enveloped them while Michael searched his mind for a reply. Emily refused to meet his gaze. "I. . . I don't need to see her," he said at last. "I just came to pick up my car."

"Your car?"

"The Volks in the driveway. Do you have the keys?"

"I—I don't know. Why don't you come in while I look? They're probably around somewhere." Emily stumbled slightly as she stepped back to allow him to enter. Her eyes were swollen, and there was a streak of mascara that followed a furrow of strain or fatigue down her left cheek. She put a trembling hand on the doorjamb to steady herself.

She's on something, he thought, a millisecond before a whiff of alcohol on her breath confirmed his speculation.

"Just wait a second, and I'll check." She went first to the kitchen and then returned empty-handed to the entrance hall. "She probably left the keys in her bedroom. I'll be right back." Slowly she ascended the stairs to the second floor, walking like an elderly woman, ignoring the banister but leaning heavily on the one arm she had extended, palm flat against the wall.

As he waited, Michael looked around the pleasant hallway. His eyes fell on a leather purse that rested on a table set against the wall. Immediately he recognized the purse as Clare's. Naturally, the keys would be inside—wasn't that where women kept everything? Why had Emily missed it? Since it was the only item out of place in the neat entrance hall, she must have been pretty far gone to have overlooked it. He wondered what had happened to make Emily, who didn't look at all like a heavy drinker, resort to alcohol. Moreover, what was she doing at Clare's this late on a Saturday night? Shouldn't Emily be home with that bastard she was married to?

He opened the purse and spied the keys resting there. He pulled them out, just opening his mouth to call up the stairs to Emily that he had found them when the words died on his lips. He saw, and immediately understood the significance of, the creased papers in Clare's purse.

"What a devil she is!" he said sotto voce. "She actually

got her hands on some of the records." He unfolded the photocopies and the copy of Clare's invoice from the Rejuvenation Clinic and studied them. How had she managed to get copies of Hahn's records? Lord, she was ingenious! He had never expected her to go so far.

"I'm sorry, Michael, I couldn't find the keys. I don't really know how soon Clare will be back... What have you got there?" Emily spoke at his side. He hadn't even heard her descend the staircase.

Reflexively, Michael whipped the papers behind his back, immediately feeling the fool. He had been caught, literally caught, with his hand in Clare's purse.

"I—I found the keys," he mumbled. "They were in Clare's purse. I..."

What else do you have there, he imagined Emily asking as she came wide awake. *You took something out of Clare's purse. I saw you do it.* How would he answer her suspicions?

"These are—are some papers that have to do with the car. Clare...Clare didn't want to drive it without the registration papers. Where is Clare? I want to talk to her." *Stop explaining yourself,* he ordered. *She hasn't asked you a single question.* Indeed, Emily seemed to have forgotten that he had sneaked something out of Clare's purse. Her eyes gazed, vacant and sleepy, at a point beyond his shoulder. Nevertheless, Michael stuffed the papers into the inside breast pocket of his jacket, worried that Emily would demand to see them.

"She's at my house."

"Your house? What's she doing there?" As he spoke, a look of misery washed over Emily's features and threatened to crumble her fragile composure. He thought again how strongly she resembled her younger sister, although Michael felt Clare was the more beautiful of the two, especially now that the fair Emily looked as if she hadn't slept in two days.

Emily bit her lower lip and hesitated. "Picking up some things for me. I'm going to stay with her for a while."

"Trouble at home?" he asked sympathetically. *Why didn't I realize it before,* he wondered. *She's had a falling out with Hahn. Probably found out about the book-keeper.*

Emily, to his consternation, burst into tears. He laid an awkward, comforting hand on her shoulder.

"Oh, Michael, the most terrible thing has happened!" She wept noisily, throwing herself into his arms. Michael's mouth fell open in astonishment.

NOT FAR AWAY, in a quiet, darkened bedroom, the voice came again.

"Don't do it," the man said. "Mmm."

Jonas! Clare's heart skipped erratically and her mouth went dry as she recognized his distinctive, deep voice. Oh, thank heaven the flashlight was off! Maybe he hadn't yet seen her cork-blackened face; maybe he wasn't aware that the intruder in his bedroom was his own sister-in-law. Could she run for it? Was there another, closer way out of the house than the long trip back through the kitchen? Jonas hadn't said her name, so he probably hadn't seen her face. She shifted her eyes to where the draperies were, closed against the cold night. Would the sliding glass door behind them be locked? Could she possibly—

She rejected the impulse immediately. Of course the sliding glass door would be locked; the alarm had been set, protecting the house from cellar to rafters. That precaution would certainly include locking the door from the bedroom to the deck. The window was out; she'd be hopelessly tangled in its voluminous draperies, and Jonas would be on her long before she found and opened the latch.

Through the hall to the main part of the house, then. Without moving her head, she let her eyes roam the darkness of the room, searching for her would-be captor, trying to ascertain if the door, the door to freedom that led from the bedroom, still stood open. But nothing moved in the quiet room. And yet, and yet... She was certain she could hear Jonas breathing. Where *was* he? Why didn't he *say* something? Why wasn't he attempting to wrestle her to the floor?

Clare heard his movement before she saw it. She whipped her head around at the sound: a rustle, a sigh, another mumbled "mmm." Fighting the scream that threatened to explode from her lips, she held her body so still that every muscle ached.

The rustling ceased. With a dawning realization of Jonas's location, Clare allowed the corners of her mouth to turn up in a half smile. Jonas was turning over in bed! He was asleep, dreaming, talking in his sleep! He had been in the room with her all along, sound asleep in his bed. While she sank to the floor as her knees turned fluid and refused to hold her weight, two of the ledgers slid off the pile of books she held and fell to the carpet with a muffled thud. Clare sucked in her breath in panic. Had he heard? Would he awaken?

There was no sound from the bed.

She couldn't believe she had been in the same room with a sleeping Jonas for...could it have been fifteen minutes?—and that she had been unaware of his presence. How would she escape?

Close the safe! an internal voice screamed. *Close the safe!* She could probably slink away even if he awoke—*if* the room appeared normal. Slowly she rose and found the safe's door with her fingers. Laying one hand on the edge of the opening in the wall, she brought the door to the recess until she felt cold steel on her skin; then she slipped her fingers out to allow it to meet the edge of the safe itself. There was a metallic click as the door found its niche. Fumbling, Clare twirled the dial, which seemed to shriek its secret to the quiet room. She sank to the floor again and listened for the even exhalations of Jonas's breath.

After a long moment, she lifted the heavy painting and raised it awkwardly. Where was the blasted wire? One, two, three times she made a futile pass with the canvas in search of the elusive hook that hung above the safe. Oh, how she ached to turn on the flashlight, if only for one second, but she didn't dare. She replaced the painting on the floor and ran an open palm across smooth plaster, finally locating the hook. With another try, she had it. The wooden stretcher rasped against the wall, breaking the silence in the room, while she nudged first one corner, then another, attempting to straighten the painting.

Thank heaven Jonas had come to his senses and returned home! Clare longed to see the look of relief mixed with wild happiness on her sister's face when she told her the boys weren't kidnapped at all, but were asleep in their beds. Yet it never occurred to Clare that she should put the ledgers and the money back in the safe. No one, least of all Clare, was in a position to predict what further aggression Jonas planned for the following day. Emily still needed protection.

Where was the flashlight? Clare couldn't remember where she had dropped it. On hands and knees, she crawled around, patting the thick Berber carpet in futile search of it. As she bent over, the money stuffed into her sweater shifted and threatened to fall loose. She grabbed the bundles and shoved them back into position. Blast, the flashlight was gone! She would have to leave it behind. How could she reset the alarm without it? Did she dare turn on a light in the kitchen? Should she leave the house unprotected?

No, she should leave the house exactly as she found it—minus the ledgers and the money. That way Jonas would have no suspicions when he awoke. There was no telling how much time would pass until he opened the safe again.

Clare gathered the remaining ledgers into her arms. Without rising from her knees, she made her way to the hall, where she stood up at last and took one look back into the black void that was the bedroom. It really was too bad about the flashlight, she thought. Would Jonas see it the moment he awakened and recognize it as Emily's?

At the back door, she peered through the glass in search of Heidi and Rolf. It was still so dark outside she couldn't be certain, but apparently the dogs had wandered off somewhere. As quietly as possible, she opened the door and stacked the ledgers on the stoop.

She was standing in front of the panel when she thought of Kevin and Ian. Should she bring the twins to Emily? Did she dare?

She shook her head. Although she longed to, she decided the physical location of her nephews was really none of her business. Jonas was bad enough in ordinary circumstances, but he would turn maniacal if he awoke to discover his ledgers, his money and his children gone. She compromised by deciding to take a quick peek in the boys' room so she could assure Emily that they were all right.

As much as she hated to go back to the main part of the house, she forced herself to do it, feeling her way along the hall with her hands and cursing silently at the panic that had made her lose the flashlight. She thought the twins' door was the third on the left; at least their bedroom was located in a wing opposite to where Jonas slept on, oblivious to the violation of his castle.

When she reached their open door, she made her way inside, praying that the floor wasn't strewn with toys. Her prayer was answered, for nothing tripped her as she crossed to a night table that separated the child-size beds. On the table, she could barely see the outline of a large lamp, shaped like a goose, that served as a night light and usually burned throughout the night. She patted the plump shape of the fat goose, finally locating the switch.

When she turned it on, she saw that both beds were empty.

"What have you done with your sons, Jonas?" Clare whispered into the empty room. But there was no time to speculate; she had to escape the house before Jonas awoke and found her there.

Clare returned to the kitchen as quickly as she could. Once more in front of the digital panel, she realized that, flashlight or no flashlight, she didn't dare reset the alarm. She had no idea how to turn on the peripheral system that Jonas had activated so he could sleep in peace. She knew only how to work the system for the entire house, inside and out. If she did that, Jonas would set off one sensor or another as soon as he left his bedroom—even before, perhaps.

In silence she let herself out of the back door, gathered half the ledgers and tiptoed to the Mercedes. After stacking the pile on the front fender, she returned with the balance—no dogs in sight, thank goodness—opened the door on the passenger side and dumped the books on the car floor. Pulling her sweater from the waistband of her jeans, she tossed the two thick packets of money atop the ledgers.

"There, Dr. Hahn," she whispered to the night. "Take that!"

Sliding across the leather seat to the driver's side, she realized that if the gear was slipped into neutral, the car would probably coast almost to the gate and she would not have to start the engine in the driveway. Maybe she could even push it through the gate....

Clare closed the gate behind the station wagon and jumped into the driver's seat. After she had pushed through the gate, the car had come to a stop with its front wheels resting against the curb opposite the Hahns' driveway. At least she was off their property, the gate was securely closed, and neither dog had run barking into the quiet waterfront lanes of Greenwich.

She reached for the ignition key. It was gone.

"Looking for this?" a male voice asked from the back-seat. Clare's heart jumped to her mouth. She dared a quick look in the rearview mirror.

"Mi-Michael!"

"What in hell are you doing, Clare? You must be out of your mind!"

She whipped her head around to stare at him. A street lamp half a block away cast a pale light on his face. She saw immediately that his mouth was set in a tight, angry line. He looked ready to explode as he eyed her cork-blackened face, her black turtleneck sweater and her attitude of total, breathless panic.

"You just broke into his house, didn't you?" His eyes impaled her and caused a thrill of fear, real fear, to shoot through Clare.

" 'Broke in' is too strong for what I did. I went in with Emily's permission. No, I didn't break in—what are you talking about?" He looked tired and bedraggled. Deep circles smudged the skin beneath his eyes, but their unaccustomed presence caused no compassion in Clare. Instead, she fumed with rage. Not only had he scared her immeasurably, he also owed her an apology for his silence of the past two days.

"There's no time for that now," he answered, his voice rough and angry. "Clare, what did you take from the house?"

"Some money and Jonas's ledgers. You were right, Michael," she said, gathering enthusiasm as her fear and surprise subsided. "There are two sets of books—one for cash, one for insured patients. I took the cashbooks—"

"Clare, you stole those books. They're no good to anyone if they're stolen. They aren't worth a hill of beans as evidence without a court order, don't you understand?" He slammed a fist into his hand and muttered a curse beneath his breath. She had never heard Michael say such a word, had never seen him so angry, not even the night he had waited for her at the carriage house. Clare frowned.

"Who's talking about evidence and court orders, Michael? Emily needs leverage because Jonas has threatened to divorce her. I just thought—"

"You thought! You thought! Who the hell are you to think—"

Clare's mouth fell open, astonished at the brutal tone of Michael's voice. "This is a family matter, Dr. Duffy. A family matter! You have no right to stick your nose in where it doesn't belong. Why don't you go back to Fairfax or Washington or whatever place lacking telephone service you've been for the past couple of days and leave us alone to take care of our own problems?"

"I'd say that's a perfect example of the pot calling the kettle black, Mrs. Eckert. Talk about sticking your nose in the wrong places!" In a jumble of arms and legs, he climbed over the seat and plumped himself down next to her, kicking the ledgers and the money savagely until he found room for his feet. "You've made a terrible mess out of everything."

How dare he imply that *she* was meddling, she fumed inwardly. Hadn't *he* urged her to discover Jonas's secret life in order to protect Emily? What was the significance of Michael's sudden about-face? Clare tried to calm down, reminding herself of his tendency to be overprotective, which could only mean he felt strongly for her, despite his failure to tell her so. But no one had ever spoken to her the way he did, and his manners raised her indignation level two notches higher.

"Where are the keys?" she asked levelly. "If we don't get out of here, we'll be arrested. I can't sit around in the middle of the night, in someone else's Mercedes that's parked sideways across the street, and expect to be ignored for long, you know. For one thing, Jonas is asleep in the house."

"He is? You went in there while Hahn was sleeping?" He gave her a look she interpreted as one of grudging admiration.

"Give me the blasted keys, Michael. Now!"

He held the keys out to Clare, who fumbled for the correct one, finally inserting it into the ignition. When the engine caught, she found the reverse gear and stepped on the gas too forcefully, forgetting she was driving an automatic transmission. The car leaped backward and shot toward the house behind them, only screeching to a stop when she stamped down hard on the brake pedal. With an attempt to calm her trembling hands and knees, she slipped the gearshift into drive and headed toward the first intersection. "How did you get here, Michael?" she asked.

"In my car," he answered. "I left it two or three blocks down the road. Drop me there, and I'll follow you home. I can't believe you actually went in there and stole all this stuff!" As he spoke, he picked up one of the bundles of bills and ran his thumb across its edge. "There's a lot of money here."

"You owe me some explanations," Clare said, ignoring the comment.

He tossed the money on top of the ledgers. "I'll explain everything to you when we get back to your place, Clare. It will take too long here. I'm afraid I have a lot to tell you, and you're not going to like any of it."

"Like what?" She turned her head toward him. Suddenly a rhythmic strobe of bright blue light illuminated the planes of his face. "What's that?" she whispered.

As Michael turned to look out the back window, he swore audibly. "It's the police," he said with disgust. "I should have known you'd gum up everything. Pull the car over to the curb before they turn on their siren."

"Oh, Lord," Clare moaned. "What are we going to do?" She thought of her face covered with burned cork, of the money lying in plain sight on the floor of the car, of the ledgers. . . . "I didn't even bring my driver's license."

"Stay where you are, Clare. I'll take care of everything." Before the car had even stopped, he had opened the passenger door and was out on the street, walking back toward the police car. She craned to watch, but the flashing blue light stung her eyes, and she was forced to close them. One of her hands, its palm suddenly wet with tension, slipped from the steering wheel. *They'll take us to jail,* she thought. *They'll take me back to face Jonas. Why did I ever decide to break into his house? Michael's right; I must be crazy.* She had to grip her icy hands together to still their trembling.

In less than two minutes he was back in the car with her. In the rearview mirror, she saw the patrol car start up and prepare to pull around the Mercedes.

"Look at me," he ordered. "Don't let them see your face. What have you got on it, anyway?"

"Burned cork."

"A regular Nancy Drew," he said with disgust. "There's my car. Drop me at the next corner."

With a leg still shaking from fear, she gently pressed down on the gas pedal. The car responded. "How did you get rid of the police?"

"I gave them fifty bucks," he said.

She pulled the Mercedes up next to Michael's Volkswagen. Fifty dollars! She hardly believed her ears. Wasn't there anyone honest left in the world? It was bad enough the police had accepted the money, but the idea that Michael had offered the bribe stunned Clare even more. She turned to him, but he already had the door open and one foot on the street. "You gave the Greenwich police— Michael, wait!"

"I'll see you back at your house, Clare. Drive carefully—I can't afford to bail you out again. I'll be right behind you. Oh, and wipe that gook off your face. You look like a burglar." He handed her a white handkerchief. "Do it now!"

"But—"

"Later." He slammed the door on her objection.

She parked the station wagon in the driveway. Leaving the ledgers and money in the Mercedes, which she locked, Clare let herself into Mrs. Sydney's house and dropped Emily's keys on the table next to her own purse. She went upstairs and into her room, found the brandy bottle, and returned to the kitchen, where she poured a stiff three fingers of the amber liquid into the coffee cup she had abandoned earlier. Emily had been fast asleep in her bed. Clare took a sip and listened for Michael's entry through the now-unlocked front door.

"I'm in the kitchen," she called softly when she heard him drop his keys next to hers on the hall table. A moment later he appeared at the door. He wore a suit, but no tie, and he had the wrinkled and disheveled look of a man who hadn't been home in a long time. When he sank into a chair at the kitchen table, Clare noticed dark shadows beneath his eyes. Two deep lines, newly appeared, ran from the sides of his nose to the corners of his mouth.

"Can I have a shot of that?" he asked, fatigue evident in his voice.

She took a clean coffee cup from the drainboard and poured out a brandy for Michael. "I'm disgusted," she said without preamble as she handed him the drink. Leaning against the counter, her back to the sink, she watched him stare into the cup.

Finally he looked up at her. "*You* are disgusted! Your feelings pale beside mine. What, please tell me, disgusts *you*?" He took a hefty gulp of the brandy.

"You, the police, Jonas, the whole damn world. Nobody's what he seems. I can't believe you bribed them."

"You'd rather be explaining yourself at the police station, I presume."

"I haven't done anything wrong," she insisted, "so I have nothing to fear from the police. Emily asked me to go to her house and get a few things for her. But you—you actually gave the police fifty dollars to look the other way. And they took it! That means law and order belongs to people with money, not to the law-abiding. It's a rotten world, Michael." Clare knew the fuss she was making had less to do with bribery than it did with the fact that Michael had disappeared and not called her. But she couldn't seem to stop, continuing to dwell on the police bribe because she recognized the incongruity of Michael's behavior but hadn't yet figured it out.

"Don't give me that Emily-asked-me-to-go routine. I'd stake my life it was *your* idea to go into their house in the first place. You talked Emily into the scheme, didn't you?"

"Me?"

"Yes, you! You're so busy meddling you can't tell right from wrong."

"Meddling! How am I meddling? I keep my mouth shut. I never said a word to Emily about that Chetnik woman, nor a word to Jonas—or to you or to anyone—about the man *she's* been seeing. I was only trying to protect Emily because Jonas threw her out of the house and told her he planned to divorce her. It's clear to me she needs some protection from him—believe me, I know what it's like to be caught without any protection in a divorce. What did I do wrong?" Her voice rose as she defended herself.

"You have no right, Clare, no right at all, to stick your nose in where you're not wanted, don't you see?" He thumped his fist on the table for emphasis. The cup jumped and sloshed brandy. He picked it up and drained its contents.

"How can you say that? It was you who gave me the idea to go to the clinic in the first place! And I found just what you suggested—two sets of books."

"Yes, I know," he said with a sigh. As he spoke, he patted the breast pocket of his jacket. "The papers were in your purse."

"And what were you doing in my purse?"

"I was looking for the keys to my car so I could stop you before you did something foolish."

"Like what?"

"Like steal all his books."

"Why would you want to stop me? If what you suspected is true, if Jonas *is* evading his income tax, when Emily has the information contained in those books, Jonas will be putty in her hands. He'll have to give her back the boys; he'll have to settle some decent money on her. He can't just throw my sister out of the house with two garbage bags and a promise of ten thousand dollars. Oh, Michael, you don't understand anything! I did it for Emily."

"Who gives a damn why you did it? You've spoiled everything!" Each word was like a slap.

"I don't like the way you're talking to me, Michael. What have I spoiled?" Clare swallowed hard. Michael was her lover; he had always been so kind and thoughtful. That very night she had admitted that she loved this angry, tired man. But the man who sat before her barely resembled the Michael with whom she had fallen in love. She had never heard him speak in the harsh, ugly tones he now uttered, and she was afraid she would cry.

He exhaled a long sigh, and the anger went out of him. When he spoke, his voice had quieted. "Sit down, Clare. I have something to tell you."

She approached the table. He reached out a hand and pulled her into a chair that sat at right angles to his. His hand was warm on her cold fingers, and she expected him to soften and give her some comfort—an apology for having disappeared without telling her, an explanation about his job, some amelioration of the painful accusations he had hurled at her. But Michael was all business. He reached across to the drainboard and grabbed the brandy bottle. Silently he topped her cup, and then he refilled his own. His blue eyes searched hers. The intensity of his stare sent a thrill of nervous apprehension through her.

"I am not a doctor, Clare."

"What?" Her eyes opened wide, reflecting bewilderment. She thought he had said he was not a doctor, but she must have heard him wrong.

"I'm a criminal investigator for the IRS. We've been trying to catch Hahn in tax evasion, and we were this close—" he held up two fingers for emphasis "—before you stuck your nose in and ruined everything. On Tuesday we were scheduled to raid his offices and his home for incriminating records. Now that *you* have them, it's all off. You've blown an entire investigation that has been going on for months."

"I—I don't understand." But she *did* understand, she realized. Like a silent movie, a rash of unrelated incidents played before her mind's eye—Michael refusing to help a sick man on the airplane, Michael driving a battered car, Michael an unknown name at Schoenfeld-Loewe. Michael, so unlike the Greenwich doctors—in looks, in attire, in speech, in topics of conversation. Michael, Michael, Michael... "How many months old is the investigation?" she whispered.

"Lord, I don't know," he replied. "Since that article in the decorating magazine. When was that—July? August?"

"Guadalajara," she said quietly. "Guadalajara was no accident?"

He looked down at the table and shook his head.

Clare felt her blood turn cold within her. She, too, dropped her gaze as the significance of his admission penetrated her consciousness. One of her hands came up to cover her eyes. She put an elbow on the table and pressed her fingers against her eyelids until tiny red pinwheels of light danced within the skin, the pressure making her eyes throb with welcome pain. Any gnawing, any torment, was better than the conclusion his words forced Clare to draw.

"You slept with me because of a tax-evasion investigation," she whispered finally, not as a question but as a statement, her guttural words echoing the anguish that ripped through her breast. "You seduced me so I would spy on Jonas." *And I did,* she told herself. *I spied on him, I sneaked into his clinic and copied his records, I entered his house in the middle of the night and stole thousands of dollars—all because a man told me pretty words and convinced me to sleep with him.*

"No, no, Clare," he said quickly. She knew he had leaned toward her because she felt the heat of his body close by, and she shivered as his warm breath blew across the skin of her cheek. He picked up her free hand and squeezed it tightly. "That was different," he insisted, his voice low and hoarse. "That had nothing to do with the investigation. You have to believe me."

Clare said nothing. Her entire world ceased to spin as she sat there. *How can I believe you? You asked me to dance, you took me out, you took me to bed—all so you could catch my brother-in-law. How can I believe you?* Slowly she withdrew her hand from his, but she couldn't look at him. Memories of Michael's hands on her body haunted her, causing her breasts to shriek with pain. Michael's kisses...his caresses...the intimacies she had granted him...all in the belief that she loved him, and in the hope that he loved her, too. Two tears of shame escaped Clare's closed lids and rolled down her pale cheeks.

"Don't cry, Clare. I love you, Clare. I swear I made love to you because I love you, and not for any other purpose. Please believe me, my darling." His voice was low and soothing; beneath his words was a note of sadness she fought to deny. "I love you," he whispered, his face close to hers. "And I had hoped you loved me, too."

She felt warm fingers brush away one of the tears, but she stiffened visibly at his touch and sucked at the air as a sob tore from her throat. At last, wincing at the light, she opened her eyes.

"Don't touch me, Michael Duffy. Michael Duffy—is that your real name?"

The hand withdrew. "Yes, it's my real name."

"Were you ever in Guadalajara before? Did you go to school there?"

"No, not school, but I was there in January to check out the city."

"So you never knew Jonas before?"

"No," he admitted.

"And you used me to get close to him and Emily."

"But Clare, what happened later—that had nothing to do with business, nothing at all. Won't you believe me? Can't we salvage. . .us from all this ugliness?"

"No!" Clare stood up suddenly, the chair she abandoned scraping harshly across the floor. "No, we can't salvage us! There's nothing at all to salvage. You lied to me, you used me, you tricked me into going to bed with you. And all for the government! So what if Jonas doesn't pay his taxes! How much money are we talking about, anyway? Do you think I care? I'm just an ordinary person, Michael. I've already lost everything I worked so hard for. The government—you!—you took it all. And now. . . You can't use innocent people like that, Michael—you just can't! It's. . .it's so low I don't even know a word for it!" Unable to stop herself, she broke into racking sobs. He rose and tried to put his arms around her, but she wrenched away from him.

"I know how it must seem to you, Clare. When we first met, I never knew what had happened to you—about your house, that is. About losing everything. You have to believe me, Clare. I—''

"Get out of here now," she said between her tears. "I don't want to see you again. Get out."

"I didn't bribe the police, Clare. I showed them my identification and explained that we—you and I—were on an investigation. At least I didn't bribe the police." She looked at him in contemptuous silence. What difference did it make now whether he had bribed the police or not? He had *used* her, violated her. He had dirtied her, and nothing could ever erase the stain.

"I'm going to take the books, Clare. I have to take them, don't you see?"

"No, I don't see! Those books belong to the Hahns— to Jonas and Emily. She needs the books to get her boys back."

"She doesn't need them now. You just told me Jonas is at home, asleep."

"Yes, he is, but the boys aren't there. I don't know where they are, but I know she can trade the books for the twins."

"They'll be at that Chetnik woman's place, then. Where else would he have left them?"

Clare was momentarily distracted from her pain. "At Angel Chetnik's...yes, of course. I wonder where she lives." Probably somewhere on Long Island, Clare thought, close enough for Jonas to have driven there and home in the short time since his violent fight with Emily. "Even so, Michael, I can't give you the books. I'd die first!"

"Angel is in the Queens phone book. Tell your sister to go there tomorrow. I'm certain she'll find her children. Anyway, Hahn is going to prison, so she'll have her boys. He won't be in any position to care for them."

"Why is he going to prison?" Clare asked. "You just told me I blew the entire investigation."

Michael sighed. "After all I've had to do, I'm not going to stop until I get him. And we'll get him. We always do."

"Bully for the IRS," Clare said with disgust. Against her will, her eyes filled up with tears once more.

In the hall that led from the kitchen, there was the unmistakable sound of keys rattling, followed by the slamming of the front door. Stunned, Clare and Michael looked at each other for a few seconds.

He raised a questioning eyebrow. "Mrs. Sydney? Did we wake her up?"

"It's Emily." Clare's hand flew up to cover her mouth. "She must have heard us."

Michael raced into the hall. "My keys—she's taken my keys!" he shouted. He ran to the door, pulled it open and stumbled down the steps. By the time Clare got there, the Mercedes station wagon had backed into Keeler Street, its tires squealing on the wet pavement. Emily threw the gear into drive and took off toward the main street several blocks away. Clare saw the window on the driver's side open and a glint of light on steel as Emily hurled Michael's keys into the night.

Chapter Fourteen

Clare was already in the bed lately abandoned by Emily by the time Michael found his keys, twenty minutes later. She had locked up the house and prepared to retire before he tried to rouse her—first with the nearly inaudible rap of his knuckles on the solid oak of the front door, then with the thud of the lion's head knocker, and finally with the obnoxious shrill of the electric bell, which rang both in the kitchen and in the upstairs hall.

She stomped to the window and threw it open with a heave that left its sash weights crashing inside the frame. Michael stood on the front walk, his features invisible in the gloom.

"Please, Clare, can't we talk?" he asked in a low, pleading voice that carried in the quiet night. For a moment she remembered the hours of happiness they had shared, but she forced away the painful thoughts.

"Go away before I call the police," she snapped. "I never want to see or hear from you again."

"Clare—"

She slammed the window shut and jumped into bed, burrowing under the blue comforter. *I won't cry, I won't,* she promised herself, even as hot tears soaked into the comforter. She turned on her stomach and buried her face in the pillow. She was still in that position when she heard the distinctive engine of Michael's Volkswagen start.

THE NEXT AFTERNOON Clare sat in the living room reading the Sunday paper when the doorbell rang. Her entire body ached as she raised herself from the chair. Dropping the section of the newspaper she had been pretending to read, she went to a window and pulled back its curtain to study the scene outside. Emily's yellow station wagon sat in front of a fire hydrant on the opposite side of the street.

She opened the front door.

"May I see you for a minute, Clare?"

"Of course, Emily. Come in." Clare led the way back to the living room and resumed her seat.

"It's cold in here. Is the heat on?" Emily, wearing a yellow cashmere pullover and matching yellow wool trousers whose cheery color sucked what life remained in her pale cheeks, arranged herself on a graceful Queen Anne footstool ten feet from Clare's chair. It wasn't the same outfit she had worn the night before, and Clare realized she had been home to change. New lines on Emily's face had aged her a decade.

"I hadn't noticed the temperature," Clare replied. Indeed, except for a pervasive pain that began in her heart and radiated to every fingertip, she was numb to cold, to hunger, to any sensation at all. Clare ascribed the pain to lack of sleep, refusing to credit Michael's deception with any power, refusing even to think his name. "I'll turn up the thermostat."

"Don't bother, Clare. I can't stay long because Jonas and I have to go to Queens to pick up the twins. I talked to them this morning, and they're fine." Emily smiled shyly.

"You're. . . picking up the twins—with *Jonas*?" Clare stared hard at her sister. What was this, a loving reconciliation? A trip together to the home of Jonas's mistress? "But—"

"Now, Clare, I know how Jonas and Miss Chetnik must look to you, but I assure you your suspicions are unfounded. She is merely his bookkeeper, nothing more."

And what about the Porsche, Emily? Did he tell you he bought a thirty-five-thousand-dollar sports car for his bookkeeper? How stupid could a woman be?

"Yes, I know it all looks terrible to an outsider," Emily continued. "Jonas even bought her a fancy car. One would think there was something sexual between them."

"One would get that impression," Clare assented dryly. "You know about the car?"

"A so-called friend told me about the car some time ago. I asked Jonas about it—not right away, but last night, when we had a long talk. He explained everything to me."

"Last night, after you left here? After you overheard Michael and me?"

"Yes. I didn't mean to eavesdrop, but I'm glad I heard what I did. And I'm sorry about Michael's keys. Did he have much trouble finding them? I assume he did find them, since his car is gone."

"Of course his car is gone!" Clare exploded. 'After the lies he told, do you think I would allow him to spend the night here, keys or no keys? What do you take me for, anyway?" She looked away, too ashamed to meet her sister's eyes. "Emily, I—"

"Don't worry, we all make mistakes. How could you have known what he was after? Although, looking back on everything, I don't know how any of us could have been so foolish. Jonas, especially. Poor lamb."

Clare's throat closed in pain. "Don't feel sorry for me, Emily. I couldn't stand it. I've had my fill of everyone's pity."

"Oh, I didn't mean you. I meant Jonas is a poor lamb."

"Jonas, a poor lamb? Jonas? After the way he's treated you, how can you say that? Don't you have any self-respect?"

"He's my husband, and he's in trouble. Wouldn't you feel the same way?" Emily toyed with the gold key ring in her hand, turning it over and over until the sound of one key clinking against another in the still room nearly made Clare scream. "I love him. What can I tell you?" She looked up and shrugged, a half smile playing on her lips.

"What about the divorce? What about the children? What about Gene?" After everything that had happened, how could Emily insist so calmly that she loved Jonas? Clare realized she hardly knew the woman who sat before her.

"There won't be any divorce, Clare. Jonas needs me. As for the children, they're fine. I spoke to Miss Chetnik, and she assured me they're apple pie. After all, the boys are used to nannies. We've had a parade of nannies for them. And Gene—I guess Gene was only a passing fancy. Thank heaven, I made Jonas recognize the truth."

"Nanny! Miss Chetnik doesn't look like a nanny to *me*," Clare insisted. "She looks like a third-rate tramp with a nose bob. You don't seriously believe their relationship is merely a business one, do you, Emily?"

"I do," she exclaimed in a tone that brooked no objection. "Not only that, I have to ask you to cease interfering in matters that concern only my husband and me. How do you know what Miss Chetnik looks like, anyway?"

"I went to the Rejuvenation Clinic and saw her. Do you know about the Rejuvenation Clinic, too, Emily? Did Jonas explain the clinic to you? I must say you're taking all this rather lightly."

"He explained everything to me. Tell me, what misguided quixotic impulse motivated you to go to the clinic?"

Clare blushed with shame. "Michael Duffy more or less suggested I do it," she replied finally, her eyes sliding away. "To protect you," she added. Her voice faltered.

"Oh, that's great." Emily rose suddenly and stared at her sister. "You really have a nerve, Clare. I would never interfere in your life before you asked me to. I would never pretend to know what's best for you. I don't like your insinuations about Jonas and Miss Chetnik, and I don't like the way your every facial expression is screaming how you disapprove of my decision to stay with my husband. Coming from a woman who let herself be seduced in the line of duty by a lousy tax investigator, I find that pretty hard to take."

Clare sucked in her breath. Emily's contemptuous reproach hit her like a slap in the face. "Emily—"

Emily held up one hand. "I told you before, I love Jonas. I explained to you that he was going through a bad time in his life, but I guess you're incapable of understanding a woman who decides to stick with her husband, for better or for worse. No matter what *you* did, that's what I promised, and that's what I intend to do."

Clare, too, rose, her eyes brimming with tears of outrage at her sister's undeserved accusation. "You're being unfair to me, Emily. You're implying I had an opportunity to stand by Teddy when things got rough. He never gave me a chance!"

"If you nosed around in his affairs as you've nosed around in ours, it's really no wonder. Why didn't you just mind your own business?"

"Emily, you are a fool. A fool, do you hear? Go back to Jonas and he'll break your heart again. Don't you know what he's been doing—not just Angel Chetnik, but his entire financial life? Don't you realize the IRS is breathing down his neck? Don't you know what they want to do to him?"

"To *us*, Clare, to *us*. To Dr. And *Mrs.* Jonas Hahn. Jonas and I are a couple, don't you see? Joint returns, Clare—did that ever cross your pea brain?" Emily turned and ran from the living room, slamming the front door as she left the house.

THE NEXT TWO WEEKS passed without a word from Emily, but Clare felt too hurt and too proud to make the first move toward a reconciliation. She knew that when a woman and her husband closed ranks, no room existed for an outsider, not even a previously close and loving sister. In her heart, Clare shakily maintained she had done nothing wrong, but self-righteousness was scant compensation for the shame she felt. To be estranged from her sister for the first time in her life was excruciating, yet the anger and hurt born of Emily's unkind words continued unabated.

She was unable to think about Michael Duffy without returning to the paralyzing rage that had followed his departure from her life. When Mrs. Sydney asked her if she had ever solved the Schoenfeld-Loewe mystery, she curtly changed the subject and refused to discuss Michael.

Pierce and Pierce, the accounting firm, offered Clare a position in its Boston office, which she accepted with alacrity. Although the money was ordinary, there were opportunities for advancement at the large national firm; between the health-insurance benefits and the tuition program, she felt compelled to accept. As she gave notice to her short list of clients, she looked forward to a change of location; Connecticut held no happy memories for her.

By the first of April she had found an apartment in Brookline, a suburb of Boston, and learned enough about the MTA to get from Cleveland Circle, where she lived, to downtown Boston without a mistake. She would have preferred an apartment closer to her office, but rents in Boston itself were prohibitive, owing to the number of colleges and universities there. She was forced to take a small furnished studio flat on the third floor of a buff-colored brick building whose stairs were worn and whose floor slanted unevenly. The apartment's dismal gray walls depressed her, but only one month's security was required. Clare felt her heart sink as she wrote a check that nearly matched what she had saved for a used car and handed it over to a new landlord. Her first activity, in violation of the one-year lease she had signed, was to paint the four walls a pale shell pink.

When she returned to Greenwich for the rest of her things, Mrs. Sydney allowed her to raid the attic of the house on Keeler Street. Clare salvaged three pairs of matching tie-back curtains and an attractive Indian throw, souvenir of one of the landlady's many trips to exotic places. The older woman also gave her cuttings from various houseplants, and Clare looked forward to the day when she could hang pots of greenery in her Brookline studio.

Mrs. Sydney promised to forward Clare's mail, but to return unopened any letters from Michael that might arrive. Clare asked her to tell no one, not even Emily, where she had gone.

With no money to waste on frivolities, Clare quickly learned that Boston was paradise for a person on a limited budget. There was no charge for walking along the esplanade on the Charles River and watching the sailboats glide by; the Charles separated Boston from Cambridge and its world-famous universities, Harvard, Radcliffe and MIT. A cup of coffee on Harvard Square cost the same as anywhere else, but the show of people who thronged the crowded Cambridge streets was free. In the Harvard Coop she found two miniature Harvard sweatshirts that would have looked adorable on Ian and Kevin, but she put them back on the shelf, telling herself they were too expensive, and allowed her nephews' fourth birthday to pass without a word from her.

She took an after-hours job doing the books of a dry cleaner near Cleveland Circle, which led to a second night job in the neighborhood. She carried her lunch to work in an insulated plastic bag. Within three months, she found herself gaining on the bills that remained from her disastrous California days, and she had enough money left over to buy an FM radio.

Clare signed up for summer-school night courses in accounting, with an eye to obtaining her C.P.A. certificate.

Between her free-lance jobs and night school, she was busy every weeknight.

But the weekends were difficult.

Men asked her out: men at work; two men she met separately on the stairs of her building. She turned them down. Vaguely she expected to date again—someday. She even wanted to marry again, to have children before she grew too old, but something within her heart—pain, fear she wasn't certain what—stopped her. It took too much of an effort to smile, to make small talk, to dress carefully for a man.

She refused to think about Michael Duffy. Once in a while she saw a man who resembled him, which was not unusual in Boston, where men routinely dressed in conservative suits and wore white or pale blue shirts and mutely striped ties. Whenever that happened, she would unconsciously slow her step. Once she even followed a man from the Parker House Hotel up toward Beacon Hill, until he turned into an apartment building that overlooked Boston Common. When she saw his profile, she realized her mistake and felt embarrassed.

Each time that happened, her heart twisted in pain, and it took a massive effort not to cry. Did she want to cry over the loss of a man she had loved? Or because her pride was still hurt at how he had used her? She refused to answer the questions, because thinking back on the sordid trick that had brought her to his bed drove her crazy. She hated self-pity in others and refused to recognize it in herself. Better, much better, to put Michael Duffy out of her mind.

One question she pondered, but could not answer. How could love turn to hate in the blink of an eye?

IN EARLY AUGUST, Clare sat on a brick bench in the center of Quincy Market, near her office. Her eyes were closed, her face turned to the sun. The insulated plastic bag that had held her lunch rested next to her purse atop her lightweight blazer, which was neatly folded on the brick seat at her side. When the weather was nice, as it was that day, she often took her lunch to crowded Quincy Market and watched the never-ending show of tourists and office workers who thronged the complex at the noon hour. There was a store in the market that specialized in exotic coffees, and Clare was working her way through every blend, cup by cup. A tiny extravagance, but one she needed. That day she had drunk a cup of Vienna-chocolate-amaretto roast and found it to her liking.

She sighed with contentment. On a hot day there was a distinctive scent in the air, an elusive olio of coffee, molasses and tangy salt wind from the sea, that she had learned to associate with Boston. Someone had told her that, many years before, a molasses-processing factory had burned in a spectacular fire not far from where she sat. From a guide book she had learned that the original warehouses on the waterfront had stored and shipped coffee for hundreds of years. She knew why the air smelled the way it did.

In Clare's past, in the days before she had met Michael Duffy, she would have fantasized herself back in colonial Boston. She would have imagined what she would have worn, how she would have spoken, what her name might have been. Ever since childhood, she had lost herself in fantasies, but Clare was aware her imagination no longer worked the same way it once had. Except for her purposeful lie to the trembling doctor at the Rejuvenation Clinic, the last time she remembered pretending to be someone she wasn't had been during a romantic carriage ride with Michael Duffy in Guadalajara. They had talked about Don Juan that night, she recalled, about Mozart and Tirso de Molina—wasn't that the name he had taught her? She felt a heaviness in her heart when she remembered the evening, and she knew something vital within her was dead.

No, I won't think about him, she told herself sternly. She had never heard a word from Michael after the terrible night she had sneaked into Jonas's bedroom and stolen his ledgers. She wondered where he was—off on another secret assignment disguised as a doctor, breaking an unsuspecting woman's heart?

She knew now that what she had done was wrong—unfair to Jonas, unfair to Emily. She had had no right to interfere in their lives. She had had no right to question Emily's love for Jonas, or Jonas's inability to demonstrate his love for Emily, if love her he did. Months of soul-searching, months of mentally reliving the events of the previous winter, had taught Clare a few bitter lessons. One was that love had no explanation. Love was irrational, love was illogical, love was...well, it was just love.

Emily had called her a meddler. Outraged, Clare had denied the ugly accusation. Now she accepted its truth. With her usual intuition, Emily had sensed a connection between Clare's behavior and her problems with Teddy. Because Teddy had been inaccessible, Clare had wanted to punish Jonas. A first-semester psychology student could have recognized her behavior for what it was. Clare didn't know the fancy psychological word, but she knew there was a name for what she had done.

Not that Jonas would ever pass as a saint—on the contrary. Jonas was odious—but only to Clare. Was it any of her business how Emily felt about Jonas or how much she could tolerate? Clare knew she owed her sister amends. Although so much time had passed that Clare felt incapable of healing their rift, she had written Emily a letter of self-reproach; it still lay on the table in her studio apartment. How would Emily react when she received the heartfelt apology?

Someone sat down at Clare's side. She opened her eyes to rearrange her purse and lunch bag, snatching a quick glance at her watch. Then she closed them again and watched the wavy red images the sunlight caused to form on the inside of her eyelids. She had lost her half-formed musings about eighteenth-century Boston, but her lunch hour was nearly over, and she had to return to the office. Despite closed eyes, she became uncomfortably aware that the newcomer was staring at her.

"Clare, is that you?"

The familiar sound of her name on the man's lips impelled Clare to reopen her eyes. Slowly she turned her head until her eyes met those of Michael Duffy, who was seated a scant ten inches away on the other side of her blazer. She looked away quickly, hoping he couldn't see the shock that stunned her and the flash of heat she knew stained her cheeks.

"How did you find me?" she whispered, afraid to speak aloud for fear her voice would betray the welter of conflicting emotions that assailed her. A roar filled her ears. *Oh, could it really be Michael, after all these months?* He didn't look the way she remembered him; he was older. Had those strands of gray in his hair always been there? And wasn't his hair longer, more the way it had been in the photograph on his driver's license?

"It wasn't easy," he said, "but I knew you'd file your income-tax return eventually."

Income tax! Clare frowned. How did he keep his voice so calm? He acted as if no time had passed since the fateful March night during which Clare had lost both her innocence and every person she loved.

"I asked for a ninety-day extension because I was busy moving. I . . . I wasn't positive what my new address would be." She had filed at the end of March while still living in Connecticut, requesting a legitimate extension. Her throat functioned beautifully, she realized; her words sounded perfectly normal to her roaring ears, although she felt as if someone else were speaking and she were merely an observer. Was she crazy? Talking about income-tax returns and ninety-day extensions as if meeting him were the most ordinary occurrence in an ordinary day?

"I had the Andover office watch for your return," he explained. "You can't hide from the government. Why did you go away without telling anyone where you had gone?" He reached out to touch her arm, then thought better of it when she shrank slightly at his move. He dropped his hand to his lap.

"Mrs. Sydney knows where I am. We write to each other." *Why am I defending myself? I owe this man no explanation.*

"She claims she doesn't. Neither your parents nor your sister know. Everyone is worried."

"No one wants to see me. And I don't want to see anyone—especially you." Clare stood up and mechanically brushed off her skirt. There were no crumbs among the pleats, but she needed to buy time until strength returned to her legs. It wasn't as if she hadn't imagined what she would say or do if Michael ever walked back into her life. She had pictured the moment many times, always with a smart retort, with a perfect insult on her lips. Now that he was actually at her side, the best she could manage was a cold facade and, she hoped, an unmistakable air of indifference. "I have to get back to the office, Michael. Nice running into you."

Why did I say that, she wondered, berating herself for having uttered the normal courtesy. Seeing him was far from nice; it was excruciatingly painful. Although she had barely glanced at his face, the way he smelled, the way the slightest shadow of beard grew on his jaw, and the strong lines of his cheekbones conjured up disquieting memories she had put away long before. She had nearly forgotten him, she insisted, knowing the very idea was a lie even as she thought it. Well, if not forgotten, at least she had learned to live with her mistake, and she barely thought of him during the busy workday. Only at night when she tried to sleep did thoughts of him return.

"You didn't run into me. I've been searching for you for months." His voice was low and urgent.

She turned to look him directly in the eye for the first time. "Why? Why did you bother? We have nothing to say to each other. I've made a new life for myself here in Boston. I'm finally on my own, totally on my own—no parents, no husband, no big sister to take care of me. While carefully minding my own business, I've discovered that I'm a very self-sufficient person. I don't need anyone in my life. It would have been better if you had never come here."

"Sit down, Clare. I have some things to tell you." He indicated the seat she had just vacated.

"I have to get back to the office."

"This will only take a minute."

Clare perched tentatively on the edge of the bench, her body poised to flee.

"Jonas is in jail."

"He is?" A vision of her elegant brother-in-law dressed in a black-and-white-striped prison suit flitted through her mind. "I can't believe it!"

"The federal prison in Danbury. It's like a country club. He won't be there for long—six months at the most."

"There's not much point in catching the offenders if they're only going to get six months, is there? Was it all worth it to you, Michael? Are the lies, the hurt, the deceit all worth it?"

He looked as if she had slapped him, but he recovered quickly. "Well, he owes his back taxes, plus interest and penalties. And the other doctors, the ones at the clinic—they turned themselves in, too, so the money is pretty substantial. But to answer your question—no, it wasn't worth it to me, Clare."

" 'They turned themselves in, too.' Did Jonas turn himself in?'' Somehow the idea that Jonas had volunteered his guilt was incredible.

"He and Emily together. Apparently she talked him into making a clean breast of things. They sold off their investments to pay their tax bill—their house, too—and Emily has a job now. Jonas's practice is for sale, as well. He convinced the Service that Emily was totally innocent of collusion, although as you probably realize, she is equally culpable in the eyes of the law.''

"What is Emily doing?''

"She and the boys live in a small apartment in Stamford, and she's working in the personnel office at Greenwich Hospital. The twins are in a day-care center, which she told me they like.''

"I'm surprised Emily even speaks to you, Michael. After all, you destroyed her entire life.'' *With my help,* she added silently.

"Strangely enough, she doesn't feel that way, Clare. She told me she was grateful she and Jonas were given an opportunity, however radical, to correct their marriage. She misses Jonas, of course, but she is not unhappy. She wants you to get in touch with her. I'll give you her new address.''

Clare fell silent as she mulled over the cataclysmic changes in Emily's life, changes for which Clare carried a heavy burden of guilt. She examined the toe of her shoe, the pattern of stones in the pavement and the heels of passersby who meandered through the market. Anything was preferable to looking into the blue eyes of Michael Duffy.

"I guess I can understand why she stayed with Jonas,'' Clare said finally. "She loves him. He's lucky to have such a loyal wife. I would have helped Teddy if he had given me a chance, but he didn't. I've made a terrible mess of my life.'' She hadn't meant to make such an admission, not to herself, but certainly not to Michael Duffy. Clare pressed her lips together, as if to stay further confidences.

He laid a hand on her bare arm, which tingled disconcertingly at his touch. "Clare, do you love me?"

Her heart turned over when he asked the question. "N-no," she said shakily. "No, I don't love you."

"Did you ever?"

"No," she exclaimed, gathering strength. "No, I never loved you." *Of course I loved you,* she raged inwardly. *I wish I didn't, hadn't; I wish I'd never met you.* She let the anger flow freely in her mind. Maybe the IRS was capable of discovering all a person's financial secrets, but the Service still couldn't read her thoughts.

"Well, I love *you,*" he said quietly. "Will you give me another chance?"

He loved her. The words she had longed to hear the previous winter now proved to be too little, too late. Why did life have to be so ill-timed? "Another chance to what? Deceive me? Seduce me?"

"Seduce you! You wanted it as much as I did."

Oh, I did, she admitted silently. *I wanted you and I loved you; I gave myself fully to you.* "But I thought you were a doctor. I thought you were an honest man. I thought—"

"I'll be anything you want me to be."

"No, it's too late!" she exclaimed, throwing her hands over her ears. *But I do still love him,* she realized. The few short moments they had been together had already convinced Clare that the attraction she felt for Michael had not diminished, despite the passage of time or the base way she believed he had used her.

"Please, Clare. Tell me what you just said isn't true. It's not too late, is it?"

What should she do? What was there to say? The roaring in Clare's ears increased, blocking out all attempts at rational thought. She didn't know what to say; she couldn't decide. She jumped up and ran through the crowded market. At State Street, without looking in either direction, she cut through a line of idling automobiles stopped for a traffic light. She ran until she reached the modern glass building where her office was located. It wasn't until she stood in the elevator that she realized her blazer, her lunch bag and her purse were back in Quincy Market with Michael Duffy.

"THERE'S AN INVESTIGATOR from the Internal Revenue Service here to see you, Mrs. Eckert," the disembodied voice on the interoffice telephone told her.

Clare, her blouse damp and sticking to her skin, hadn't been back at her desk ten minutes before the call came. *Should I have stayed? Should I have told him that I loved him? No, let him go away,* she urged herself with a quick shake of the head. *He lied to me. It's too late for us.* "What's his name?" The hand that held the telephone trembled.

"Michael Duffy."

Clare glanced toward the reception area, some fifty feet away. Although his back was to her, she could see Michael casually studying the pattern of acoustical tiles set into the ceiling.

"I can't see Mr. Duffy today," she said. "I'm much too busy."

"Mrs. Eckert," the receptionist said in a stage whisper, "it's the IRS!" No one at Pierce and Pierce ever avoided the IRS. It simply was not done. Few things were as important as a cordial working relationship between one of the nation's largest and most prestigious accounting firms and the Internal Revenue Service, its sworn enemy. The receptionist's voice reflected her outrage.

"Nevertheless, I'm busy," Clare repeated, depressing a lighted button to break the connection. She placed an elbow on the desk, a hand over her eyes, and waited. Either her supervisor or Michael Duffy himself would appear at the door to her tiny, glass-walled office within twenty seconds. She prayed it would be the supervisor, a kindly middle-aged man who had befriended Clare on occasion. She couldn't tell him the entire story, but she could say Michael was a...a...masher. Yes, "masher" was a word he would understand.

"You're under arrest, Mrs. Eckert."

Clare looked up. Michael, carrying her purse, lunch bag and blazer, blocked the door. What was worse, behind him stood a knot of curious coworkers who had gathered to see what the fuss was about. On most occasions, word traveled fairly quickly from the reception room through the office, but when a junior clerk refused to see a representative of the IRS, rapidity turned to speed of light. Clare blushed to the roots of her hair, but made a quick decision to remain calm, no matter what Michael did.

"I'm under arrest," she repeated tonelessly; out of sight beneath the desk, her hands opened and closed nervously. "What am I charged with?"

"Evasion," he answered. Only she could see the twinkle in his blue eyes and the almost imperceptible twitch at the left side of his mouth. "Refusal to provide viable answers to questions posed by an official representative of the United States government. Fleeing said representative, not once but twice. These are extremely serious charges. Get your things and come with me, Mrs. Eckert."

"What rot!" she said, sputtering. "How dare you come in here and embarrass me in front of everyone! If anything, I've overpaid my taxes. Go pick on a conglomerate, Mr. Duffy." She doubted he was empowered to arrest anyone. "Besides, you already have my things," she added.

"Why, so I do. Shall we go? Inform your superiors you won't be returning today."

"I haven't done anything wrong. You can't take me out of here."

"She'd better go along with him," said an unfamiliar voice from the crowd.

"She needs a good lawyer," another said. Clare thought the latter voice came from the managing partner.

"Now, now, Mrs. Eckert," Michael chided. "We don't want to make a fuss in front of our coworkers, do we? Why don't you simply come quietly and we'll go somewhere and discuss this matter of evasion."

Oh, he was infuriating—supercilious, sarcastic and imbued with that air of self-importance that government employees seemed to cultivate from their first day on the job. It enraged Clare that her coworkers lacked the spine to object to the power of the IRS. Although their professional lives were dedicated to slipping around the thousands of tax rules and suggestions that spilled like confetti from Washington, they were as cowed as the average taxpayer when actually faced with a government representative.

"Make me," she said. There was a simultaneous gasp of surprise from various open mouths behind Michael. Clare heard their mumbles and whispers, but she could no longer make out the words because of the roaring in her ears. "Show me a court order or something."

"Oh, I'll show you, all right. The Service always gets what it wants." He threw her blazer on the floor and the purse and lunch bag on the desk, then strode purposefully to where she sat. He began to lift her.

"W-what are you doing?" an outraged Clare squeaked.

"I'm going to carry you out of here. You're going to talk to me."

The faces outside the office door pressed closer to hear every word. Even the receptionist, earphones still clamped in place, had abandoned the switchboard and joined the throng, the telephone jack forgotten in one hand. With one quick movement Michael scooped Clare from her chair. He fully intended to do as he threatened, Clare realized; he fully intended to lift her like a sack of potatoes and carry her out of the staid Pierce and Pierce office.

"Wait, wait, I'll walk!" Clare cried, pushing at his chest. His expression poker-serious, he lowered her, feet-first, to the floor.

With as much dignity as she could muster, Clare bent and retrieved her blazer, which she made an enormous show of brushing and shaking before putting it on. Then she took her purse, checked its contents and slung the strap over her shoulder.

"I'm ready now," she announced finally. With head held high, she preceded Michael from her cubby-sized office, carefully avoiding the eyes of her coworkers. Silently she walked through the large outer room and past the receptionist's desk, stopping only when she reached a heavy wooden door that led to the elevator hall.

Michael swept open the door and held it, inclining into a half-bow as she went through.

"I'LL NEVER BE ABLE to go back to my office," Clare muttered. "How can I ever explain being arrested by the Internal Revenue Service?"

Michael negotiated his rented car through the traffic on Commonwealth Avenue while Clare hugged the door on the passenger side, her face reflecting an unidentifiable jumble of emotions. She seemed thin and pale to him, subdued almost, as if some of her vitality had drained away during the months they had been apart.

"I don't want you to go back," he said. "I want you to come and live with me in Fairfax. I want to marry you." He kept his eyes on the road, barely breathing as he awaited her response. She stared at him in silence for a long moment.

"I would never marry an IRS investigator," she said finally. "The very idea of what you do for a living makes my skin crawl!"

"I could get another job," he mumbled. "I could even go to medical school. I think I made a fair physician, don't you?'' He ventured a quick look at her face and a tentative smile. Later he'd explain to Clare that he was no longer an investigator. Later he'd tell her about the long memo he had written, criticizing the undercover program. Of course, the memo meant nothing; even if his ideas were taken seriously, nothing would happen for a dog's age. Changes in the Service came slowly, if at all. Later he would tell her that he had taken a desk job he hated, but with which he intended to live until something better came along. The trouble was, he didn't know what he wanted to work at; but he knew that if he wanted to be Clare's husband, he needed a new occupation.

"You're not a very convincing doctor. I was on to you from the first."

"Revisionist." He glanced in her direction again, smiling broadly when he realized she no longer looked as if she planned to jump out of the car at the next stoplight.

"No, really. You were too nice, too much of a gentleman. You had other interests besides real-estate trusts and condominium investments. You read books. You talked about fascinating artists—Mozart, Tirso de Molina.'' As she said the Spanish name carefully, she moved a scant inch closer to him on the seat.

"I'm still nice, still a gentleman. I don't give a hang about condominiums, and tomorrow I'll tell you about Garcia Lorca, another Spanish playwright." *Oh, tell me there'll be a tomorrow for us, Clare.* He reached across and laid his hand over hers. She did not remove her hand.

"But you lied to me. You're responsible for my sister's predicament."

"Oh, no. I may have lied, but I was—"

"Just doing your job." Clare mocked him. "That's a weak excuse."

"I *was* doing my job," he stated emphatically. "That wasn't my first time as a doctor. I played a lot of different roles, most of them quite successfully. The only difference was that I never fell in love before. As for your sister, she knew what she was doing."

"No, she didn't. I can't believe Emily would purposely cheat anyone."

"She signed those joint returns, Clare. That makes her responsible. She knew, or should have known, what was going on, whether she admits it to herself or not. Emily chose to look the other way. If we didn't have voluntary compliance in this country, no one would pay his taxes— and then where would we be? In all fairness, you cannot hold me or the IRS responsible for the trouble the Hahns got themselves into."

"Jonas made her do it," Clare insisted stubbornly.

"Just as your ex-husband 'made' you sign a bunch of loan applications. Did he beat you? Twist your arm behind your back? Threaten you with bodily harm?" Later he would tell her that Theodore Eckert had recently undergone a dreaded Taxpayer Compliance Measurement Program audit. The TCMP was a taxpayer's worst nightmare come true, a grueling review in which an agent scrutinized every line of a return and demanded written proof for every answer. Checking off the box marked "single" meant Eckert had to produce his divorce certificate. Deducting a cash business lunch in Peoria meant he had to produce a dated, accurate restaurant receipt. Eckert had done very poorly indeed, especially on line twenty-seven, where he had claimed an enormous deduction for alimony, which he could not prove he had ever paid.

"No, but... I didn't understand what I was doing," Clare said. "I didn't know anything about Teddy's investments."

"It's your business to find out such things. It's every person's responsibility. I can't believe how blindly trusting some women are. No wife of mine—"

"I never said I'd be your wife."

"Is that an out-and-out no?"

She moved another inch closer. "I'm interested in your proposition."

"My proposal," he corrected her. "I'm certain we could file a lovely joint income-tax return. Your tax bite decreases, you know. Think of the deductions: home mortgage interest, energy credits, real estate taxes...."

"And exemptions," she added. "Dependents..."

"At least two, besides you and me," he concurred. "Don't forget child-care credits."

"I'd do the taxes, of course. Allow me to remind you that my services as an accountant are deductible."

"Do I detect definite interest? Is that a yes?"

"Interest, yes," Clare said, smiling shyly at him. By now her body pressed close to his on the front seat of the car, and he thanked his stars he hadn't rented the Chevrolet a Hertz agent at the airport had first offered him, with its intrusive gearshift that separated driver from passenger. "But I've already paid the price of admission," she reminded him. "No more penalties."

"No, no penalty." Michael slowed the car to a stop in the middle of a block, unaware of the truck that screeched to a halt behind him. He slipped his arms around Clare and touched his lips to hers, sighing with contentment as he felt her body melt into his and her lips respond. Behind him, a horn began to honk, then another. *Let them wait,* he thought. He'd waited a long time for this moment with Clare. Nothing was going to spoil it.

IRS SETS UP GUIDELINES TO LIMIT
AGENTS' USE OF PROFESSIONAL POSES
By Leslie Maitland Werner
Special to *The New York Times*

WASHINGTON, May 30—In new guidelines for undercover operations, the Internal Revenue Service has forbidden agents to pose as lawyers, doctors, clergymen or reporters unless they obtain specific approval from top officials.

John Rankin, acting assistant commissioner for criminal investigations, said in an interview that the IRS had decided to issue "more restrictive" guidelines because its use of undercover techniques was growing. . . .

He said that the Service had recognized that impersonating such people raised particularly sensitive questions [and] a significant risk that another individual might be led into a professional or confidential relationship with the undercover employee.

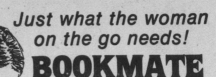